# Grown-Up Second Chance

by

## Casey Dawes

Mountain Vines Publishing

# Chapter One

A bison stood in the middle of the road.

"What are you going to do?" I hissed at my sister Kathleen.

"Wait it out."

"Can't you just nudge it a little with the RV?" It had been a long day.

"It's not a cat." Kathleen turned to look at me. "You *have* been out of Montana a while."

"Oh? And just how many buffalo roamed across the ranch while I've been gone?"

"There's the one by the bank."

"It's a *statue.*"

Kathleen shrugged.

The bison turned its massive, horny head and looked at us.

"You'd better not charge us," I told it. "We just bought this rig."

The animal studied me as if considering its choices.

It was a long few minutes.

On the couch behind us, Liz continued her valium-induced sleep, totally unaware of the crisis.

With a snort, the beast turned its head and trotted into the vegetation.

Kathleen put the RV in gear and continued down the highway toward the first stop of our epic adventure: a park in West Yellowstone.

I had to admire the way my gray-haired sister handled our new-to-us motorhome. It was forty-three feet long, and we were towing Liz's beloved forest green Jeep so we'd have a car once we got to our destination. A lifetime of wrestling incalcitrant farm machinery into line had given Kathleen an edge up over us when it came to getting a license to drive the rig. It had taken me three tries for a license. Liz had given up after two.

And we'd let her stop trying. Just like we'd always let her take the easy road. Even when we were kids we protected her from the hard knocks of life, somehow knowing her life was always going to be difficult in spite of our efforts.

I shook off memories and indulged in the scenery. Montana would never get old for me. It was home, no matter how long I'd lived in the San Francisco Bay Area. In this stretch between Bozeman and West Yellowstone, the pine trees descended close to the road, except for the huge expanse of the Big Sky resort with its ski slopes and resort community which we'd left behind a half hour ago.

"Maybe we should try skiing next winter," I suggested to Kathleen.

"I thought the whole point was to get away from snow," she said. "Although why *you* need to do that, I can't imagine. You haven't spent a real winter here in decades."

"We visited Tahoe in the winter," I shot back.

She just turned her stink eye on me.

It was an ability she'd inherited from our mother, then honed to a high performance with her own two children.

I shut up and stared at the trees.

"Where is the turnoff?" she asked a while later.

After consulting the map on my phone, comparing it with the paper map we carried because Liz didn't trust phone directions, and verifying it by calculating the time we'd traveled from the last small town consisting of a post office, a church, and a bar, I told her.

"About twenty minutes on the left."

"And you double-checked the reservation? They're expecting us? Because we're not going to find anywhere else around Yellowstone in mid-June."

"I got a text from them yesterday." And an email the week before. And another email the week before that. The RV park wanted to make sure we were showing up. "And I double-checked the reservation email they sent us. We're scheduled to arrive today and leave mid-July."

"Do you think we're staying too long?" she asked. "Will

we have enough time to get south before the snow comes? I'm not driving this rig in the snow. I told you that."

A million times.

"We're good. We'll get to snowbird country by the time the bad weather hits. I've made sure of that." I hoped. Climate change had messed the weather up so much that nothing could be relied on anymore.

But I wasn't telling her any of that.

Behind us, Liz stirred and sat up. "Are we there yet?" she asked.

"Almost," Kathleen said.

"Good." Liz scooted to the end of the couch closest to us. "Any coffee left in the Thermos?" she asked.

I reached my hand out for her travel mug. Somehow both Kathleen and I had never gotten over treating Liz like a porcelain doll, even though we were now all in our sixties.

Keeping one eye on the road ahead to make sure we weren't running over any rough spots, I poured the coffee. It wouldn't do to have a big ol' coffee stain on our recently detailed rig. Kathleen would ignore it, Liz wouldn't even see it, but it would bug the crap out of me.

I checked my phone again. "Five more miles."

"I'm so excited," Liz said. "I haven't seen Yellowstone since I came down here with my high school buddies. That was a trip." She laughed.

"Mom and Dad grounded you for a month," Kathleen reminded her.

"It was totally worth it," Liz said, her gaze soft with memories.

I checked my phone. "We're almost there. It's coming up on the left in about a mile."

"Be sure to give me plenty of warning," Kathleen said.

"I just did."

"When you see the sign. Make sure to tell me when you see the sign."

"What if they don't have a sign?" Liz asked—unhelpfully, at least in my opinion.

"Then you'll just need to tell me when you see the street."

"What if it isn't—"

I raised my hand to stop Liz's endless stream of "what-if" questions. She'd developed the habit at seven and had never given it up.

It's too bad she'd never considered using the questions on her own life.

I leaned forward and stared through the windshield at the road ahead. Patterns of sunshine and shadows made it difficult to quickly discern what I was seeing. A break came in the trees and centered in its space was a big, vibrant, blessed sign.

"There," I said, pointing. "Turn left there."

Kathleen turned on her blinker then slowly rolled to a stop, peering down the road for oncoming traffic.

The road north was empty.

She turned the wheel and the rig made a slow turn into the roadway.

Behind us, a long row of cars streamed past.

I was too busy looking backward to notice the stop sign until Kathleen braked suddenly, and I was thrown against the seatbelt.

"Kathleen!" I yelled.

"It's a stop sign," she said. "I stopped."

I took a deep breath and checked to see if Liz was okay.

She'd apparently seen the sign and had braced herself.

"There's the office." Kathleen pointed to a stained log structure.

I picked up my purse. In the division of duties, reservations and checking in had fallen to me as I was deemed the most internet and financially savvy.

The office was part of the store, which was filled to the brim with everything an East Coast tourist could want, including candy masquerading as bear poop and hats with moose antlers. Here and there were actual treasures: locally handcrafted pottery and watercolors of the Grand Canyon of the Yellowstone.

"We're checking in," I told the woman behind the counter and gave her the name and confirmation number of the reservation.

"Ah, yes. Welcome to Happy Trails Resort," the woman said with a perky smile.

Why did park owners use lame names and hire well-preserved cheerleaders to staff the counter? The woman didn't appear to be too much younger than I was, but her hair was colored and styled, make-up fresh. Pretty earrings dangled from her lobes.

My gray hair needed a cut and I had no idea where my make-up bag was.

I could also stand to lose a few pounds.

I'd start every morning with a brisk walk, I vowed.

"Ah, here you are," she said.

A few minutes later, I walked out with a map, a list of rules, and several brochures of things to see in the area that weren't Yellowstone National Park.

After clambering back into my seat, I told Kathleen how to get to the site. The places were laid out in rows with a big loop that encompassed the entire area. We had a site at the end of a row that contained sites numbered twenty-one through thirty.

"Turn there," I said when we got to the row.

Kathleen sailed right past.

"You missed it."

"You didn't give me enough warning," she huffed. "I'll get it on the backside."

We made the loop and she entered the row marked thirty-one through forty from the other side and pulled into our site.

"All the other RVs are pointed the other way," Liz observed.

"So we're rebels," Kathleen said. "Can you check to see if we're too close to the hookups to put out the sliders?"

Muffling my sigh, I once again got out of the rig and looked around our space. There was a picnic table, but that was it. Nothing that held a large outlet or spigot.

I stood on the steps that automatically came out when the door was opened. I loved this feature. In fact, I had opened and closed the door several times before we bought the rig just to marvel at this mechanical wonder.

"There are no hookups," I announced to Kathleen.

"That can't be," she said and shook her head. "I swear, Diane, I can't count on you for anything." Her tone went back to our teenage years and brought the same reaction from me.

Mentally, I gave her the finger. Then I stepped aside to let her prove her own idiocy to herself.

"Huh," she said, hands on her hips.

She walked around the other side, and I followed, peering around the rig as she stared at the post with the hookups she'd been looking for.

Then she returned to the side with our picnic table.

"Huh," she repeated

Across the way at the next site, an older man sat in a camp chair in the shade of his rig. He was pretending to look at his phone, but his gaze flitted between it and the woman standing by the picnic table.

"Guess we better turn it around," Kathleen said, stomping back to the RV.

On this model, the RV door hissed gently closed. A good thing because back in the day Kathleen had been the master of slamming doors.

She pulled out and went around the top of the loop and into the row marked twenty-one through thirty.

When she got to our spot, she brought the rig to a halt and stared.

We were at the wrong angle.

With a huff, she pulled to the end of the row and stared ahead.

I held my breath.

Liz was quiet, too.

Finally, Kathleen pulled out, turned right, went all around the loop, then pulled into the correct row and parked.

I looked over to where our new neighbor sat.

He gave a thumbs up and a grin.

Kathleen hesitated a few moments before following me out of the RV.

"Glad to see you finally figured it out," the man called

over.

She ignored him and opened the compartment door to get the wheel chucks.

They were thoroughly pounded in next to the tires while I used the automatic devices to level the trailer before hooking up the electric and cable.

Water—both sides of it—were Kathleen's department. She'd told us she'd been dealing with manure for decades, so dumping the trailer's black water and gray water holding tanks into the RV park's sewer was just another day's work.

I was more than happy to let that chore go.

But guilt nagged at me as well. For almost three decades, Kathleen and her husband had managed the family ranch, a ranch that belonged to all three of us. She and Michael had received a salary from the living trust that owned the property, but I'd walked away from Silver Bow County after high school and was content only to show up for the odd holiday and our parents' funerals.

I'd pushed for the year-long RV trip to renew the close feelings I'd once felt with my siblings.

I only hoped my plan worked.

# Chapter Two

"Our first dinner together on our trip!" Liz announced as she put a bowl of salad and another bowl of her homemade baked beans on the small dinette in the RV. "Ham was on special at the IGA before we left, so I got a big one and cut it up."

"You are one to spot a bargain," Kathleen said with a smile.

"And look, there's even biscuits!"

"You made biscuits from scratch?" I asked. "We haven't been here that long."

"No, silly, from a can. They were on sale, too."

"Liz cooked for me and Michael most nights," Kathleen said. "Especially during calving season and roundup. Although she was a good hand to have around when we had to get those cattle to go where we wanted."

"Remember that one time?" Liz began as she sat down. "That cow was having none of the chute. She'd get up close, just enough to think you had her this time, then veer off at the last minute."

"You had to lasso her and lead her down the chute while Michael pushed from behind." Kathleen laughed. "We had some good times during roundup. We sure did."

Abruptly, her laughter stopped and she reached for the baked beans.

Michael had been gone a little over a year. It was obvious she still missed him.

On the other hand, I didn't miss my ex one bit. Not one iota. Not even for a nanosecond.

Life was much better without Larry's constant put downs or the rising volume of the TV as his hearing gradually worsened. Nope. I didn't miss him and had no intention of repeating the experiment again. I was done with men in this lifetime. Only a fool would take up caring for a man at sixty-five, and my mama didn't raise no fools.

"When are we going into the park?" Liz asked as she helped herself to a hunk of ham. "I want to see the geysers and the mud pots. All that power under the ground. Do you know Yellowstone is actually one big volcano? It would be awesome if it ever blew. Terrible. But awesome."

"I can skip that event," Kathleen said, as she passed the beans to me.

After putting a small amount on my plate, I put the bowl back on the table. It wasn't that I didn't like Liz's beans; I liked them too much. The doctor had already put me on high cholesterol medication, and I didn't want it to get any worse. In fact, I was already up to two pills a day, not counting the vitamins I downed daily.

"Stop counting calories," Kathleen muttered.

"Well, I can't eat like you. I've got a desk job."

"We've all got desk jobs now," Liz said. "That's why it's going to be important to walk around a lot. There are lots of boardwalks by the mud pots."

"Mud pots stink," Kathleen said.

"Maybe," Liz said, undaunted. "But we're going. That first guy—well, white guy—that stumbled across the geysers and all, he thought it was hell."

"Colter's Hell," I said. Facts had always had a special place in my brain. The more useless they were, the more they tended to stick.

"That's it!" Liz shook her head. "I never know how you remember all that stuff."

I took a bite of the baked beans. They were better than I'd remembered. I must have groaned because Kathleen gave me the side eye.

The next bite I took was bigger and almost finished what was on my plate.

I was definitely going back for seconds.

"So from here we're going to Jackson Hole for a few days, then to Moab, then head east to see the foliage, right?" Liz asked.

"Yes, we're all set for reservations," I responded. For

months before we left I was calculating miles and making reservations. We were set through the fall when we hoped to be in New England, the cradle of the revolution. I was looking forward to it. Every school kid in Montana knew pretty much everywhere Lewis and Clark laid their weary heads, but Boston could be in the middle of the Atlantic for all we knew.

"And the Hudson River," Liz said softly. "I want to see where those painters worked. And maybe do some of my own. We have enough time, don't we?"

I smiled at her. "We have plenty of time. You can paint to your heart's content."

"There will be enough time then," she said.

For a moment I wasn't sure she was talking about painting.

"What are you working on these days?" I asked. "Have you sold anything recently?" I knew Liz made her living selling her paintings, but I'd long been fuzzy on the details.

"A few things here and there," Liz said vaguely. "I'm trying a new style, but the gallery that usually buys is being resistant. I've sold a few from my website."

Website? My sister had a website?

"Don't bother looking for it," Kathleen said. "She paints under an assumed name. I've tried for thirty years to get it from her, but she should have been a spy, she's so tight-lipped."

"For heaven's sake, why?" I asked.

"Because it's the way I want it," Liz said firmly. "Now make sure you eat your salad. Got to get some greens in you."

I obediently put a heaping helping of salad on my plate and passed the bowl to Kathleen.

"Is she always this much of a tyrant?" I asked.

"Uh-huh."

"Then why were we protecting her all those years?" I asked. "Who's protecting us from her?"

"Good question," Kathleen said. "Maybe it should be a cucumber shoot-out at dawn to see who can take her down?"

"Tomatoes would be better."

"Not tomato season yet."

"Good point."

"I'm ignoring you!" Liz sang out, then dug into her salad and chewed away while staring at us, her expression rather like Peter Rabbit's after he'd once again escaped the wrath of Mr. MacGregor.

Kathleen and I looked at each other, shrugged, and stuck forks into our own greens.

It was good to be back with family.

~~~

"Are you sure you know how to operate this thing?" Kathleen asked as I set the smokeless fire pit up in the center of our chairs.

I was especially proud of my new acquisition. It had been pricey, but I had envisioned hours around the campfire with my sisters, talking about our childhoods and catching up on the missed years as adults. And maybe roasting a marshmallow or two.

YouTube videos and the excellent instructions provided by the manufacturer made me confident.

"I'm sure I can handle it."

Using the logs the camp store had delivered that afternoon, I set up the teepee just as I'd been taught in Girl Scouts. I'd purchased the special fire-starter material at the same time I'd gotten the grill. Around the logs I carefully tucked what looked like a mass of Ramen noodles from one of the cheap packages college students consume.

I was just about to start the fire when our neighbor came around the front of his RV. He was carrying a can and accompanied by a small furry dog. Our neighbor had arrived.

"I got just what you need," he said. "I was out walking my dog ... this is Hooch ... remember from the old TV show? Anyway, I saw you settin' up this fire, and I said to myself, Henry, I know just what these gals need."

He paused.

I was almost afraid to hear what came next. What
~~~

exactly was it that he felt "us gals" needed that only a man could provide?

I shuddered.

"So I brought over my can of trusty lighter fluid. It'll start anything," he said. He took a step toward my brand new smokeless never-use-an-accelerant fire pit.

I rose from where I was sitting and held up my hand.

"Don't come any nearer," I warned, holding up my lighter stick. "I'm armed."

His face whitened, and he stepped back.

The dog started yapping.

I glared at it.

"Shh ... shh," he said. "Don't go botherin' the lady now."

"Oh, she's harmless," Liz said, standing and putting a hand on the man's arm. "It's so nice to meet you. We have an extra chair. Why don't you sit for a bit?" She led him to the chair and pried the lighter fluid from his hand, putting it on the picnic table.

"Where are you from, Henry?" she asked as she resumed her own seat.

"Oklahoma. Went up to Casper to work the oil fields there for a bit. I wanted to see the park before I drove home. Wonder of the world, you know. There weren't any sites south of here. Got one up here last minute. But I'll be headed home soon. The wife misses me."

"I bet she does," Liz said.

I rolled my eyes as I went back to work on the fire.

Soon the fire blazed and was almost smokeless.

"Well, I'll be darned," Henry said, and some of my testiness thawed. He'd meant well.

Proudly, I handed out the marshmallow sticks I'd also purchased and produced the bag of marshmallows. There was even a stick for Henry. I'd bought the large package in hopes we'd have guests. One of the things I'd hoped to do on this trip was make new friends.

In spite of living in one of the most vibrant areas of the country for the last two decades, my world had been shrinking every year, but had rapidly accelerated in the last ten. Because Larry and I had never had children, I'd never developed a clique of mommy-friends that lasted well beyond the kids leaving home. Building my accounting business meant spending time working, and my employees were the only circle of friends I had.

When I'd down-sized the business, my friends had downsized too.

After Larry retired, he demanded more of my time. I was constantly running errands, making meals, or doing laundry while he had to be reminded to take out the trash and arrange to have the lawn mowed.

And there were always the comments. Even though we'd done a few fertility tests before Larry said he wanted to stop, he took every chance he got to remind me that I wasn't a complete woman.

After a few years of therapy and the discovery of some papers Larry had hidden, I went directly to the sharpest divorce attorney in town, and she got me everything I'd asked for.

I left Larry his television.

"Your marshmallow is burning!" Liz said.

I yanked it from the flame and blew it out.

"I like it this way," I lied.

"No you don't," Kathleen said flatly.

I contemplated eating it anyway; I'd been raised on "waste not, want not."

"Don't you dare," Liz said, a fierce look in her eye. "It's *one* marshmallow."

It was a struggle, but I used a napkin to pull it off the stick and put on a fresh one. Then I returned it to the flames, keeping a good eye on it this time.

~~~

After two marshmallows, the cloying sweetness got to me. "I'm going for a walk," I announced in a tone that indicated I was doing it alone.

I walked away from the main part of the RV park, away from the lights and the people. This is what I'd missed most after I'd left Montana: the ability to quickly get away from
~~~

civilization and breathe in the sweet air of nature. Above me, stars twinkled clearly, and the Milky Way scattered solar systems like so much pixie dust. If only I could feel as mentally unencumbered as the animals that must be nearby. My mind was constantly beset by worry. What if there isn't enough? Enough water? Enough time? Enough laughter?

Enough money?

I'd always been excellent at saving for a rainy day, quite sure one would come someday. But what would life be like if I could let go of that sense of emergency always nipping at my heels? Wonderful? Or terrifying?

I shook my head free of wonderings and turned back toward the camp. As I did so, I caught site of a man sitting by his Airstream RV, leaning back and staring at the sky much as I had done. He must have sensed my presence, because he looked over.

Something about the way he moved was familiar.

Nah, just my tired imagination working overtime.

I gave him a friendly wave and turned away.

# Chapter Three

"Is tomorrow a good day for the mud pots?" Liz asked as we shuffled through the sinks—thankfully there were two—and toilet to get ready for bed. Liz and Kathleen shared the bedroom in the back, while I was stuck making the sofa into a bed every night.

It had seemed logical at the time because I'm a restless sleeper, but the reality was already something I wasn't looking forward to doing every night for the next year.

And it was only the first night.

As I put on my nightly moisturizer, I answered Liz's question. "I've got a call with a client tomorrow to go over his quarterly taxes," I said. "He couldn't schedule it any other time."

"I thought you were giving up your clients," Kathleen said as she emerged from the tiny toilet room.

We'd probably get used to being on top of each other all the time, but I was willing my bowels to behave until the other two went to bed so I'd have the illusion of privacy. My body had always made noises at the most inappropriate times, and age hadn't improved its disposition.

"A few of them wouldn't take no for an answer," I said. "Besides, I enjoy the work. I can't see myself sitting around all day crocheting doilies." As soon as the words were out of my mouth, I regretted them. A decade ago Kathleen had taken up both knitting and crocheting. She produced amazing garments to wear, and had even sold some at a local artists' consignment shop.

"You should take up a hobby," Liz said before things could get out of hand. "Then you wouldn't be bored. Unless you need the money."

The toothpaste tube in my hand protested as my grip tightened. The lid, which I'd already loosened flew off and pinged into the other sink, just missing Liz.

She looked down, then shook her head.

"No need to get all dramatic about it," she said with a grin.

"Sorry," I said, retrieving the cap.

"So," Kathleen said, "are you really worried about money? I thought you made out in the settlement."

"I'm not worried about money," I declared, putting a large dab of toothpaste on my brush. "Like Liz said, I just don't want to be bored. And having an extra bit of cash around doesn't hurt." I tried to make my voice light, to hide the tight fist of fear that lived in my gut. The one that made me constantly aware that things could, and would, go wrong. I'd adopted Murphy's Law as part of my catechism years ago. "We'll go see your mud pots the day after, okay? What's so exciting about them anyway?"

"The colors," Liz said. "The way the heat interacts with the composition of the soil produces these incredibly subtle hues. Imagine hundreds of shades of brown." Her face lit up with the possibilities. "I want to look at them closely, take some pictures, then play with them in my paintings. It will be like going to an art class."

I loved my sister. I didn't always understand her, but I loved her enthusiasm for the art world. Even when we were kids she'd produced the most amazing drawings and paintings.

"Will we get to see these experimental pieces in brown?" I asked.

"Maybe."

Why was she so secretive about her work?

"I hope so," Kathleen said. "Now will you two stop hogging the sinks so I can get in there?"

~~~

My sleep had been dominated by hissing water bubbling from the ground, a world from which I couldn't escape. I was grateful when sounds from the back bedroom woke me, although it took my brain a while to clear its mind from the
~~~

fog of sleep and grapple with the unfamiliar surroundings. Outside, doves were cooing their repetitive song and in the distance, a meadowlark trilled. Soft conversations from other RV sites drifted through the window.

I stretched and swung my legs out of bed. After pulling some pants on under my nightgown, I swiftly changed it for a T-shirt.

By the time I got done in the bathroom, Liz was starting the coffee maker. She was still in pajamas.

"Bless you," I said. "I forgot to hit the switch."

"Tough night?" she asked.

"Crazy dreams about mud pots."

"Sorry about that." She grinned. "Kathleen's up, too. She claimed the shower first."

"That's because she's memorized how much hot water we have," I said.

"Probably. I don't mind going last. I like to read in the morning and do some stretches."

"Where are you going to do them here?" I asked, eyeing the cramped quarters.

"I'll take my mat outside. I mean, sun salutations were meant to be done in the sun."

"I suppose." Yoga had never appealed to me. Kathleen and I had gotten our father's squatter body shape, while Liz had developed more like our mother: petite and thin.

Not that I was jealous at all.

"I know we said we'd take care of our own breakfast," Liz said. "But since today is our first day, I decided to make us pancakes. You up for that?"

"Bacon too?" I asked as she took the package from the small fridge.

As I'd gotten older, bacon had become as seductive as rich dark chocolate.

"Yes," she said. "Now get your coffee and leave me alone."

"Yes, ma'am." Pancakes *and* bacon. Too bad Liz didn't want to do that every day. Probably just as well. I didn't need the ten extra pounds I'd gain.

"Ah, coffee," Kathleen said as she emerged from the

back bedroom, dressed in jeans and a T-shirt, not dissimilar from my outfit. Our mother hadn't been a fashion guru, and neither were we. I'd don the basic business casual for my job and business events in California, but I was only too happy to give up the uniform for comfort.

"After breakfast, I'm going to go into town to get some things," Kathleen said as she sat in one of the dinette chairs. "Henry told me about a bunch of little gadgets that will make working with the water and sewer lines easier."

I bit my tongue to keep from asking how much these gadgets were going to cost. Instead, I grabbed clean underwear and headed to the shower, before beginning my work.

Despite my offer to help, Liz cleaned up the kitchen then went outside to do her exercises. As tall men walked by with their short dogs, they took a moment to check out her positions.

When I finished work a few hours later, I leaned back in the chair, my back muscles stiff from its unfamiliar curves and angles. A walk would do me good.

Liz was long done with her yoga and shower. She'd muttered something at me as she'd left the rig with a satchel of some kind, but I'd been deep into trying to understand why the balance sheet for my client had bad numbers. I had no idea what she'd told me.

Once I pulled up the shade, I saw Kathleen ensconced in her chair, coffee mug in hand, her e-book lying on the table next to her as she chatted to a woman who'd taken over my seat. I smiled. It was good to see my sister enjoying herself. Tending to her husband as Michael slowly succumbed to cancer had been hard on her. Although something I'd seen or heard had given me the sense that all hadn't been well with the pair for a while before he was diagnosed.

Automatically, I slid my phone in my back pocket and headed for the door, passing the trash which was threatening to overflow.

Oh yeah, that was my job.

I bundled it up, then walked out the door, stopping a few moments to chat with Kathleen and her new friend.

"Any idea where Liz is?" I asked.

"Off drawing or painting somewhere. It's the same routine she followed at home. If the weather was nice, she was out right after breakfast and didn't return until lunch. Sometimes in the summer, she'd be gone as soon as the sun was up."

"Your sister's a painter, then?" the visitor asked. "Is she famous? Would I know her?"

"I have no idea," Kathleen said. "She paints under another name, and we've never been able to pry it out of her."

"That's odd," the woman said.

It was stranger now than when I'd first learned about it. We were her family. Why couldn't she tell us? Why was it such a big secret?

I held up the bag of trash. "I'll be back." I headed down the loop to where I believed the big dumpster would be. Kathleen called out something, but I ignored her as I puzzled over secrets.

There were a few of my own I hadn't shared with anyone. The pain of my marriage, how deeply Larry had cut me when he blamed me for our lack of children. The therapy I'd gone to again and again to cope with the news that I'd never be a mother. My dalliance with alcohol and valium to dull the ache.

No one needed to know that. It was in the past.

I absently waved and nodded to people as I made the loop, trying to remember where I'd seen the dumpster yesterday as Kathleen circled the park.

Kathleen. What had I heard about her and Michael? They'd been high school sweethearts, and their marriage had seemed solid. Had Liz said something? Or was there something on a social media site an old friend had posted that made me suspicious?

My normally fastidious mind was failing me.

Where was that dumpster?

I stopped in my tracks and looked around. As I did so, a pickup truck with a fifth-wheel behind it came roaring out of one of the rows. I barely made it off the pavement before the truck could hit me.

"Watch where you're going!" the driver yelled from the open window. "I coulda hit you!"

My hands on my hips and my mouth open, I stared as he continued his mad dash to the exit, ignoring the posted signs for a speed limit of ten point one miles an hour—cute but obviously not effective.

Jerks were everywhere these days. We weren't going to escape them in an RV park.

And from what I'd read online about visitors to Yellowstone, we weren't going to escape them there, either.

"We're not all like that," a man said as he washed the huge windows in the front of his motorhome. "I knew as soon as he got here, he was going to be like that. You can tell by the way people get into their site. Newbies are hesitant. Couples who've been on the road too long yell at each other. Jerks spin gravel as they run their rig back and forth to make sure they're in the optimum place."

"We're newbies."

"Yeah," he said with a grin. "I kinda got that the third time you guys went around the loop."

It didn't look like we were going to live that down.

"Don't worry. You'll get the hang of it." He waved and went back to his window.

I continued my walk. Where was that damn dumpster? Were the O'Sullivan sisters going to be condemned to go around this loop forever?

There it was.

As I walked toward it, I realized there was a man standing in front of it. He was absolutely still, as if caught in a trance. He must have heard me because as I got closer, he turned.

Twenty-seven years had passed since I'd last seen him, but there was no doubt who he was. To paraphrase an old movie.

*Of all the dumpsters in all the towns in all the world, he's staring at mine.*

"Joe Kelly," I said. "What are you doing here?"

# Chapter Four

"Diane O'Sullivan," Joe said, his voice rich with wonder. "How wonderful to see you. It's as if I conjured up the best thing that could have happened to me simply by wishing on a lucky charm."

Wow. Just wow. Who says something like that? And why did it feel so good?

Then I remembered where we were.

"Garbage is your lucky charm?" I asked.

"Treasure can be found in the oddest places."

I gazed at the rusted blue container, brimming over with plastic bags, boxes from Amazon, and large boxes used to lug home groceries from warehouse stores. The box nearest to us had been used to contain four gallon jars of bread and butter pickles.

Who needed that many pickles?

Joe grinned and began to recite:

> "There once was a pile of trash
> Made all campers dash
> But if you just held your nose
> And wiggled your toes
> The bottom was loaded with cash."

I had to laugh, bad as it was. "That was really horrible," I told him. "You haven't improved since high school." At least once a week Joe would come up with a really bad limerick that he'd recite in the middle of class or torment me with on the bus ride home.

"My students thought they were funny."

"Funny? Or did they just groan?" I asked.

"Groan? Diane, you cut me to the quick!" He pounded his fist against his chest and opened his mouth in dramatic excess.

I reverted to being a teenager and rolled my eyes.

"Yeah. You're right. They groaned." He grinned again.

I looked at him for a few moments, taking in the sight of him, comparing him to the young man who'd sat next to me in senior year history. The guy who'd taken me to senior prom. The guy I'd never looked at again after that night.

The line of his jaw was softer, but the planes of his face were still strong. In spite of his undeniable Irish roots, something about the profile of his face resembled the visage of Alexander the Great on old Roman coins.

He'd been kind, smart, and in love with me. Or at least I had thought so.

"Here, let me help you with that," Joe said and tugged the trash from my hand. He tossed it to the top of the heap. "It's really good to see you. How are you?"

"Good," I said. "Fine."

"I'm glad." He started walking away from the dumpster. Then he stopped. "You coming? Or do you need to spend your own meditative time with the trash?"

"I'm coming," I said with a laugh and caught up with him.

"Want some tea?" he asked. "I've got some sun tea back at the site. We could sit and catch up."

"I really should—" I stopped abruptly as I spotted a bunny from the corner of my eye. Yanking my phone from my back pocket, I prayed it would stay put until I pulled up the camera on my phone and took the picture.

It was a cooperative rabbit.

After a few snaps, I put it back in my pocket.

"You still like to take pictures," he said as we ambled away from the dumpster. "I always thought you'd become a great photographer someday. You had a really good eye."

"I owned my own accounting firm," I said.

"Accounting's good, too. We need someone to figure out taxes. Lord knows I never could. Thankfully, Patti did. She was good with investments, too."

"She's your wife?" I wasn't sure which tense to use.

"Was. She passed away about ten years ago. Cancer."

His Adam's apple moved as he swallowed.

"I'm sorry."

He waved it away. "It was a long time ago."

"You must have loved her very much."

"I did. I still do in a way." He glanced at me. "Not in a way that keeps me from living my life, but you can't forget someone you spent decades with, no matter what happened."

I nodded, although I didn't really understand.

"And you?" he asked.

"Divorced. Two years now." I hoped the terse tone would keep him from asking any more questions.

He touched my arm and pointed to a limb high in a nearby pine. At the outside edge of a branch, a familiar shape perched. I reached for my phone, but knew it wasn't going to be possible to get the shot I really wanted. Still, it was sweet of Joe to point him out.

I took a few pictures of the eagle.

"Let me see," he said.

Even he would be able to tell the images weren't in a sharp focus.

"You still have an eye," he said. "What you need is a camera that suits it."

"It's just a thing I do," I told him. "No need to spend a lot of money on something that's only a hobby." As I said the words, I recognized the echo of my ex's comments.

But he'd been right. Spending several thousand dollars on a camera and lenses didn't make sense if I was an accountant.

"It's not just a thing you do." Joe turned to face me. "It's a gift. Talents shouldn't be ignored. Not everything has to make money just to be worthwhile."

I forced a shrug, then started walking again, my mind grasping for a different topic.

"Did you have children?" I blurted out, before remembering what a mine field that question was.

"Two," he said proudly. "Joe teaches English at the university in Dillon. Tess is finishing up her masters at MIT."

"MIT?" I asked. "Cambridge, Massachusetts? *That* MIT?"

"Yep." If there had been buttons on Joe's shirt, they would have popped right off. "Got her smarts from her mother. Joe takes after me."

"Joe Junior?"

"The third. He hates it. But my dad was pleased as punch."

"You always got along with your dad."

"Still do. He and Mom still live in the same house. Neighborhood's one of those places stuck in time. Know what I mean?"

I nodded. There were those places everywhere in Montana. Even in big cities like Butte, one could easily identify the time periods when houses were first erected. Joe had lived on the outskirts, in a section built in the 1940s, while our ranch was further out of town. In high school my bus route had been changed to pick up the kids from his neighborhood, and our friendship, established in junior high, had deepened.

"Your folks?" he asked.

"Gone for a while now. Kathleen—my younger sister— took over the ranch. Liz—she's the youngest—has a small house on the property, too."

"Who's taking care of the cattle while you're RVing?" he asked.

"We sold the cattle, kept the two houses and acreage. Someone's managing it for us. Now we're on our great adventure." I clutched onto the present. No more meandering around in the mucky murk of maudlin memories.

I'd put my purple prose up against Joe's limericks any day.

"What's so funny?" he asked.

"Inside joke." I grinned.

"Have it your way." We walked down the park road, and, in spite of my vow, the past crept back in. Joe and I had walked forever through the mountains next to Butte. We were just friends meeting up on a Saturday morning to get outside.

At least that's what we'd told ourselves.

We reached his spot. Somehow I wasn't surprised to see that it was the Airstream RV I'd noticed the night before. A big jug of sun tea was sitting on the picnic table.

"I'll get glasses and ice," he said, indicating the camp chairs he had set up. "Have a seat. Make yourself comfortable."

As soon as he went inside, my phone buzzed.

"Where are you?" Kathleen asked. "Did you fall in?"

"Ha, ha," I replied. "Just taking a walk."

"I can see you. You aren't walking."

I swiveled in my chair. Sure enough I could see the back end of our RV from where I sat.

Kathleen waved.

I didn't wave back.

"MYOB," I typed, proud of my awesome texting skills.

Joe came out of the door with two glasses filed to the brim with ice.

My phone dinged.

I ignored it. Then I got up and shifted my chair a little so my back was to Kathleen.

I'd forgotten how nosy she was.

"Here you go," Joe said placing a glass on the small table next to me before sitting in his own chair and taking a long drink from his glass.

He'd aged well. While his figure wasn't the painfully taut ropes of an obsessed athlete, he didn't have the small pot belly that many men carried at our age. He still stood erect and seemed to move about with the kind of ease I remembered from when he was a kid.

"You look good, too," he said.

"What do you mean?" I asked, flustered. I reached for the drink, something to hold onto, but I missed and instead set the glass rocking back and forth. I managed to grab it before it fell over completely.

My phone dinged.

I was going to kill Kathleen.

Joe laughed.

I might add him to my mad rampage.

"Come on, fess up," he said. "You were checking me out, weren't you?"

"Not in the least," I said.

"You're a terrible liar, Di. You always were." He gave me an appraising look. "You're looking good."

"No, I'm not," I said. "I'm overweight, my hair needs a styling, and I didn't get my make-up on."

"Don't do that," he said. "Don't put yourself down. Those things aren't important at all. What's important is the smile I saw when you realized who I was. The years fell away."

An ache bloomed in my gut, one that threatened to spill over with tears.

I went on the offensive.

"You always were over the top," I said. "Some people kiss the Blarney Stoney. You were born on top of it."

His laugh roared out.

"I've missed you," he said. "You were the only one who could dish it out like that."

"Like what?" I said innocently. "I don't know what you mean."

"Liar. You used to get me into all kinds of trouble in class."

"It was the other way around," I said. "You'd make some comment about what the teacher was saying and make it so I had no choice but to respond."

"You always had choices," he said.

"Not when you said something funny."

"Oh, so now you admit I was funny. You didn't like my limerick before."

"You should stick to things that don't rhyme."

"But rhymes add a zing ... a little like bling!"

I shook my head and took a sip from the glass I'd been clutching since I rescued it from myself.

"How long are you here?" I asked.

"About three more weeks. You?"

"About the same." I smiled. He'd be a fun companion when I needed to get away from my sisters.

"We'll have to do some things together then. Like old times."

Yes. Like old times. We could keep it light and friendly, just like we had when we were younger, never discussing anything more serious than whether we should take the left or right fork of the trail.

# Chapter Five

"I can drive," I told Liz as we prepared to leave early the next morning for Yellowstone. We'd been warned about the summer crowds by numerous people in the park.

"They've been worse since the pandemic," one of the park's employees had said. "It's like they think being outdoors in the park will save them from ever catching a virus." He shook his head. "I've been working here for the last ten years, and I've never seen it so bad. It's like people have lost their minds. They think the animals are pets. And that it would be fun to take a swim in the 'hot springs.'"

"No cure for stupid," Kathleen had replied.

"You got that right," he'd said before driving off in his maintenance cart.

We got our lunch cooler in the car and took our places with Liz riding shotgun, to make sure I treated her Jeep with loving care, and Kathleen sat in the back. The senior park pass I'd purchased as soon as I'd turned sixty-two sat in a cup holder, ready for entry.

There was already a buildup of traffic at the entrance gate, but it wasn't as bad as I'd heard it would be later. And that didn't count the visitors who were already in the park, camping or staying at one of the hotels.

After about fifteen minutes we were through and driving eastward toward the road that looped through the park. The magic of Yellowstone began to seep into my bones. No matter how many people overran the terrain, there was no place like it on earth. Even Disney couldn't compete in my mind.

"An eagle!" Liz said as she pointed.

"Two," I said as I spotted the white heads high in the branches of a lodgepole pine. As we drove by, one of the pair pushed off from the branch, soared for a moment before diving across the road in front of us and reaching toward the earth with its powerful talons.

Like every other human in the park, I slowed down to watch, earning a glare from a driver who sped around us. I pulled onto the shoulder.

Beside us the eagle twisted this way and that, before delivering the final blow with his sharp beak. A moment later he rose, the massive wings straining to achieve liftoff, a limp rabbit in his talons. We watched him land on a tree where he secured the carcass in the fork of two branches before preceding to eat.

"It's kind of brutal," I said.

"It's just nature," Kathleen said. "Like gutting a deer."

While I'd never developed a love for hunting, for years my sister had gone out and gotten her deer for the freezer. She'd also gotten into the habit of spending a few days a month fishing during the season. Her rods and gear were packed into a storage compartment in the RV.

I pulled back onto the road.

There was a short wait at the stop sign where the road to Old Faithful intersected, but soon we were parallel to the Gibbon River.

"Are we going to stop at the falls?" Liz asked.

"I thought you wanted to go to the Artists Paint Pots," I said.

"I do. But I want to see this, too," Liz protested.

"The parking lot is on the right hand side. Might be easier now," Kathleen added.

"The parking lot near the pots fills up fast," I reminded them. "It's why we left early. But it's up to you."

"We can get back to this pullout later," Liz said after a few moments of hesitation.

The falls were visible from the car and my sisters rhapsodized over their beauty as I kept my eyes on the road. With no regard for traffic, a man dashed into the road, causing me to slam on my brakes.

"Idiot!" I yelled.

"Better get used to it," Kathleen said.

I took a deep breath and started up again.

The parking lot was half full when we got there.

"God, it stinks!" Kathleen said when she got out.

"Sulphur," I said. "We are at the edge of the volcano." Right before we'd reached the lot, a sign had announced the edge of the caldera. "It's a half mile hike. We should take water. And make sure you have your phones."

"What are you, the Girl Scout leader?" Kathleen asked.

"She's the oldest," Liz said. "It's in her job description."

"Did you ever listen to her?" Kathleen asked.

"Well, yes."

"But then you did what you wanted anyway," I commented.

"I'm not doing things just because you say so anymore, Bossypants," Kathleen announced before grabbing her water bottle and shoving her phone in her back pocket.

Without any more comments, we walked to the beginning of the path that led to the boardwalk surrounding the field of bubbling mud, steam vents, and whatever else the earth was spewing forth. Steam rose from beyond a screen of trees. When we reached the edge of the field, I stopped.

Spread out before me in circles, ripples, and splotches was the most amazing landscape I'd ever seen. While I'd been through Yellowstone a few times, I'd never stopped to give it the attention it deserved.

"Oh, my," Kathleen said.

"I have to paint this," Liz said. "I don't know how, but there has to be some way."

I reached for my phone, knowing in my heart it wasn't going to do the place justice. I needed a better camera to capture the depth and textures I saw. But a camera was just one more thing to lug around. Larry had been right about that. A phone did just fine.

We started down the path, stopping as every new wonder was laid out in front of us. Mud tinted with blues and greens, mottled with sections of orange and yellow that oozed beside us. Bacteria gave it color, a nearby sign told us. White crusty earth surrounded a vent with water tinted a baby blue. Gentle steam rose from within, making it look like an inviting hot tub.

Another informative sign reminded us that it was 185 degrees Fahrenheit, close to boiling. Not much could live in that temperature, and we were instructed to stay on the boardwalk.

In spite of the smell, the place mesmerized me, and I could see Liz was totally immersed. Kathleen looked around, but I could tell her practical soul couldn't see the point of it all.

A pond of bubbling gray-white mud caught my eye. It looked like a monster was roaming around under the slime, blowing bubbles that occasionally burst into thick droplets. I crouched down to take a picture with the phone, once again longing for a camera. I tried a few different settings with the phone and was about to get up when I felt the boards shake as someone pounded down the boardwalk at a rapid pace.

I looked over my shoulder. A lanky, awkward teen was striding toward me, his head down as he stared at his phone. Behind him, his parents strolled, seemingly unconcerned about their child.

He ran into me when I was balanced precariously, getting up from my crouch.

My arms flailed as I tried to regain my footing, images of a painful death by boiling water running through my mind. I clutched my phone desperately, determined not to lose it.

Someone grabbed onto my arm.

"I've got you!" Kathleen yelled. "Stop moving!"

"I'm trying," I said, trying to compensate as she tugged me in a direction opposite from where my body had been intending to go. I threw myself back in her direction and landed on my butt.

"Oh!"

"You okay?" Liz asked.

I never knew my posterior could hurt so badly.

"Yeah, I suppose," I said, trying to determine the most graceful way to get up without completing my tumble into the cauldron. My options weren't pretty.

"Looks like you took a tumble," a man said with false

humor.

"No thanks to your son." Kathleen moved so she was nose to nose with him. "And not even a sorry or an offer to help. He just kept walking."

"Well, you know teens these days ..." the woman said with a twittered laugh.

"Hmph. What I know is parents these days. Get your kid some manners." As she stood there, Kathleen seemed to loom bigger than she was.

"And we don't need your help," Liz added, holding out her hand to me.

I shook my head and flipped to my hands and knees before struggling to a standing position.

The three of us stood shoulder to shoulder, forcing the couple to walk single file around us.

We stared after them.

Beyond, a ranger had caught up with the boy and was giving him a stern lecture.

We high-fived and continued on our way.

~~~

We'd been able to snag a picnic table by Gibbon Falls. As usual, Liz had prepared a feast. She insisted we lay out the handspun tablecloth and arranged a selection of sandwiches on a plastic plate. Bowls of potato salad and green salad sat along shallow dishes of two kinds of pickles and olives. A choice of ice tea and fruit drinks lay next to a promise of brownies for dessert.

"You took up the wrong occupation," I said. "You should have been a caterer."

"It's simply art in a different form," she replied.

I took another look at what she'd laid out and realized even the placement of everything had an artistic touch.

"Well, you two can admire the food as much as you want. I'm hungry." Kathleen reached for a sandwich.

Liz and I laughed and dug in as well.

It was only as I was going after a second helping of potato salad that Kathleen launched her ambush.
~~~

"So how is Joe Kelly these days?" she asked with a fake casualness that told me how long she'd been planning the attack.

"Who's Joe Kelly?" Liz asked.

"Diane's old boyfriend."

"He was not," I protested. "We were just friends, that's all."

"Keep telling yourself that. But now that you've run into each other, you can give him a second chance. You could never see the poor boy was nuts over you."

That's what I'd thought too. But on the night of the senior prom, he'd proved me wrong.

"Just a coincidence," I said. "We'll be here together for a few weeks, then he'll be on his way. I doubt I'll ever see him again."

"But what an opportunity," Kathleen said. She picked up a pickle spear and held it partway into her mouth before snapping off the end with her teeth.

I shuddered at the image that crept into my mind.

"You should go out with him," Liz urged. She'd obviously missed Kathleen's obscene action. "It's been a while since you and Larry divorced."

"I'm beyond all of that," I said. "Done with men. Besides we've got the next year planned for our adventure."

"Oh, don't say that," Liz protested. "I know you and Larry weren't all that happy. I think the right man is waiting out there for you."

While I wanted to tell her to mind her own beeswax, I could never be harsh with Liz. She'd always seemed a little fragile.

"I'm sure you two could find something to do," Kathleen said.

She would not let it go.

"We did talk about doing a few things together," I said. "I'll be sure to announce it when we take a walk so you can get there ahead of us to spy."

"I wasn't spying last night," she protested.

"Right." I pushed my plate away. I didn't need any more potato salad. Just as well she interrupted me.  "We were friends then, and that's all we're going to be now."

"There was a disappointing lack of kissy-face," she said with an exaggerated sigh.

I looked over at her. How far was she going to push this?

Liz started laughing.

"You guys," she said with a shake of her head. "I'd forgotten how you two could get." She looked at me. "Don't put any rules on your relationship with Joe. We can adapt, no matter what." Then she turned to Kathleen. "And you. Leave her alone."

"Spoil sport," Kathleen said.

"Hush."

I let a smile return to my own face, but inside I strengthened my resolve. This year was for me and my sisters. No man was going to change our time together.

# Chapter Six

Kathleen's comment about Joe being nuts over me in high school played over in my mind as I drove back to the RV park. It forced me back to a time I'd firmly put in the rearview mirror decades ago.

Joe and I had been seated next to each other in junior high English; the teacher's effort to maintain some classroom order by putting us boy-girl-boy. He'd been a bit of a cut-up, clearly quick with words and a sense of the depths language could plumb. I hadn't been quite sure what to make of him.

In pre-algebra, our roles were somewhat reversed. Numbers always came easily for me, and manipulating letters as if they were integers seemed logical. It had been an alien world to Joe. When we realized we were in the same study hall, we petitioned the teacher frequently to study together.

The next year we'd gone our separate ways in classes, only to have our classes intersect again in high school social studies. This turned out to be a shared passion, each of us willing to drill down to see how actions of the past had created the present. Somewhere in our senior year during an honors class on current events, we'd both come to the conclusion that it took a great deal of effort to get humanity out of its circular rut of war, treaties, a short peace, broken promises, and a return to war.

Those were the topics that had kept us talking during our long walks in the three mountain ranges surrounding Butte's valley.

Had we held hands?

It seemed to me we had, but the memory was vague, as if the event was a natural outcoming rather than a momentous event.

But there had been a kiss, hadn't there?

No, no. The only kiss had been the disastrous one on our last night together after prom.

"Don't forget to turn," Kathleen said as I idled at a light in West Yellowstone.

I flipped on the turn signal.

"Other way," Liz said from behind me.

"Fumes must have gotten to her," Kathleen commented.

"Or the blow to her rear end reverberated in her brain."

I ignored them. My head wasn't in a space to play verbal badminton.

But I did pay more attention to where we were going.

Once we returned to the RV and cleaned up the lunch debris, Liz gathered her art papers and paints and departed to a solitary spot she'd found to try to capture the colors she'd seen on paper. Kathleen dug out a book and parked herself in one of the camp chairs.

I sat inside the camper, grateful for some time alone, but unsure what to do with myself. During my marriage, I'd either been doing everything I could to build the business, tending to the basics of living, or trying to figure out the right glue to finally stick our marriage together permanently. Occasionally, Larry and I traveled to see his relatives in Nevada, or up to see mine in Montana. We tried cruises, camping, and cities, but both of us had been more homebodies than travelers.

This trip was totally out of character for me.

But in the two years since I'd been divorced, I'd realized I'd spent my adult years being responsible. Larry did the minimum when we traveled, but the planning and details fell to me, mainly because I was good at it. I'd lost any sense of my needs or wants, or even the possibility of who I could become if set free.

No wonder I couldn't remember the details of my walks with Joe.

I picked up my phone to look at the pictures I'd taken during our day trip. I was glad Liz had gotten going to the mud pots out of her system, but I really wanted an early morning outing to the Lamar Valley, sometime before the hordes of people arrived and the big animals were still foraging for breakfast.

But as I looked at the pictures on my phone, my spirit deflated. They were okay, and some even better than that low bar, but they lacked the vision I'd seen in my mind's eye. I'd never be able to capture what I wanted with a simple phone.

A better camera was required.

The same excuses and resistance came up. I wasn't a photographer. I didn't deserve such fancy equipment. The phone would capture the animals well enough.

And good enough was fine for me.

Putting the phone down, I lay my head back on the headrest.

~~~

"I can't figure out how to light your campfire thingamajig," Kathleen complained as she woke me up.

"What?"

"The campfire in a can," she said. "It doesn't make sense to me. Why can't we just light a fire."

"First, because it keeps the smoke down." I ticked off the reasons I'd already recited a dozen times. "Second, it insures the fire is contained. Third, it's easier to clean. Fourth—"

"I got it," she said. "But you need to light it."

"Why?" I was comfortable right where I was. Maybe I could find some news on the television. See what was going on in the world.

"It's cocktail hour. And cocktail hour requires tradition."

"We've only been here a few days."

"See? It's tradition already."

I groaned and heaved myself out of my chair. If I didn't, my sister would just go on and on until I relented. May as well cut to the chase.

A half-hour later we were seated in our chairs, drinks in our hands, each with plates of nibbles that Liz had conjured out of nothing. At other sites people were settling into their
~~~

own end-of-day routines. Some, like us, were enjoying pre-dinner drinks; others were already preparing meals.

Then there were the amblers, the couples who took their cocktails and dogs on a walk around the loop, intent on making new friends wherever they could find them.

Kathleen waved at everyone who passed by. Some ventured closer and started up conversations. Liz kept talking about the amazing colors of the mud while Kathleen never missed an opportunity to retell the story of my fall. The noise my butt made when it hit the ground got louder with every retelling.

I sipped my cocktail and listened to the animated conversations, but my mind was still grinding away at the question of Joe Kelly. When the man himself appeared, I wasn't particularly surprised.

"Why, Joe Kelly," Kathleen said as if she hadn't known he was at the park. "Pull up a chair and join us. It's so nice to see someone from home out this way."

"Kathleen O'Sullivan," he said. "You haven't aged a day."

"Go on with you," she said, echoing the Irish lilt my dad had employed until the day he died.

He stopped in front of Liz. "I don't know if you remember me."

"Of course I do," she said. "You were Diane's friend."

"Still am, I hope." He favored me with a smile that brought a flash of heat to my entire body.

I shrugged. "It was a long time ago, but I'm sure we'll still get along."

Reserve masked his features for a second, then he smiled again. But it wasn't quite as bright and easy as it had been a few moments ago.

The sequence took me aback. Was he still interested after all these years?

Unimaginable.

"So where have you been off to today?" he asked, settling into a chair.

"We saw the mud pots!" Liz hadn't lost any of her enthusiasm. As she told Joe, in extreme detail, the colors and aspects of what we'd seen, he listened intently.

A memory arose. I'd been upset at something another girl at school had said to me. It had been mean and hit me to the core. I'd thought she was someone who'd liked me, and her betrayal hurt.

I'd finally blurted it all out on one of our walks. He'd sat me down on a nearby rock and listened. He didn't say much, or try to fix it, or worse, dismiss it like other people often did.

No. He'd sat there, sitting still with his gaze on me, just as he was doing for Liz right now.

He looked up at me then, and something stirred within my heart. It was as if I'd been sleepwalking through the last forty years and had been jolted awake.

His lips turned up at the edges, then he returned his attention to Liz.

I leaned back in my chair and stared up at the blue sky. What had happened?

Liz finished her story, and Kathleen immediately recited the tale of my almost-tumble into the boiling caldron.

Joe laughed at her description.

I glared at him.

"Can't help it," he said. "She tells it too well."

"That's because she's had hours of practice." I switched my gaze to my sister.

Kathleen simply shrugged.

"I'm laughing at the story," he said. "But I'm glad you're okay. There are too many people in the park who aren't aware of their surroundings, or even how to interact with the environment they're in. They come from a city or suburbia and expect the animals to behave like the neighborhood cat."

"True." Kathleen nodded. "Even in our area, especially with the hunters in the fall, some of them don't even understand basic courtesy. They think they can go blasting their guns anywhere without a friendly knock at the door."

"Montana's changing," Joe agreed.

"What were you up to today?" I asked, interrupting Kathleen's inevitable rant about how the state had deteriorated since we were kids in the 1970s.

"This and that," he said. "I got up early and went fishing."

"Fly or casting?" Kathleen asked.

"Fly. It's great when I catch one, but it isn't the purpose of fly fishing, is it?"

"So you got all duded up with that gear from Orvis and such?"

"Nah," Joe said with a grin. "Basic Bob Ward's waders. I've got a rod of my dad's. Some of the other stuff I picked up used here and there. Flies are about the only thing I buy new."

"I'm a casting gal, myself," Kathleen said.

I was tempted to close my eyes and take another nap.

"To each his ... or her ... own," Joe said gently. "Fly fishing is something my dad and I do whenever we get together."

I'd never had that. Kathleen had shadowed my dad, and Liz got her artistic talent from my mother. I'd been the odd kid out, in spite of being the oldest.

"How long are you planning on being on the road?" Liz asked him.

"Until mid-September," Joe replied. "That's when I get to move into my new cabin in Ennis."

"Big change from Butte," Kathleen said.

"It is. But I've been planning it for a while. I wanted a slower pace. And there's good fishing around there, too." Joe grinned as he rose from his seat. "Nice chatting. See you around." He nodded at Kathleen and Liz. "Don't forget we're going to see some sights together," he said to me.

With a wave, he headed back down the park road, giving me another chance to admire how he'd maintained the easy walk of his youth.

And the way his jeans fit.

"Ooooh!" Kathleen said. "There's still something between you two."

"You have an over-active imagination."

"I don't think so," she replied.

I got up and refreshed my drink. "Don't you have better things to do?"

"Not really," she said. "Without the ranch to take care of, I have all the time in the world to meddle."

"Well, meddle somewhere else. I'm done with men and love. I'm even taking a pass on lust."

Kathleen laughed. "I saw how you watched him walk down the road. You are soooo not done with lust."

"I don't need another project. And a man is *always* a project."

"You got that right," Kathleen said, raising her glass. "Here's to the O'Sullivan sisters, single and loving it for the rest of our days."

We drank, but Liz didn't join in.

"Is there something we don't know about?" Kathleen asked.

"Oh. No. Nothing." She took a sip of her drink. "It's just that ... well ... I'm not sure. I think ... no matter how old or sophisticated we think we are, love isn't ever done messing with us."

I had a sinking feeling she was right. The look I'd exchanged with Joe made me realize there was unfinished business between us.

# Chapter Seven

"We're on our own for breakfast this morning," Kathleen said as Diane came out of the bathroom area. "Liz got up early, said something about the light, and drove off."

"She warned us that was going to be important to her," I replied, making my way to the kitchen space. A quick breakfast of toast and jam, accompanied by a few mugs of good, strong coffee suited me fine. Maybe I'd finally catch up on past online copies of the San Francisco Chronicle before handling the work my remaining clients had sent me.

"She was like that at home," Kathleen said, settling into one of the armchairs that were created by spinning the driver's and passenger's chairs. "She'd be up before me in the summer and come home late. Even in the winter she was out late at night, trying to capture the right light."

"You ever seen any of her work?" I asked.

"Nope. She must sell well, though, because money is never an issue."

"Wonder why she won't show us her paintings?"

"I'm not sure. She said something once about disappointing Mom, but when I questioned her, she told me I'd misheard."

Hmmm. I plucked the toast from the toaster and slathered the Amish butter we'd brought with us from home. A dollop of raspberry jam, a product of my sisters' efforts in the brambles and kitchen, went on next.

The television clicked on.

"Got to catch up on the news," Kathleen announced as she picked up her knitting.

"Uh-huh." I took my breakfast outside, more than happy to leave the mayhem of the TV news behind. In California, I hadn't been able to escape it. Larry was a television addict, needing the drone of the talking heads on the air all day, whether he was watching it or not.

Even starting a conversation about what to have for dinner could be a challenge. If I tried to get his attention when he was zoned out on something, he'd throw down the remote as if he'd had to stop brain surgery to answer my irritating question.

The ink on the divorce papers was dry, but getting over the constant small hurts was taking a lot longer than I'd thought it would. I'd be ill-advised to get involved with anyone again, no matter how good he made me feel. I knew from experience how poorly things could turn out, no matter how much effort you put into a relationship.

With a few clicks, I got to the current version of the Chronicle, picked up my mug of coffee, and began to read.

~ ~ ~

A snap close to my ear made me jump.

"What?" I turned my attention away from the in-depth article I'd been reading about the merits of live musicians versus the technologically-produced music in the play, *Frozen*, and glared at Kathleen.

She snapped the blue glove on her hand again. With a malicious grin, she held out another pair of latex gloves. "Someone besides me needs to know how to do this."

"Not me. It's your job."

"What if I get sick? You don't want me out there puking all over the sewer hose."

"You never get sick."

"There could always be a first time." She gestured again with the gloves.

Over her shoulder I could see Henry headed our way.

"Why don't you let Henry help you? I'm sure he knows everything about sewers," I said.

"I thought he was hurrying back to his wife," Kathleen commented.

"Maybe he's not as fond of her as he made himself out to be."

"Or maybe she's run off with the Fuller Brush Man."

"Give me a break," I said. "Fuller Brush Men didn't come around even when we were kids."

"Liz said they came by once a month," she countered. "And the last one was still delivering products in 2013."

"Why do you know this stuff?" I asked.

"Good morning, ladies," Henry said with a smile. "It looks like it's dumping time."

"Um, yes," I said. "So Kathleen says."

"Well, let me help you with that." He snatched the extra pair of gloves from Kathleen's hand and snapped them on. "I'm an expert dumper. I can show you all the tricks of the trade."

"That's kind of you," Kathleen said. "But my sister and I have it handled." She snatched the gloves back and thrust them in my direction.

I hid my sigh as I took them.

Kathleen led me to the hole where the bright orange and brown sewer pipe led from the bowels of the RV to someplace deep in the earth. A momentary flash of a great big tank swarming with all kinds of unmentionable objects under my feet made my stomach flip.

"Cut it out," Kathleen said. "It's no different from city sewers."

But city sewers didn't require me to get up close and personal with them.

"I see you got one of those splitters like I told you. Good girl," Henry commented.

No, he didn't say that.

Kathleen stiffened.

Yep. He did.

I cleared my throat as I finally pulled the blue gloves on. "We've got this," I told Henry.

"I'm sure you do," he said, actually patting my arm. "I'm only here in case anything gets ... um ... stuck." Then he roared with laughter and slapped his thigh. "Get it? Gets stuck! Ha!"

Kathleen crouched down by the Y where the two sewer pipes connected. "This one's gray water. This one's black. Most of the time, all we need to do is dump the gray water.

That's what I'm going to do today."

"Can't wait too long on the black water. Don't want things getting stopped up," Henry said. He laughed again.

The muscles in Kathleen's arms flexed. Henry may have worked the oil fields, but my money would be on the woman who yanked calves from their mothers for over forty years.

I turned to Henry. The sewer lesson could wait a moment.

"It looks like all we have is the gray water today," I said to him. "And I'm not too worried about it. Kathleen's been handling shit for decades. She's more than capable." I took a step away from the RV, hoping to herd him back to the pasture where he belonged.

For a moment he looked longingly at Kathleen and the sewer line. Then he took a step in the right direction.

"So, how long are you here again?" I asked. "You said you needed to get back to your wife in Oklahoma."

"Um? What? Oh, yes. I need to get back. She called me last night. She's anxious to see me." Once again he glanced back at Kathleen.

Unfortunately, my sister had maneuvered herself into a position where her ass was broadside to us.

"How long have you been gone?" I asked.

"About eight months. I tried to make it back for the holidays." He shrugged. "But you know how that goes."

I knew exactly how that went. The girlfriend won out over the wife. Road warriors of all stripes were far too tempted when they were away from home. In my forties, I'd fended off more than one conventiongoer who'd suggested we have a little fun.

Taking his arm, I steered him back to his rig. "My sister just buried her husband of forty years," I said in a confidential whisper. "She loved him very much. It's going to take a long time before she considers another relationship. If she ever does." I shook my head in mock sadness.

"Oh, dear. That's too bad."

His feet drifted but I yanked him back in the right direction.

"I guess you'll be leaving this week," I said. "I'm surprised you got a spot for long. We booked way in advance for this one."

"I have to be out by Friday. I tried to get it extended." His pace slowed.

"Oh, look," I said practically dragging him along. "There's Hooch waiting for you."

"Yeah. He's a good doggie. Aren't you, boy?" He shook free of me and headed to the dog.

I smiled to myself. Sometimes a woman's greatest talent was to manipulate a man into doing what she needed done.

I pivoted back to my lesson in sewage.

~ ~ ~

I finished up with my clients about ten minutes after Kathleen went off to do laundry. We hadn't been gone long, but I think she was restless from having too little to do. She was used to being a ranch wife, and after Michael had gotten sick, she'd done everything herself.

It was funny how life turned out. While Kathleen had always seemed destined to become who she was, all bets were off when it came to Liz. She'd always found it difficult to focus except when it came to art. Mom tried to guide her into believing that being a housewife would be enough if she found the right man. She could do her art on the side for "pin money." Such an old-fashioned term that lived on in our rural household where, even though we were loved and cherished, our work was valued a little bit less than the same task done by a man.

I'd gotten over it long ago. My parents did the best they could for the time and place they lived in. They loved and provided for us, cared for each other deeply, and held to a clear moral code. Not everyone was as lucky.

But still, I wondered. What would it have been like to be free to imagine all the possibilities of life, not simply "women's work."

Space fascinated me as a child. I was a kid when men first walked on the moon, not much older when the Apollo program ended. But if we'd made it to the moon, what was next? Mars?

I tried to get my parents to send me to space camp in Georgia, but that was a non-starter. My dad allowed there might be jobs for me in the new world of technology, but his advice was to make sure I took the practical bookkeeping courses alongside calculus.

Picking up the heavy copy of Ron Chernow's *Grant*—I'd never lost my fascination with how historical figures intersected with each other and changed the trajectory of the country—I headed outside. Since Kathleen wasn't there, I chose her chair.

Across the way, Joe was sitting at the picnic table outside his trailer. Several open books lay around him, and he'd read some, then scribble on the pad of paper in front of him. It was exactly the way he used to prepare for papers in the library, his quick mind assembling nuances about historical events and turning them on their head to produce something that was different from anything else I'd ever read. We'd always exchanged papers for final editing for our history class. The teacher had taken points off for what he termed "grammatical sloppiness."

It had been a rigorous training ground for critical thinking, the one high school class that had stuck with me my entire life.

I was being ridiculous about hesitating to do things with Joe. What could be the harm? He was only here for a few weeks; we weren't going to be plunging into a lifelong—what there was left of it—relationship. We could have some fun. He'd always been easy to be with.

But Larry had left scars. I'd thought I was entering a partnership, only to find that I was still responsible for laundry, meals, and cleaning the inside of the house while he took care of the outside and barbecued. He'd been a traditionalist in every fiber of his being. It didn't matter that I'd spent long hours building a business. There was "women's work" and "tasks for the man of the household."

But worse than that was the emotional burden. Any discussion of feelings was off the table. If a tragedy occurred, like the death of his mother a few years after we were married, I was expected to do the mourning for both of us, while he simply added a second beer to his nightly ritual.

And I'd endured it. Because that's what women did, wasn't it?

I refocused my attention on the man across the way. Joe and I had talked about everything under the sun, including his feelings when a classmate's older brother died at the tail end of the Vietnam War.

Joe was nothing like Larry. We'd only be together for a few short weeks. What was the harm?

At the picnic table, Joe lifted his head and saw me staring. With a grin, he raised his hand and waved, then gestured for me to come over, pointing to the sun tea jar.

Why not?

I pushed the clamoring voices with a dozen answers to that question away.

It was time to have some fun.

# Chapter Eight

"What are you working on?" I asked after Joe and I were seated with our ice teas. A small stand of aspens close to Joe's site had leafed out and provided a delicious respite from the glare of a high-elevation sun.

"I haven't decided."

"Well, you must have some idea," I replied. "Otherwise, how do you know what's important?"

"I know I want to write something about women's suffrage in Montana."

"For heaven's sake, why? Isn't that a topic women usually pick up?"

"Yes. But I've got a very vocal daughter. Tess has been a challenge every step of the way, but she makes me look at things with a very clear eye. Just because a human being may come in 'a different format'—her words—doesn't mean they shouldn't have equal rights and opportunities. Any kind of discrimination never made sense to her."

"Sounds like an interesting child."

"Right from the get-go. After my son was born, Patti had her first bout of cancer. They told us she'd never have another child. We'd accepted that, especially once Joe turned ten. We'd gone to Hawaii for our anniversary—a very delayed honeymoon trip. By the time we came back, she was nauseous all the time. We thought she'd gotten food poisoning, but instead she'd gotten pregnant."

"That's wild," I said, while at the same time my gut was twisting. No matter how much I'd longed for it, I'd never had a child.

Mother's Days were hell.

"How old is she now?" I asked with a polite smile.

"Twenty-nine. Like I said earlier, she's finishing up another degree at MIT."

"She must be very smart. Takes after her dad."

"Could be. But she's also on the Asperger's scale, so developing relationships can be difficult. She wants to be loved so much, but doesn't know how to go about it. She's working with someone in Boston, but it's going to take time."

"It's tough to watch our children in pain." I knew that much, even though I'd never experienced it.

He nodded.

"But enough of that. She'll work it out."

"Suffrage is a big topic," I said, grateful to turn the conversation away from children. "How are you going to write about it?"

He laughed. "I can't even decide whether it should be fiction or non-fiction. Non-fiction gives me research creds—and you know how much I like research."

"You always had the most footnotes of any of us. Mr. Droble was always commenting about it."

"Yeah. I was in competition with myself. I always had to have ten more than the last paper."

"No wonder your daughter is at MIT."

"Yeah. Probably. Apples and trees and all that."

His grin caught me and transported me back to a time before ... before growing up and learning how little control we actually had on the world around us. A time of possibilities.

*Hello, hope. It's been a long time since I've seen you.*

"On the other hand," he said. "Fiction makes history so much more accessible. A story makes anything go down better, especially when you're teaching."

"Did you like being a teacher?"

"Loved it. Being retired is the weirdest thing I've ever experienced. I spent my whole life preparing for work, then working at getting better at teaching, taking more responsibility at school. Then all of a sudden it was over. I have to admit, I rattled around a bit before I got my act together. The kids were out of the house, Patti was gone, and I didn't seem to have a purpose anymore."

"What did you do?"

"Got some therapy and went back to church," he said.

"I did the therapy part," I said. "About a year during and after my divorce. It helped."

Joe nodded, but seemed to be expecting something more.

"I quit going to church when we couldn't get pregnant. I tried, but I just couldn't." I hardened my heart and my tone. If Joe had turned into some religious nut, we weren't going anywhere together. God hadn't delivered, and I'd never forgiven Him.

"I get it," he said softly. "More tea?"

My glass was empty, but I shook my head. "I've got to get back. There are ... um ... things to do before dinner."

I stood, and he rose with me.

"I meant what I said about going into Yellowstone together. Maybe we could plan something for next week?"

"I'll see about it," I said. That would give me time to come up with excuses as to why it should never happen.

"Maybe we could get up early one morning and go to the Lamar Valley. Or at dusk. They say if you get there at the right time, you can see wolves."

That stopped me. I shouldn't encourage him.

*But wolves. To see one of those elusive creatures ...*

"I'll let you know," I said and hurried to our RV, like a deer running from the pack.

~ ~ ~

I huddled inside the trailer, making up busywork on my computer, until Kathleen and Liz returned. Both were bubbling with enthusiasm. Kathleen had met a rancher from the eastern part of Montana at the laundromat, and Liz had had a successful day painting, although she wouldn't show us her work.

Liz had brought fixings for dinner and insisted that we help her chop up the vegetables she needed for a stir fry.

"You get the red peppers," she said.

"I hate peppers," I replied. "Those little seeds get all over the place."

"You could do the carrots." She held out a tapered orange root.

"Nope." Liz had exacting demands from carrots in a stir fry.

"Crybaby," Kathleen said, pulling the vegetables from Liz's hands. "How about you pour the wine and let's get this party started."

"What are we celebrating?" I asked.

"Don't need a reason to celebrate anything except being alive at our age," Kathleen said. "We're healthy and on a grand adventure. It doesn't get better than that."

"I thought marriage was the great adventure," I said. "At least that's what Mama always said."

"That's because she was totally in love with Daddy," Liz said. "And why not? He treated her like a princess when he could. Most men aren't like that." She turned back to the counter.

"But you and Michael were happy," I said to Kathleen.

"Yes. But ..." A shadow crossed Kathleen's face so quickly I almost missed it.

"But what?" I asked.

"Nothing to discuss. He's gone. No more romance for me. Just the open road!" She concentrated on the carrots.

Why did I feel like there were too many secrets lurking in this RV? There were things about my life I'd kept from my sisters. They knew Larry and I couldn't have children, but not his machinations to prevent it.

They didn't know I'd been robbed of my chance to be a mother, something I'd always taken for granted.

"What about you, Liz?" I asked. "You've never married. I'm not sure you ever got serious about anyone. You haven't ever said."

"There was someone ... in college," she said with her back still to us. "But it didn't work out." Even with a T-shirt, I could see how rigid her back muscles became.

*Secrets.*

"Well, I'm done with men. I declare this a male-free RV!" I said, raising my glass.

My sisters raised their glasses with varying degrees of

enthusiasm. Kathleen's glass was high, Liz's didn't make the height of her shoulder. She quickly drank and then declared, "Music! We need music!"

Picking up her phone from a nearby counter, she dashed to the back bedroom.

As we continued to slice and dice, the sound of cabinet doors opening and closing echoed through our space. Suddenly Captain and Tennille singing "Love Will Keep Us Together" blared from the back room.

Liz sashayed down the corridor, electronics high over her head. Kathleen and I put down our knives and held our arms in the air, dancing in circles and bumping hips just like Mama used to do with us in the kitchen. It didn't take long before the trailer was rocking with our beat as we sang out the lyrics along with Tennille.

Joy surged inside me, and the years fell away. We weren't slightly misshapen, mostly invisible aging women anymore. We were young, energetic teens with our lives ahead of us, bursting with hope at the brave new world we were determined to create. Our parents were old-fashioned, and we hadn't been awash with cash, but damn we'd been happy.

Kathleen's grin was one I hadn't seen in years. The end with Michael must have been harder than she'd let on. It was as if she was finally free of a burden no one knew she was carrying. Liz was still guarded, and I had the feeling she was faking some of the craziness she was portraying.

And me?

For the moment, I was determined to forget the past and shelve worry about the future. Now. It was simply now. I was dancing and singing with my sisters next to one of the grandest national parks in the world, and it didn't get much better than that.

The song ended, transitioning to Glen Campbell's "Rhinestone Cowboy." We slowly stopped moving and took up our tasks. But as the playlist continued, I was amazed at how many times one of us would join our voices to the recorded song, playing with harmonies as we'd done as kids when Dad dragged out his old six-string guitar.

We were on our second glass of wine when Liz returned to the topic of men. Well, not men in general.

Joe.

"I kind of remember Joe in high school," she said. "He was a cross country runner, wasn't he?"

"Yes," I said.

"He was a funny guy," Kathleen said. "I mean, not like a class clown or anything, but he could say things that struck me as funny. Usually a pun of some kind."

"He liked words," I said.

"And limericks," Kathleen remembered. "They were soooo bad."

"Still are. He told me one the other day."

"Old habits die hard," Kathleen said.

"I remember something else about him," Liz said. "He was really good at making bad situations better."

"Yeah," Kathleen said.

They were right. I'd seen Joe in action a few times. Sometimes I thought a fight that was brewing ended before it began because Joe talked so much they were tired of hearing him. Other times, he used his gift with words to lighten a mood that was threatening to go black.

I remembered a girl I didn't know very well, staring at her locker. Not moving. Not opening it. Just staring.

Joe was coming down the hallway. I'd always noticed him whenever he was near, but had never thought much about it. He spotted the girl and veered to stand next to her. I couldn't hear what he said, but soon he got her to bump fists. He stood there while she opened her locker and walked her to her next class. I'd asked him later what was going on, but he'd shaken his head and said it was private.

A few days later, I saw her again, hesitating as she looked for a place to sit. A few of the sports guys started snickering and looking at her.

She reddened and looked ready to bolt.

I'd walked over to her. "Hey," I said. "Why don't you come sit with me and my friends? We've got room."

"Really?" Her eyes widened.

"Really," I'd told her.

"I'd like that."

As we walked toward the table, I noticed Joe watching us. He gave me a big grin and thumbs up.

The girl didn't become part of our circle, and I never did find out what happened, but whatever good came of that situation, it had gotten better because of Joe Kelly.

No matter what had happened between us, I had clearly missed an opportunity.

# Chapter Nine

I was soaped up in the shower the next morning when the water turned freezing cold.

"Dammit!" I yelled. "Who used all the hot water!"

Walls in RVs give a new meaning to the word "thin," so I got an immediate response.

"You were the first one in the shower!" Kathleen yelled back.

I shivered as I got the soap off. Stepping out, I toweled off and pulled on my clothes.

"I guess I'll wait for my shower, since you hogged the hot water," Kathleen said.

"Not me," I replied. "I was only in there a few moments when it went cold."

Kathleen frowned and put down her coffee. She went to the sink and flipped on the water. Her frown deepened.

"It can't be the water heater. This thing is almost brand new."

"What else could it be? I mean, I had water. Just no heat. Sure sounds like no water heater to me."

"Stop being so logical," Kathleen said. "If it is the heater, we're going to have to take our showers in the main building. It'll take a while to get any parts."

Ugh. I hated showering where other people had been. My own dirt I could handle. But someone else's?

My coffee threatened to return to my mouth.

Liz came into the RV. From the covered canvas under her arm, I assumed she had been painting.

"Can I see?" I asked.

She shook her head. "I'm not comfortable showing them."

"Are you painting nude geese or something?" I asked with a grin. Not being able to see Liz's paintings was beginning to bug me.

"Ha, ha," Liz said, and continued to the rear.

"She's never shown you anything?" I asked Kathleen, who was still staring at the faucet as if attempting sorcery to get the hot water to work.

"Huh?" she said. "Oh. No. Never."

"Weird."

"I stopped asking. It's her work."

Hmmm. I was going to crack this case one way or another.

But first we needed hot water. I was *not* showering in the public showers.

I stood and joined Kathleen staring at the faucet.

"Are we having a séance or did someone die," Liz asked as she came back up front.

"Water heater," Kathleen and I said together.

"Oooh. Does staring at the faucet fix it?" she asked. "I'll help."

The three of stared for a full minute before Kathleen turned away and left the RV, the two of us trailing behind like little ducklings.

She retrieved her tool kit from its compartment, then opened a different compartment on the side of the rig. Then she started to stare at the water heater.

We crowded around her.

"Don't you two have something else to do?" she asked.

"Well, I do have to go shopping this morning," Liz said. "Since it looks like I'm not getting a shower, I could go now."

"Good, take Diane with you."

"I don't need to go shopping."

Kathleen turned on me, using the expression I'm quite sure had quelled any thought her children had had of rebellion.

"I'll go with her," I said.

"Good idea." Kathleen turned back to the water heater.

Liz and I went inside to make a list.

~ ~ ~

When we returned an hour later, Kathleen was still at the water heater, but she was surrounded by four men, including Henry, who were pointing, talking, and shaking their heads at each other. We stowed the groceries, then Liz said she was going to take the car and go to a small space she'd rented in town where she could paint.

"How did you ever find it?" I asked her.

"There's an app for that," she said. "Kind of like an AirBnB for artists."

Of course there was. There was an app for everything these days. I wondered when someone would build one that our parents logged us into when we were born, and it guided us through life for the rest of our days.

Maybe it would be smarter in the affairs of the heart and I would have married Joe instead of Larry.

As if I'd conjured him, Joe wandered into our site with his coffee mug in hand. He looked at the small group by the water heater, grinned, and sat down to observe the action.

I grabbed my own coffee.

"So you think you can come into our site and have a seat?" I asked after sitting down next to him. "Didn't you read the list of rules?"

"There seemed to be plenty of interlopers here already," he said. "Watching Kathleen do her stuff is pure entertainment."

"What do you mean?"

"Sometimes I'd run into her at Murdoch's back in Butte. The first time it happened, she snared me. Gave me an idea of what she wanted to do, then asked my opinion. Of course, any time a man offers an opinion to a woman at a hardware or ranch store, there's bound to be another guy with a different one. Kathleen would get us all going, listening carefully. See? Like she's doing now."

Sure enough, my sister was paying close attention to what one of the men was saying. I could almost see her taking mental notes. Kathleen had a prodigious memory, even better than mine when she chose to use it. While she didn't remember odd facts, she remembered important things, like when I owed her money.

Beside me, Joe started to chuckle.

"Who's the bowlegged guy with the weird shorts?" he asked.

"Oh. That's Henry. He lives next door." I pointed.

"Bet he thinks he knows everything," Joe said.

"Why do you think that?"

"Expression on Kathleen's face. She's going to cut him off at the knees. Wait for it … wait for it …"

I watched carefully as the expression on her face changed. Henry had been wearing at her nerves for a while.

Finally, she tilted her head and said something to Henry.

He frowned for a moment.

The other men in the group looked at him with sympathetic smiles.

Kathleen said something else, and Henry shook his head and took a step back.

She turned back to the others and asked a question. Henry stayed with the group, but it didn't look like he offered any more opinions.

"I've heard her cut a loud blow-hard down to size," Joe said. "It's magnificent to watch. I wish I had her skill with some people."

"Your students?" I asked.

"More often their parents," he admitted. "Way too often, if I'm having problems with a kid and ask to meet their parents, it's game over. I don't even have to ask any questions. The minute they show up I know why the kid is the way he or she is."

"Wonder what Henry's kids are like."

"You probably don't want to know," Joe said, as the men around Kathleen started to disperse.

"Probably not."

My sister came over to us.

"I bet you thought that was funny," she said to Joe.

"It's always interesting to watch a master at work," he replied. "Do you know how you're going to fix it?"

"Yep. I can even get the part at the local hardware store." She looked around. "Drat. Liz has the car."

"I can take you," Joe offered. He looked at me. "Why don't you come too? Westmart has everything you need, even things you never knew existed."

"I don't know."

"Get out of your chair, and let's get moving," Kathleen ordered.

"God, you're bossy."

"Learned it from you."

Joe laughed and walked to his car while we trailed behind.

It was a glorious day for a drive. The temperatures had softened from the nineties of the last few days to a moderate upper seventies. A slight breeze kept the bugs to a minimum. The pines were full of twittering and cawing birds, and a doe peered out from the depths of the woods.

Although it was during the work week, the town was bustling mid-day. It looked like many locals were out and about, readying themselves for the months of onslaught from tourist mobs.

How did people manage in a place like this?

How had I dealt with the crowds in the Bay Area all these years? I'd intended to move back to the region when our little adventure was over. In fact, I'd kept my condo, renting it out for the year.

But the room to breathe in Montana had reminded me there were more things in life than acquiring. So much was available for free. I just had to open my eyes and appreciate it.

The three of us were quiet. I glanced at Joe's hands on the steering wheel. They were strong and sinewy, like they'd been when we were teens. Capable of managing anything. Now the skin was a little looser around the tendons and the knuckles a bit rounder, but they still looked like they were strong.

How would hands like that feel on my body?

God, why was I thinking anything like that? Granted, Larry and I hadn't had sex for years before we divorced, but surely I was past all of that now. Didn't a woman's libido simply settle down and fade out of existence after a while?

Margaret Mead may have believed in post-menopausal zest, but I'd found it to be a huge disappointment.

After my period ended, life went on. A few more hot flashes, but the basic structure was the same.

I took a second look at Joe's hands, then quickly looked away as we pulled into the parking lot.

The store was a neighborhood hardware establishment on steroids. There were the normal sections of paint, lumber, flooring, electric, pipes, and the like, but there were also areas for all types of gardens, outdoor living, and stuff geared to the tourist looking to haul something "authentic" home with them.

Kathleen asked the employee at the front door for what she was seeking. He immediately pawned her off to another employee who whisked her off to a far section.

Joe led me in another direction. "While we're here, I wanted to show you something."

The pizza ovens distracted me for a moment, but soon we were in the fishing section.

"I don't fish," I said again.

"Only because you've never tried."

"Of course I have. My father made sure we did all the outdoorsy things: camp, fish, hunt. It only took with Kathleen."

"Your father taught you cast fishing."

"Of course. He wanted to actually catch the things, not look pretty doing it."

Joe chuckled. "Indulge me. I want to see what kind of flies they have."

He led me to a spot with rows and rows of brightly-colored feathers and fur tied to deadly-looking hooks.

"Does someone actually need all this?"

"No. The best lures mimic what's happening in a place at that time of year. For example, caddis and mayflies will be hatching soon. So I need a lure that will make the trout think they're getting a nice fat meal."

I looked at the lures closely. "Some of them are so intricate."

"Come over here," he said. "These are hand-tied lures.

Ah, here are some made locally that are what I'm looking for." He selected a square box with six tiny lures.

"And a fish will go for that?"

"Every time. These are beautiful. I like to buy local hand-tied flies wherever I go. There's a veteran up our way who does amazing flies. He's in a wheelchair, but still fly fishes with adaptive equipment. A group called Project Healing Waters got him interested, and now he's ... well ... hooked."

I groaned.

Joe laughed.

"There you are," Kathleen said, walking up to us. "I got what I needed. Are you done?"

"Soon as I pay for these," Joe said.

We were soon headed back to the park.

"What are you doing tomorrow?" Joe asked as we drove. "I was thinking of going into the park, seeing if I could catch Old Faithful erupting."

"What a coincidence," Kathleen said from the back seat. "That's exactly what we're doing tomorrow. Come with us. It'll save gas."

Damn her sharp hearing.

"Yes," I added. "Sure. Come with us."

He glanced over at me.

"If you're okay with it, I'd love to."

"It will be great to have you along," I said, forcing a smile.

I hoped.

# Chapter Ten

Joe was too close. I could feel the heat from his body, sense his arm mere inches away from my own as we shared the back seat of Liz's Jeep.

Wait. Wasn't there an armrest in this thing?

Peering carefully, I saw where it had been hidden to blend in with the upright portion of the seat.

"Looking for something?" Joe asked.

"Got it," I said, and yanked down the rest. "I needed someplace to put my arm."

He stared at the barrier between us. "If you say so."

I plunked my arm on it. "There. That's better."

"Good idea." He put his arm on the other half.

I turned my head to the window and pretended everything was fine. It should be. I shouldn't feel this way around him. Not around any man. I was in my sixties for god's sake. Sixty-year-old women shouldn't be lusting after a friend from high school.

Didn't normal people give up sex by our age?

"What are you thinking about?" Joe asked.

"Um ... nothing." I smiled brightly at him. "It's a beautiful day, isn't it."

He shook his head. "Nice try, but you weren't looking at the scenery."

I tried to move my arm so the fine hairs on his skin would stop touching me, but there was no room. I fanned myself with my hand and placed it in my lap.

"What'd you do in California with all those people?" he asked.

"Their taxes."

"Funny. I mean, wasn't it crowded?"

"Only if you tried to drive anywhere. Sometimes Larry and I would take a trip to Yosemite or Carmel if it was a nice weekend."

"Along with everyone else?"

I shrugged. "I got used to it." I looked around. "Now I have to get used to all this space again."

"Well this is a good place to do it. There are too many people here too. I want to come here in the winter. Do some cross country skiing."

I shivered. "I bet you enjoy ice fishing too."

"Sure. Can't live in Montana without enjoying the winter."

"A good reason not to move back."

"You've become soft." He grinned. "With a little time, your sisters and I will get you toughened up again."

"Right. Just what I want to be, a tough old bird ready for the soup pot."

"Oh, you'll never be that," he said, his voice soft.

I gave him a sharp look.

"No fooling around back there." Kathleen's voice was loud and strong.

"Oh, darn it," Joe said. "And here I was, just about to make my move."

I squished myself as close to the door as I could. California. Definitely going back to California. Ironically, lots of people meant more privacy. Small towns bread nosy people who were only too happy to tell you what to do.

~ ~ ~

We stood by the Old Faithful sign that predicted the next eruption. That time had come and gone, but the geyser bubbled away.

"It used to be regular," Kathleen said.

"So did we all," I said without thinking, then clapped my hand over my mouth.

There was a moment of silence, then the three of them chuckled.

Joe struck a pose, and I knew what we were in for.

"There once was a geyser in Yellowstone
For years she'd faithfully blown
Till the earth shook her core
And said with a roar
Old Faithful's schedule has flown."

"That wasn't bad," Liz said.

"It was kinda good," Kathleen added.

Joe looked at me.

"Yeah," I said. "It was okay."

"Okay? Okay? You cut me to the quick!" He mockingly stabbed himself with dagger and staggered back.

"It should be soon, even if we can't rely on it," Kathleen said. "There's a little bit of space at the end of that bench. I think we'll fit over there."

We squeezed into the too-small space, and once again I was crammed next to Joe.

I tried to concentrate on the geyser, but all I could think of was the feel of the man next to me and the effect he was having on my body. Tingling feelings I remember from decades ago were making their presence known. I'd thought they were gone for good and had already bade them good riddance. Overactive hormones had made me do crazy things in my twenties and thirties, one of which had ended in my marriage to Larry.

Nothing good could come of these tingles.

Down! Down!

Joe and I were old friends. That's it.

If I kept telling myself that, maybe I'd believe it.

The ground beneath our feet rumbled.

Murmurs circled the geyser as water gurgled and spat a few feet into the air. The sulfur smell increased slightly as the shaft of water drove higher and higher. Soon, it shot high in the air, close to two hundred feet of steam and boiling water droplets bright against the backdrop of distant dark pines.

The geyser dropped down to half its size, then shot up again. Up and down it went, varying its height, putting the dancing Bellagio fountains in Las Vegas to shame.

All too quickly the show was over. People sat still for a few moments, hoping a glitch would occur somewhere in the ground beneath us, and the geyser would begin again. When it didn't reappear, everyone stirred. We stood up and moved away from the benches.

"Everyone ready for a hike?" Kathleen asked. "There are a lot more small geysers to see."

"Definitely," Liz said. "I'm hoping to find some more scenes to paint."

"I'm game," Joe said.

Everyone looked at me.

After being sedentary for so long in the Bay Area, I'd been walking every day to get ready for this trip, but hiking still didn't bring me the same joy it apparently brought everyone else. But I pasted a smile on my face and said, "Sure. Let's go."

After crossing the aptly named Firehole River, we once again followed a boardwalk over gurgling mud, while a short distance away steam streamed from deep within the earth through cracked vents. Myriad colors threaded through the area, sometimes surrounding a blue so transparent it looked like the sky right after dawn released her pastel pinks, oranges, and yellows.

Liz had her phone out and was snapping photos that she'd later transform into whatever art she created.

I longed for a decent camera and the time to stand and play with settings to achieve the pictures I saw. Not only the full photo of what lay before me, but the detailed shot, picking out the variations in dried mud, or the moment a bubble popped out of a gray mass.

Joe didn't hover when I stopped to play with my imaginary camera, but stayed somewhere between my sisters and I so we didn't lose track of each other. All around us steam misted the air, and water leapt from the ground unexpectedly as pressure built and released. At the far edge of the steamy mess, a few bison grazed, their hides damp with moisture from the air.

I could feel it myself, the thin film on my skin that wasn't quite water.

About halfway through the trail we'd decided to follow, the three of us waited for Liz while she cataloged the Castle Grand Area, home of three geysers: Turban, Grand, and Spasmodic.

"So, Joe," Kathleen said. "Are you seeing anyone these days?"

"You mean, like dating?" He looked startled by the question.

"Exactly. Are you dating?"

"No, not at the moment. After my wife died, I was too busy raising my kids. And once they were gone, well, there didn't seem to be anyone interesting."

"Good," was all she said in reply.

Joe and I looked at each other, and he shrugged. I knew what Kathleen was driving at, and I didn't like it one bit. Not at all.

If I wanted to go out with Joe, it would be on my terms, not because my sister egged me on. Besides, there was not going to be any real dating. We were living different lives. Ships crossing in the night and all that.

Once Liz caught up with us, with unspoken agreement, Joe and I let my sisters go ahead.

"You don't have to guess what she's thinking, do you?" Joe said.

"Nope."

"So what do *you* want to know, Diane O'Sullivan? My life's an open book to you."

"No need," I said. "We've caught up on what's important. The only thing left is to exchange addresses so we can send each other a Christmas letter once a year."

"Surely there's more than that," he said, stopping and leaning against a rail that kept unwary tourists from falling onto the fragile crust of the surface below.

"Why?" I moved to the rail to get out of the way of tourists, but kept distance between us.

"Because ... well ... I guess because I want to know more about what makes you tick."

"And you figure it's a fair trade if I learn more about you," I said.

"Something like that."

I considered the internal turmoil of the earth reflected on the surface below me.

"As far as I'm concerned," I said slowly. "The past can stay in the past. After these few weeks, we'll rarely, if ever, run into each other. No need for deep confessions."

He nodded.

"So let's just have some fun. We'll go to the park together a few times if you want, take some walks like we used to do, then go our separate ways. Okay?"

He fisted, then flexed his hands, a gesture I remembered from when we were kids, and he was trying to make a decision.

Closing the short distance between us, he said, "Sounds like a plan for now."

"For now?"

"You never know what the universe has in store."

Oh, I had a good idea. The universe was a sneaky woman with nothing good in store for anyone.

I shrugged. Joe had always believed there was something special and new around the corner. It appeared even his wife's death hadn't changed that viewpoint.

My experience had been different, but there was nothing to stop us from having some fun. Maybe being with Joe again would resurrect some of the things I'd felt as a kid, like hope for the future.

# Chapter Eleven

The dining room at the Old Faithful Inn reminded me of the one at the Ahwahnee in Yosemite. A big stone fireplace dominated one end, and immense beams loomed overhead. Because we were early, we were lucky enough to get a table by the window where we could keep an eye out to see if the geyser erupted again. The sky was still light enough to make the entire geyser area visible.

I went for the salmon, Liz the quail, while both Joe and Kathleen chose the buffet. Joe came back with bison medallions plus an assortment of vegetables and mashed potatoes. Kathleen went for the meatloaf and mashed potatoes, along with a token serving of green beans.

My ranching sister may have believed in meat and potatoes, but our mother's reminders to eat our vegetables obviously took.

"What kind of art do you do?" Joe asked Liz midway through the meal.

"Oh, this and that."

"I like to browse the galleries in Butte," he said. "Has your work been shown in any of those?"

"No," Liz dissected her quail with her knife and fork. "I have representation in New York," she said. "My work is mainly displayed there and in their partner galleries in London and Paris."

My fork clunked on the table as I stared at my sister.

"I had no idea you were that good," I said. "I thought it was something you dabbled in."

"Oh, no. Not dabbling." Liz continued to work the bird.

"But don't try to get any more out of her than that," Kathleen said. "I've been working at her for years, and all I get is silence. And I've never understood it. I mean it's not like I haven't seen every naked and gross thing there is to see on this planet. Hard not to while you're ranching."

"Huh," I said. "So what's up?"

Liz looked up, her green eyes sharp. "I'm not ashamed of them. They're private, that's all."

"Private paintings that you share with strangers in New York, London, and Paris," I replied.

A hand touched my thigh briefly.

"Art can be deeply personal," Joe said. "Sometimes it's easier to share it with strangers than your family."

"Thank you for understanding," Liz said.

"Well, I don't," I said. "And I don't think Kathleen does either."

"Why don't we let it be for now," Joe said. "And enjoy this wonderful meal." He glanced out the window and grinned. "Even Old Faithful says we have better things to do." Outside our window, the geyser shot into the skies.

"It must be awesome at night with the lights shining on it," Liz said.

"It's still pretty spectacular now," I said. It didn't matter that we'd just seen it a few hours before. I'd never get past seeing what nature had to offer, from the thundering falls in Yosemite, to the first shooting stars blooming in a Rocky Mountain spring.

Once the show was over, I steered our conversation to other topics. Joe was right. It was up to Liz to decide what she wanted to reveal and what she didn't.

But I was damn curious as to what she was hiding.

~ ~ ~

Once we finished our dinner, we wandered over to the gift store. Without a lot of room, our window shopping was more practical than it would have been. I picked up a T-shirt with an image of Old Faithful. We stopped at the Monopoly game and debated about buying it.

"It brings back a lot of memories," Kathleen said. "You were always the banker," she said to me.

"And Liz always won."

"That's because she cheated."

"Did not," Liz said. "I just, um, improvised."

"Rules were a suggestion for her," I told Joe.

"But it's not going to be the same without Park Place and Boardwalk," Kathleen said.

"Or without the boot," I said.

"Or the iron," Liz agreed.

We moved on to the posters and artwork they had for sale, including some small woven baskets and prints by Native Americans. A simple, but striking piece caught my eye. It depicted a winter scene on a blank background, the images almost skeletal in their rendering. The colors were striking, especially the blues against all that white.

"It's quite amazing, isn't it?" Joe said. "I've seen his work before."

I nodded. Something about it drew me in. I could feel the wind dancing along the Rocky Mountain Front, sense myself connecting to the earth and nature all around the figures in the print. It took speech from me and replaced it with the spirit of something greater than myself.

Joe let me be, but stood beside me, protecting me from those who would penetrate the space I occupied.

Awareness returned, and I reluctantly left the painting. Kathleen was over by the bookshelf, and I walked toward her, ready to break the spell of whatever I'd been under.

She'd already picked up three books: one by C.J. Box, another by Craig Johnson, and a third by James Lee Burke.

"God, you're bloodthirsty," I said.

"What? You expect me to read trashy romance novels?"

"I suppose not. You never were one for the tales of princes and rich businessmen."

"It's not real. Marriage is a life-long endeavor, not some silly chase and catch game. Besides, they promise things that never happen."

There was a bitterness in her tone that surprised me. I'd always thought she and Michael had been happy right up to the end, but my faith in that certainty was dimming. I left her to her tales of mayhem and drifted to the cozy mysteries. Joe was studying the non-fiction section.

"I think I have enough," I said to Kathleen, clutching a

few books, my T-shirt, and a hand-made coffee mug.

"Me, too." Her stack had increased to five books.

Only Liz left the shop empty-handed. The last to leave, Joe had a bag containing a few things.

"What did you get?" I asked.

"A couple of books," he said, although the bag looked like it held more than that. "Let's have a drink by the fireplace," he suggested.

"I'll stick to seltzer," I said. "I'm driving home."

"Then I'll have to treat you another time," he said.

We settled ourselves in four empty chairs with Joe and Kathleen on the wings. Liz offered to get the drinks, and soon returned with wine and my seltzer.

It didn't matter whether or not I was drinking; the view by the fireplace was amazing. The staggering arrangement of stairways, catwalks, and log beams that soared overhead looked like a childhood fantasy of a jungle gym made of tree trunks.

Joe pulled a book on Old Faithful from his bag and thumbed through it. We leaned close as he gave us a synopsis. "The architect of this building was Robert Reamer—only twenty-nine."

"That's amazing," Kathleen said. "It's a rare young person who has this kind of vision."

"Shorter life spans," I said. "They needed to get crackin'."

"Well, he certainly did that," Liz said, her mouth slightly open as she stared up through the kaleidoscope of wood.

"The book said it was designed after a childhood fantasy," Joe said.

"Ghosts?" I asked. I'd always loved a good ghost story. Being scared to death was even more fun than making sure a company's books balanced.

"Oh, lots." Joe grinned. He knew about my fondness for scary stories. When we were younger, he'd collect them and dole them out to me like special treats.

I'd forgotten all about that. I smiled at him, and our gazes slammed into each other's awareness. All of a sudden, I was short of breath and needed to pull in air.

He looked back down at the book.

"The most popular one is the ghost of the headless bride," he said. "Seems she married a man her father opposed because her father believed the man was only after her money. Turns out Dad was right. The man left her while she was here."

"Did he ... um ... you know ..." Liz was wide-eyed.

Joe shrugged. "No one knows. She was found in her bathtub. Well, at least her body was. Her head was found up there in the Crow's Nest." He pointed toward a platform several stories over our heads.

The three of us stared upward.

"They say she walks those stairways, her head neatly tucked under her arm," Joe finished.

Chills ran down my arm.

I let my gaze follow the convoluted stairways down to where I couldn't see them anymore, then sipped my seltzer. "You're good," I told Joe.

"I aim to please." He took out his phone and scrolled through the photos he'd taken during the day. "Most of these aren't worth saving, but I should get a few to post on my blog."

"You have a blog?"

"Just started it. I figured it would be fun to do while I toured around. It's easier to come up with something to say than to take a good picture. Let me take a look at yours."

I pulled out my phone and tapped my way to the photos. I scrolled through them, reliving the hike we'd taken around the boardwalks.

"You're really good," Joe said.

I waved the compliment away with my hand. I'd learned not to take photography seriously.

"No, stop," he said. "Look at that. It's interesting." He'd found a picture I'd taken of lime green lichen on a protruding rock amid a bubbling morass. "And the one before was beautiful."

I stared at the photo of a small patch of clear baby blue water, steam misting over the crusty surface around it.

"I kind of like that one, too," I confessed. "I just wish ..."

"What?"

How could I explain the feel of a traditional camera in my hand, the weight of the body, the natural fit of my fingers around it, the off-center feel of a long lens? I'd taken some courses in college with a camera I rented from the department. I'd intended to get one once I had a well-paying job, but I'd put it off.

"I don't know how to explain it to you," I said.

"Try me."

"When I have a camera in my hand ... well, this is going to sound bizarre ... but it's as if I see things differently. I'm aware of light and shadow, contrast. I want to learn how to sharpen the image I see in my head. I want to learn about f-stops and ISO and shutter speeds. I want a really long lens so I can take pictures of the birds that only look like black dots through a phone." I stopped. It already seemed over the top.

"Do you have a camera like that?" Joe asked.

All of a sudden, my throat closed and tears beckoned. Even though I'd wanted one all my life I'd let it go, thinking there was something more important. If I only sacrificed myself enough, my marriage would be happy again, and God would bless me with a child.

Instead I only had ashes.

Unable to speak, I shook my head.

Instead of asking why I didn't, Joe took my hand and gave it a gentle squeeze before releasing it.

I wiped a tear from the corner of my eye.

"Everything okay?" Liz asked.

"Of course," I said.

"I think we're all tired," Joe said. "Maybe it's time to finish up and head home."

"That sounds good," Liz said. "I want to get up early and get into the studio. I'm bursting with ideas."

"I'm ready," Kathleen said, pushing herself up from the chair. "I feel like the kid in the Far Side comic who asked to be excused because his brain was full."

"There's a lot to see here," Joe agreed, collecting our glasses. "You're smart to take it in small bits."

There were murmurs of agreement as we gathered our things. As soon as Joe returned from taking the glasses back to the bar, we ambled out the front door and into the evening air. Ahead Venus was just rising above the horizon, and at the edge of the parking lot, the large rack of a bull elk was visible over the car roofs.

Nature's serenity eased the tension inside me. I glanced over at Joe who smiled at me and nodded.

It was a beautiful evening.

# Chapter Twelve

Somehow, before he'd gone back to his RV the night before, Joe had conned me into fly fishing lessons. And there was no other word for it. I'd thought he was having a friendly conversation as I drove home, but no. Pretty soon he was talking about the joys of fishing, how quiet and peaceful it was. How it gave him a chance to slow down and enjoy the world beyond him.

And then I found myself nodding my head. Sure, I told him, sounds lovely.

Then poof! I was committed to meeting him at four the next afternoon for my first fly fishing lesson.

Even my lack of a pole or any other equipment wasn't a deterrent.

At three-thirty I walked over to Joe's trailer, steeling myself against the torture to come.

Joe roared with laughter when he saw my face.

"It's fishing," he said. "Not execution at dawn."

"Same thing," I replied.

"C'mon. Let's teach you how to cast." He picked up a long thin rod. He started across the park road to a large field that had just been mowed.

I stood where I was.

He turned back. "Are you coming?"

"There's no water over there."

"I know."

"So we're going fishing where there's no water ... and presumably no fish."

"No," he said.

"No?"

"I'm teaching you to cast. You don't need water for that."

I plodded across the road and followed him into the weeds.

"Fly fishing is all about learning how to cast. Do it right, and it's pure elegance. Wrong and it becomes a tangled mess."

"I'm not coordinated at all," I protested.

"That's not true," he said. "I danced with you at prom, remember? Not true at all."

"Ha! That was a long time ago. I've got age-related clumsiness."

"That's not a thing."

"If it isn't, it should be. And I have it."

"Just watch, Diane. Stop overthinking and watch."

After pulling a section of line from the pole, he arced the pole back and the line unfurled in a soft wave before it flew forward with the same grace and drifted to the grass. Before he did it again, he explained what he was doing.

"You have to keep your wrist straight," he said.

"No limp hands," I said flopping my hand around like a headless dying chicken. "Got it."

He chuckled.

"The back stroke is as important as going forward."

"Learn to swim on my back. No drowning," I deadpanned. Two could play at puns.

He shook his head.

"Point the tip of the rod down, pull it up slowly at first, accelerate, then come to a complete stop."

"Got it," I said. "Drive badly."

The rod dropped in his hand. "Do you ever stop?"

"You bring it out in me," I confessed. "You always did."

"I remember," he said as he brought the rod forward, causing the line to puddle on the grass in front of him. Then he demonstrated the entire cast again.

I had to admit, it did look beautiful when he did it. I just had no hope of imitating such grace.

He showed me a few more times, reiterating his instructions.

"Your turn," he said.

There was no escape route.

I padded over to him.

He handed the rod to me. "Grip it here." He pointed.

I wrapped my hand around the pole.

"Not quite." He placed his hand on mind and arranged my grip to his satisfaction. "I'm going to stand behind you and guide you."

He moved into position.

Close. Too close. I could feel his body heat. And it stirred up old feelings, sensations I'd forgotten for decades. My body core softened, and the tips of my breasts tingled.

Fishing. That's all we're doing. I'm fishing. God only knew why, but that's what we were doing.

Fishing.

That was it.

He must not have felt a thing because he was still teaching.

"So, point your rod down," he said, guiding me into position. "Then slowly … now faster, faster, stop!"

My body was so invested in the backward cast that it kept going even as my arm obeyed his command and stopped. I wobbled back and forth.

He put his hand on my waist to try to stop me from falling.

It felt like a hot brand. I dodged away from it.

And plopped onto the ground.

He dropped to his knees. "You okay?" he asked.

I took a mental inventory. "Yep."

"Let me help you up."

"No, no. That's okay." I did *not* need him touching me again. I flipped to my knees and boosted myself up. As I did, I saw a few of the RV campers looking our way.

An audience. Just what I needed.

"Maybe that's it for the day?" I asked hopefully.

"I never thought of you as a quitter," he said.

I wasn't one.

"Okay. I'll try. But why don't you stand over there." Somewhere you can't touch me.

"Sure." He backed off.

I ran through a mental checklist. Tip on the ground, slowly lift it up. Go faster. Stop.

The line draped over my shoulders.

Joe was trying not to laugh as he walked over and untangled the line.

"Keep your eye on what you're doing. The tip of the rod needs to be behind you before you stop. And then you need to immediately reverse the process." He flipped the line out in front of me. "Again."

I tried again and managed to get the pile of line behind me this time.

"Hopeless," I said as he set up the line again. "I'm a klutz. Let's do something else." Like coffee. Coffee was safe. You could sit on opposite sides of a table. Far away from each other.

"You can do this. I know you can." He lifted my chin and looked into my eyes. "Stop thinking so hard and trust your body. You've got this."

The next five tries weren't any better, but he refused to let me give up.

Tip down, lift, speed, stop, reverse.

To my surprise, the line unfurled behind me, then arced in front to land in the grass ahead of me.

"I did it!"

"You did!" Joe hugged me, and we high-fived. Scattered applause came from the watchers.

I grinned at them and took a bow.

"Are we done now?" I asked. "Please say we're done."

"You are ... for today. We'll practice more tomorrow."

"But I've got it," I protested.

He laughed. "Now you have to learn how to make the fly go where you want it to go."

"Oh, that."

"Yes," he said. "That." He rewound the line. "Let's grab a thermos of tea and go to the river. Do you have your phone?"

"Yes, why?"

"I thought I'd do some fishing, show you some of the spots where the fish like to hang out. You could take pictures." He looked at my feet. "Or if you wanted to wade out with me, we could do some casts together."

"Don't I need waders?"

"Water isn't all that cold, and we won't be in it that long," he said.

"Sure." Liz was off painting again, and Kathleen had set up the loom she'd brought with her, so I was on my own. Spending time with Joe was easy.

Except for those moments when he got way too close.

~ ~ ~

I sat on the bank of the river, watching Joe cast. The late afternoon shadows drifted over the water rushing from one place to another. It seemed to whisper as it moved along the banks, telling its secrets in a voice so soft I couldn't grasp its meaning.

Birds I had no hope of identifying flitted from one branch to another, some as silent as their shadows, others declaring their territory in loud, raucous notes.

The greens of the newly-leafed cottonwoods faded back into the darker notes of lodgepole pines and spruces. The grass was high, and every so often a curious doe stopped by to check out the show.

Tension eased from my shoulders. No one demanded anything from me right now. Joe was content in his world, and I was satisfied watching him. Although I'd been unable to define it when I was a teen, there had always been something incredibly masculine about Joe. It was a quiet trait with no need to boast itself with bulging muscles, sexual conquests, or vulgarity.

His hair had thinned, and his forehead elongated, but they added to the character of his deep laugh lines.

All in all, he was a good-looking man.

And I shouldn't care a bit.

But I didn't seem to be able to stop staring.

I pulled out my phone and took some pictures of him. As we traveled apart, I'd want to revisit the memory of a time when everything seemed right with my particular world.

Tearing myself away from the view, I stood and wandered the riverbank, taking pictures of flowers and scenes around me. I was even able to catch a shot of the shy deer.

I tested the water. Joe had been right, it wasn't icicle cold like most of the trout streams in Montana. The water was placid, less likely to knock me to my knees. I may as well go in.

After putting my phone next to Joe's on the bank, I cautiously waded into the river, careful not to examine my motives for doing so. It certainly wasn't to learn to fish. Once he left my life, I wasn't going to dash to a store and buy a rod and tackle.

"You decided to join me," he said.

"Figured I'd look at the pro up close and personal."

"Far from a pro. I've been casting for a good twenty minutes and not even a nibble."

"You still look like you know what you're doing."

"Oh, you've been rating my casting skills?"

"Something like that," I said, averting my gaze to the end of the line which was bobbing up and down. "Why is it doing that?"

"Because a fish is nibbling." He shifted the rod back and forth gently.

Suddenly, there was a splash, and the fish took the bait.

As Joe fought the fish for control, he let the line spin out, then pulled it back toward him. Every time the fish made a run for it, there was less line pulled until finally he was close enough for Joe to net him.

"Beautiful," he said as he got the fish back in the water and worked the hook from its mouth. The fish immediately darted off.

"Doesn't that hurt him?" I asked.

"According to most people, no." Joe shrugged. "But no one's been able to get a clear answer from the fish. We've always thought catch and release caused no harm, but now some scientists are questioning that as well."

"What we know changes all the time," I said.

"Yes. And it can be hard to let go of long-held beliefs." Joe held out the rod. "Your turn."

"I can't. I'll snare it in the trees."

"I'll stand behind you and guide you."

I hesitated.

"C'mon. It will be fun. I promise."

I moved in front of him, and he placed his hand on mine, subtly guiding me to cast back and then forward, landing it in the exact spot he'd indicated.

"Perfect!" he said, going to give me a high five.

I turned slightly to match his hand. My foot slipped into a depression, throwing me off balance. One arm cartwheeled while I kept a death grip on the rod with my other hand. Nonetheless, down I went, Joe helping to break my fall, but losing his own balance in the process.

Kerplunk! Both of us ended up on our asses in a couple of feet of water.

We looked at each other and laughed. I handed him the rod.

"Sorry. It got wet."

"No problem. It's meant to."

The giggles overtook me again, and Joe joined in. We started splashing each other and played until we were both exhausted.

I took long breaths trying to recover my equilibrium.

He was quiet.

I looked over to see him staring at me.

Everything within me stilled at the expression in his eyes.

He leaned toward me and stopped, his gaze questioning.

I didn't dare move.

He must have taken my paralysis for a negative reply because he drew back and leveraged himself to his feet before lowering his hand to help me up.

"I guess it's time to call it a day," he said.

"A day," I replied, knowing even as I said it that a joke we'd shared often as kids had fallen flat on its face.

"Bad."

"I tried."

"Yeah."

Silently we walked back to the road.

"See you," he said.

"Yeah." As I started to walk away, he stopped me.

"Di? Want to go to church with me tomorrow?"
I shrugged.
"Sure. Why not?"
"Good," he said. "Good. I'll see you in the morning."
I gave a small wave and returned to the RV.

# Chapter Thirteen

I stood damp and naked in front of the vanity mirror. In high school I'd been what they called athletic, even though I avoided exercise like the plague. It was a polite way of saying I'd descended from strong peasant stock, the kind of people who'd populated much of the plains once we'd pushed the Native Americans out. In my case, it was the stock of the Irish who came to Butte to toil hours a day in the pits beneath the earth.

The Treasure State. That's what they'd named Montana as they pulled out her copper, silver, and coal, sold them to the highest bidder, and sent the profits to eastern banks. They hadn't realized the true treasure was the people who'd come to Big Sky Country and stuck it out.

In high school, I was one of many with a body like mine.

California, with its blonde surfer girls and LA obsession with all things fit, had done me in. No matter what diet I followed or how many gyms I joined, I was always going to have the body I did.

Larry started making comments about my looks after we found out I couldn't have children, and I internalized them. The scale determined my mood for the day. The expression of my doctor at my annual physical, with his not-so-gentle suggestions that I eat less and work out more destroyed what little positive body image I had left.

And I started making jokes. *It wasn't over until the fat lady sings ... what do you expect from a woman who can't see her own ankles?*

I sighed and put my clothes on.

"Other people have to get in there." Kathleen pounded on the door.

"All yours." I pushed the pocket door out of the way.

"Why are you so dressed up?"

"I'm going to church."

"Since when did you become an un-lapsed Catholic?"

"Joe asked me."

"Wow," Kathleen said. "A church date. It must be serious."

"Ha. He asked, and I figured why not." I gestured for her to get out of the way.

She moved, and I walked past her.

"Di?" she said.

I turned around. Her face was serious.

"Be careful. I know we've teased you about Joe, but I also know you had a rough time with Larry."

"What do you mean?"

"He wasn't a nice man. I never liked him. Yeah, he liked to joke, and he was funny, but his jokes often had an edge to them. He made you look small. And you didn't deserve that."

She didn't know the half of it.

"Joe's not like that," I said.

"I know. He's one of the good ones."

"So?"

"Be careful."

No matter what happened, it was good to have sisters.

I grinned. "Don't worry. I'll try not to stand by any candles to encourage the church to burst into flame at my entrance."

"You do that." But Kathleen's face was still troubled.

"Don't worry. It will be fine. I'll stand up and down a few times, maybe make a joke with the priest. You know, usual stuff."

"Yeah," she said. "Have fun."

I could think of other words for it.

~ ~ ~

Our Lady of the Pines was a rustic A-frame set amid its namesake trees. The sharp roofline gave it a dramatic flair, especially in the morning light, and the interior, with its open polished log beams and rustic pine pews, was welcoming.

Joe was already a regular, in spite of the scant few weeks he'd been attending. He'd always been easy with people; something about him made others want to open up and spill their troubles.

I was welcomed robustly, then walked with Joe to an empty pew. Shortly after we sat, Joe went to his knees, as naturally as if he'd turned on the television with a remote.

I studied the order of service I'd been given. Not much had changed since I was growing up. Change in a centuries-old religious organization came slowly, if at all.

Joe returned to his seat, but I continued to be quiet, sensing his need to remain still.

The clearing of throats let me know the processional had begun, and I rose with the others.

The routine was familiar, and it was soothing to go through the same motions I'd known since childhood. Stand up, sit down, kneel, stand, sit ... Church calisthenics. See? I could exercise.

But when Joe went up for communion, I shook my head. I hadn't gone to confession, and had no intention of doing so, but the ritual stuck. Communion without confession wasn't something I was able to do.

"Good to see you again, Joe," the priest, a stocky man whose face disappeared in the arc of his smile, said. "And who is this?"

"My old friend, Diane O'Sullivan."

"Welcome, Diane,' he said, engulfing my hand in his. "I'm Father Tim. Are you here long?"

"Only a few weeks."

"Well, come back and see us next week then. Joe, you make sure she does."

"I will."

"Oh, and here ..." The priest reached into his voluminous robes and handed me a card. "I noticed you didn't take communion. My number is on the card. I'd be happy to hear your confession any time."

"I don't think you have that long." I smiled.

*Joke with priest. Check.*

"Nice meeting you," I said and walked down the steps

with Joe.

"Lunch? Brunch?" he asked.

"Food of any kind sounds good," I said.

"The Running Bear Pancake House is my go-to," Joe said. "They serve more than pancakes, including cinnamon roll pancakes." He grinned and rubbed his stomach. "But there's also chicken-fried steak with eggs and hash browns if you're really hungry."

The image of my naked body in the mirror rose in front of me.

"Do they have anything less ... um ... filling?"

He frowned. "Don't do that to yourself," he said.

"What?"

"Whatever is going on in your head. Brunch is to be enjoyed, like old friends and fine wine. Order what you want, eat until you're satisfied, and take the rest home. Or not. Brunch is a judgement-free zone."

As the prize-winning member of my mother's clean-plate club, it was hard to fathom leaving food on the plate. All those starving children in Africa!

"If you say so." I got in the passenger seat.

Minutes later, we were in front of a freshly-painted modest eatery. Several plate-glass windows gleamed. Joe gave his name to the man behind the podium who promised him a wait of only a few moments.

The business of saying yes to coffee and deciding what to order took up several minutes, but then we were left with each other.

"You said you were going to Mt. Rushmore from here."

"I'm only stopping there briefly," he said. "I have mixed feelings about the place. The entire Black Hills area is sacred to the Lakota Sioux, and we come along and deface some beautiful hills just to build a tourist destination and one-up Georgia for Stone Mountain. The land itself was stolen with treaty sleights-of-hand. And the guy who did all that drilling? He supposedly had ties to the Ku Klux Klan."

"I get your point. Still, I'd like to see it someday."

"Yeah," Joe said. "It doesn't feel right to go through South Dakota without seeing it or stopping at Wall Drug."

"Or the Badlands."

"Yes. That's where I'm planning to spend some time. Like Yellowstone, it's a place that is fun to explore in small bites. There are lots of trails to hike, and hidden places to explore."

"Sounds fun. Except for the hiking part."

"We'll help you get your Montana legs back," he said. "Liz isn't going to let you sit around."

"No, she isn't."

The waitress came by with our food, and we dug in. In between bites of the amazing food, we continued to reminisce, easily flowing from past to future and back to present.

"I'm planning a trip into the park at dusk sometime this week. I hope to see some wolves. Interested in coming with me?"

"Oh, yes! That sounds amazing."

"We may not see any. They're easier to spot during the winter when they venture away from the woods."

"But we might," I said, hope rising within me.

"Yes, we might. I've got a pretty good spotting scope, and I've been practicing using it."

"I'd love to get a picture."

"Probably not happening with a phone. I've seen those guys out there. They have mega lenses on their cameras. And patience. They'll prop their lens on a tripod and spend hours hoping for a good shot. I don't think I could ever wait that long for satisfaction."

Could I?

I was never going to find out unless I actually bought a camera. I'd put the dream of owning one away a long time ago when Larry found excuse after excuse to dissuade me from the purchase.

But now, reminded of life's possibilities by spending time with my high-school best friend, the time might be right.

# Chapter Fourteen

"This place is a damn pig sty!" Kathleen's roar made me hit a wrong key. Suddenly, the client's spreadsheet disappeared from my screen.

Did I save it? Please god, let me have saved it.

"Cleaning day today!" Kathleen announced. "Liz! Finish up with whatever you're doing!"

"But I was planning on going into the park to paint," Liz said, coming from the back.

"Aren't we supposed to be having fun?" I chimed in, more to annoy my sister than anything else. Kathleen had always claimed I was the bossy one, but I couldn't hold a candle to her.

"We went to the falls yesterday. We'll do some more later this week. But look around you, ladies. It's time to get a handle on this."

I glanced around and immediately saw what the problem was. True to form, Liz's belongings had begun to take over every surface. Not only her personal things, but items from the kitchen had drifted into the main space. I plucked a jar of bay leaves tucked behind the computer desk and held it out.

"Like this?" I asked Kathleen.

"Like that," she replied.

"Do you have to be so regulated?" Liz complained as she snatched it from my hand and returned it to the spice rack.

"Do you have to be such a slob?" Kathleen shot back. "I always figured you'd grow out of it, but ..." She shook her head sadly, reminding me ever so much of Eeyore, the depressed donkey from Winnie-the-Pooh.

"I'm not a slob." Liz waved the silk scarf she'd looped around her neck. "I'm artistic."

Kathleen and I laughed.

I had been so close to finishing my work. She was one of my more demanding clients and had been pestering me for a week to complete the analysis.

"Can it wait a half hour?" I asked.

"No," Kathleen said firmly.

"Since when did you become the boss?" I shot back, reverting to old behaviors from childhood.

"We have to share this space. I like things clean and tidy. Is that too much to ask?"

Boss to martyr in thirty seconds.

It wasn't worth the time to argue. I knew my sister. She was relentless. If a calf went missing, she'd ride day and night to find it, no matter what the weather.

"Let me recover this file, and I'll get on it."

"Diane," she growled.

"Can it, Kathleen." Fortunately, the file was easy to recover, and I shut down before Kathleen could build up too much of a head of steam.

Starting with the living area, I collected things that didn't belong and moved them. Soon there was a pile on Liz's bed in the back room. She'd always been like that. I remember Mom complaining about it. Liz had originally shared a room with Kathleen, while I'd gotten my own room as the oldest.

Boy, how I'd loved my room.

But Kathleen's complaints grew too loud, and I'd been forced to switch places with Liz.

As I moved her stuff out of the common areas, including a bra draped on a towel rack and socks that had missed the laundry basket, my resentment grew.

When I found my favorite moisturizer—one of my few indulgences—on her nightstand, I lost it. I stormed to Liz and confronted her. "Leave my stuff alone!" I yelled as I stood toe to toe with her.

"Jeez, Di, chill." She stepped away. "I only borrowed it. You don't have to lose it."

"Yes, she does," Kathleen said. "You have no boundaries. You never have. If we're going to travel for a year in this thing together, you're going to have to respect our stuff and our common space."

"Now you're both ganging up on me?" Her eyes widened.

Great. Now we were going to have a teary meltdown, Liz's other favorite tactic when airy-fairy artist didn't cut it.

"Stop. Right. There," I said. "I put up with all kinds of crap when I lived with Larry. I divorced him so I didn't have to deal with it anymore."

"So what?" Liz asked. "Are you going to divorce me, too?"

The idea didn't sound half bad.

"Nobody is divorcing anyone," Kathleen said. "We're trying to establish some ground rules. That's all."

Liz dropped into the nearest chair like a deflated doll. "I know. You're right. It's not that I don't care ... I get distracted. My mind jumps from one thing to another. I start off in one direction and then find myself going in the other. The only thing that keeps me focused is my painting. The only thing."

She sounded like the weight of the world was crushing her.

Kathleen and I looked at each other.

"Have you ever been tested for ADD?" I asked.

"Yeah. My college advisor told me to check that out. They gave me some pills, and I took them for a while, but then, well, things happened. I stopped taking them."

"Did they help?" Kathleen asked, sitting down in another chair. She looked up at me and gestured to the couch.

I sat down. If there was a real medical problem, then standing over Liz wasn't going to help.

"They kinda helped. But I didn't feel like me," Liz said.

"Would you be willing to go back to the doctor?" Kathleen asked.

Liz lifted her head and gave us a wan smile. "If it means you won't leave me by the side of the road in the middle of the country, sure." She leaned toward Kathleen. "I don't mean to drive you crazy." She glanced over to include me. "I love you guys. You're family."

Loving feelings built up in my chest. She was right. We were family. No matter who else came and went, we would always have each other.

"We love you too," I said, meaning every word. I hesitated a moment. As much as I loved her, I knew her habits would get to Kathleen and me over and over, especially in this small space.

Liz looked around. "Well, what are we waiting for? This place isn't going to clean itself. And when we're done, I'll go to the store and get fixings for lasagna. You guys love lasagna."

I stifled my groan. The kitchen was going to be disastrous when she was done, but she was right. Her lasagna was amazing.

"Group hug," I said.

We came together and wrapped our arms around each other.

Family. It was the best.

~ ~ ~

The lasagna was delicious, and the kitchen was the disaster I'd predicted. Once Kathleen and I were finished cleaning up, I decided to take a walk. I loved my sisters, but I needed a break from them.

My feet naturally went in the direction of Joe's trailer. He was outside in his chair, making notes on a pad of paper.

"Ah, there you are," he said. "I was wondering if I'd see you today."

"Hard not to," I said, sitting down in his spare chair. "It's a small place."

"True."

"What are you doing?"

"Oh, this?" He pointed to the pad. "I'm stuck on a plot point. Sometimes sitting down with a piece of paper and brainstorming all my possibilities helps break through the logjam in my mind."

"Plot points?"

"I've decided to make the book fiction, not non-fiction.

I think more people will read it."

I frowned. A mystery set in turn-of-the-century Montana?

"Historical mysteries are doing really well right now." He hesitated. "I ... well I sent some queries to agents. But I used different pitches. Some historical fiction, some non-fiction, and a few about a mystery."

"And?"

"The one who said he'd take a look at it said he couldn't guarantee anything. It may be too specialized."

"Sounds interesting to me. He'd be a fool not to take it."

"Thanks for your support." Joe smiled. "But you've always been a history buff." He put down his pad. "In fact ... I may have something you may like. Found it in a used bookstore."

He went into his trailer, then returned with a book which he handed to me. "Cover's a little cheesy, and the writing is old-fashioned, but the story is fascinating."

The book was *The Kemptons: Adventures of a Montana Ranch Family*. It claimed to be a true story. As I skimmed the text on the back, my curiosity awoke. "Does look interesting. I'll return it when I'm done."

He shook his head. "Pass it along. There's not enough space in an RV for books to pile up. And they're heavy."

What did heavy have to do with it?

He pointed to his pickup. "When you're towing, you need to watch how much weight you're carrying, especially going up and down the long, steep slopes we have around here."

"I've never thought about that," I said. "But then, there's a lot of things I've never thought about before. Like poop."

He laughed.

"All my life," I said. "I just flushed. Never thought about it. Now there are hoses, flushing, seals, and dozens of blue latex gloves."

He laughed harder.

The sound lifted my spirits.

"The other day I saw a guy standing over the sewer, watching. I asked him if anything was wrong. No, he said.

He was watching it go down to make sure there wasn't a problem. A problem? I don't even want to think about it."

I joined Joe in his chuckles.

"Yeah," he said. "Some people get very serious and obsessive about it."

"Some people don't have a life."

"Probably not. But speaking of living, are you up for going to Yellowstone tomorrow and seeing if we can spot some wolves? We could pack some food. There are some great places to hike in the Lamar Valley. We could snare a spot on the road where everyone parks, have a picnic dinner, and watch."

"Sounds like old times," I said. We'd often pack sandwiches when we went on our long walks together, especially once Joe got his license. We'd drive to an interesting spot and find a trail. Our walks weren't strenuous, we stopped too frequently to point out something interesting. Joe would look for birds, and I'd take pictures with my trusty Instamatic.

Whatever happened to that old camera? Or the pictures? Kathleen might know.

Our friendship had deepened on those long-ago walks. People were always teasing us about being a couple, but I'd never thought of ourselves that way. We were friends, nothing more than that. I'd never thought about kissing him.

Not until the prom.

And that had turned out to be a bad mistake.

"Stop overthinking," he said now. "It's a walk in the woods, nothing more."

"If you say so."

"I do."

"Then it sounds like a plan." We'd revert to old habits: simply two friends exploring new territory, sharing a sandwich when we were hungry.

"Do you think we'll see some wolves?" I asked him.

He shrugged. "You never know. We might get lucky. Or we might have to make a date to come back in the winter sometime and try again."

"You really going to move down by Ennis?" I asked.

"Once I get done with this trip," he said. "It seems like a good time in life to make a fresh start. I like to fly fish, and it's a beautiful area."

"Sounds perfect for you."

"What about you? Are you going back to the Bay Area when you are done with your rambling?"

"I have no idea." What *was* I going to do with the rest of my life?

# Chapter Fifteen

As promised, Joe picked me up after an early lunch. We chatted briefly while we drove the short distance to the park's entrance and waited in line to present his senior pass. Once we cleared the traffic, we settled into companionable silence.

A few eagles perched on the tops of pines, their sharp eyes searching for the day's sustenance. One must have spotted something because his wings unfurled as he pushed himself off the limb. Behind him, the top of the tree swayed. The awkward movements of his wings smoothed out, and he whirled about to swoop down in a nearby field.

Joe pulled over, and we watched as the huge bird zoomed to the ground, talons outstretched, and landed hard, causing puffs of dust to rise around him. He plunged his beak toward whatever was snared in his claws. The muscles at the top of his wings bunched, and he rose in the air, wings cutting the currents, a small animal in his talons.

After watching the bird disappear from sight, Joe put the car in gear and merged back onto the road.

So much to capture with a camera: the power of the wings, the dust-up when he landed, even the effort to become airborne. Something in my soul longed to create an image that would make a person pause in their busy life and consider it.

If I wanted to do that, I was going to need to spend the money on a decent camera. And to do that, I was going to need to get rid of the voices in my head that told me it was impractical and egotistical to think I could show anything to the world it hadn't already seen.

"There is so much to see," Joe said. "This is my tenth trip to Yellowstone, and I see it differently every time."

"Tenth?"

"Yes, we came here every year we could while the kids were growing up."

"It must be pretty special to you," I said. "A lot of memories." Was that jealousy I was feeling? Sorrow that someone else—his wife—had gotten to create those memories?

"True." He looked at me and smiled. "But I'm always ready for new ones, like the ones we're going to make today."

Yes, that's what we were doing, making memories. My shoulders relaxed.

We traveled north on the same road I'd taken with my sisters to the Artists Paint Pots. All around us steam escaped from vents and geysers burst without any attention to schedules. It was a powerful reminder that we were driving through a cauldron.

"Have you spent time at Mammoth Springs yet?" Joe asked as we approached the area.

"We're going next week, I think. Kathleen has some sort of schedule."

"I thought you were the organized one."

"I used to be. I guess raising two kids and running the ranch required Kathleen to start getting her ducks in order."

"Life with kids tends to do that," he agreed, and glanced at me. "We won't stop at the hotel today, but head straight to the valley."

"Watch out!"

Joe flipped his gaze back to the road and slammed on his brakes.

A bull elk, paying no mind to the traffic, sauntered across the road.

"Magnificent," I said.

"Yep."

There were multiple scars on the fellow, evidence of past battles.

"We came here one fall," Joe said, as he started moving forward again. "As night fell, the bugles of elk echoed around us. Often we could hear the clatter of antler against antler. We only saw one battle, and that was between mule deer. But we felt like we were in the middle of a giant battlefield."

"Probably because you were," I said.

"You've got a point."

We wove our way through the roads, cars, people, and stray elk and bison that surrounded the old hotel at the hot springs. The springs themselves had cooled over the centuries, leaving behind layers of calcium carbonate that always reminded me of tiers on a wedding cake.

"This park has gotten way too busy," Joe said. "It was bad before the pandemic, but it got worse during those years."

"Everyone trying to do fun activities without risking getting sick."

"Except this new crop doesn't seem to understand they're in a national park. They're still acting like they have Disney's minions to clean up after them, and that a bison is merely a cuddly human in a suit."

I shook my head. Humans.

We went back to enjoying the beauty of the park as we drove through the Blacktail Plateau, past the turnoff to Tower Falls, and down into the Lamar Valley. A stretch of grassland lay before us, sunlit under the cerulean sky. Puffs of wind made golden stalks dance, a rippling effect poised for the opening strains of *Fanfare for the Common Man*. Black smudges in the distant landscape took on the shape of massive bison, while deer edged closer to the forest. With a few additions from an earlier time—Native tipis, a wagon train in the far distance—the valley could serve as inspiration for a Charles Russell painting.

"When we get close to the bison, can we stop for a moment?" I asked. "I'm not going to be able to get much with the phone, but I can get something."

"Sure thing."

Fortunately, there was a spot to pull off near the heard. Interspersed with the shaggy dark brown shapes, small reddish calves explored and played, a couple of young males butting heads with each other. One was with his mother at the edge of the pack. I got out of the car and slowly moved closer, but stopped well beyond the twenty-five yards the rules of the park required. Bison could move deceptively fast, and this mom already had her eye on me.

As I was returning to the car, a door slammed behind me. I turned and watched as a thin man with a bushy beard, a little girl in his arms, climbed the bank toward the herd. His wife trailed behind him, shoulders hunched and her brow knitted in concern.

"Don't get too close," the wife said, her words coming out like a misused bow across violin strings.

"Amy says she wants to pet the baby," Dad said. "It's little. It will be fine. We've seen people go right up to the big ones with no problem."

Was he nuts?

Joe came up behind me.

"Did he say what I though he said?" Joe asked.

"Yep."

I scanned the area. No official vehicles.

We looked at each other and moved in the direction of the man and his daughter, getting far closer to the herd than I wanted to be.

"Sir," Joe said, his voice calm and friendly. "I can see by your license plate you're from Pennsylvania. I've heard that's a pretty state."

"Sure is." The man smiled at me. "Not as majestic as all this, but pretty."

"But not a lot of bison," Joe said.

"Only in the zoo. It's great to see them out here in the wild."

"Sure is," Joe acknowledged.

The man took a step closer.

"The thing is," Joe said. "There aren't any bars here. Or moats. Or anything to keep a wild animal from harming you … or your family. You've got to be respectful. These guys? They may look harmless right now, but they can move quickly and they're pretty agile."

"My daughter wants to pet that cute little red calf. And what my daughter wants, my daughter gets. Don't you, sweetie?" He smooched his daughter on the cheek, and she giggled.

"Hon," the wife said, "I think what this man is trying to

tell you is not to get too close. It isn't a good idea to let her pet the calf. It's dangerous."

"Nah. We'll be fine."

I'd been keeping an eye on the bison mom whose gaze flitted between her calf and the two-legged intruders. She shifted her feet and snorted.

"We need to move back," I said. "She's getting restless."

"We'll be quick." He took another step closer.

The bison lifted her head and snorted.

The little girl screamed and buried her head in her father's shoulder. "I don't wanna. I don't wanna," she repeated.

The man soothed the girl and took another look at the bison.

His chin dropped a little from its position of bravado. "It's okay. We'll go back to the car. Wave bye-bye."

"No," she said, her face pressing closer against his shoulder.

As he walked down the hill, his wife turned and mouthed, "Thank you."

"That was close," I said.

"I agree." Joe nodded at the mom. "And we need to leave too so she can settle down and care for her calf."

In their car, the small family zipped past us, the man's shoulders rigid as he drove.

"I hope they can stay out of trouble," Joe said.

"You were great," I told him.

Joe shook his head. "If that little girl hadn't balked, I'm not sure what would have happened."

He was right about that.

~ ~ ~

The hike had been a blissful reminder of times when we were kids. We reminisced about some of the places we'd gone together, caught up on a few more things, and dissected the current state of American politics.

By six, we had snagged a good spot at the edge of the road where small RVs and big pickups were already starting to gather. Scopes were set up and handshakes exchanged. This was obviously a group of people who'd spent time together.

"This is how a lot of them spend their summers. A few do it year round. A couple of fairly famous photographers show up now and then."

I stared at the mass of equipment stretching along the side of the road.

"When are you going to break down and get a camera?" Joe asked. "You're looking at those lenses like some women look at shoes."

I laughed.

"You certainly have a way of looking at things," I said.

"Don't avoid the question," he said. "What's stopping you?"

I hesitated.

"You can tell me," he said as he unrolled and set up a small table, waving away my efforts to help.

I sat in one of the folding chairs we'd already set up.

Beyond the bristling tripod-mounted scopes and camera lenses, the prairie stretched beyond us, similar to many other areas in surrounding Montana and Wyoming. But there weren't fences here, or Black Angus being fattened for market. Nature still had the upper hand ... to an extent.

The sun was warm, but it wasn't the blistering heat of late July and August.

Joe handed me a glass of wine.

"Wow," I said. "A proper dinner."

"It's still a picnic," he said, pulling containers from a cooler and laying them on the tablecloth he'd already placed over the table. "But it's a picnic with class. Only the best for you."

"What's stopping you from getting a camera," he asked again. "You were always taking pictures in high school. I'd half imagined you'd be one of the professionals by now."

I sighed and sipped my wine.

"Part of it was the times we grew up in," I said. "And my dad was a practical man. Kathleen's a lot like him. A camera was fine. If I'd wanted to open a studio for family portraits, graduation photos, and weddings, he might have gotten behind that."

"You would have hated it."

"Yep."

"And your husband?" Joe sat down and turned his total focus toward me.

How could I explain the power Larry had had over me, a situation I hadn't even realized I was in. I'd considered myself a strong woman. Independent. Yet he'd kept me in a cage of invisible walls. I hadn't realized it was there until I opened the door and walked out.

"Let's just say he wasn't supportive of anything that didn't contribute to our welfare."

"Meaning his welfare."

Surprisingly, tears formed in my eyes, as an echo of the constant ache I used to feel in my chest returned. I couldn't speak, so I nodded.

"I'm so sorry," Joe said. He put his hand on mine, but didn't say anything more.

We sat there quietly for a while, as I let the warm comfort he offered seep in through my bones. When the time was right, he took his hand away, and we settled into dinner and a non-consequential discussion.

We had just finished when people began to stir, moving toward their scopes as if someone had sent an urgent memo. Fingers pointed toward the edge of the trees in the distance.

Abandoning dinner, we joined them. Joe chatted with the nearest person, and the pointing resumed. He moved the scope ever so slightly a few times, then stopped. With a smile, he gestured for me to come over and showed me where to look.

It took a bit for my eye to adjust to the optics, but then I saw him, a magnificent canine who could only have been the leader of the pack. His fur was dark black, contrasted with the golden eyes that seemed to peer back at me through the lens. No wonder wolves were feared. They could see into one's very soul.

Joe and I traded places back and forth for a while as other members of the pack emerged.

"Shall we finish our dinner?" he asked after some time had passed.

I nodded.

We ate silently, trading looks and short sentences as we absorbed the miracle we had seen together. Wolves in Yellowstone. An ecological balance created.

After we cleaned up, we returned to the scope and watched until we could see no longer. People around us packed up and left until we were almost alone.

"That was amazing," I told him. "Thank you."

"It was." He turned to me and brushed my hair from my face. "And so are you. Don't forget it." He smiled. "I screwed this up the last time. If you don't mind, I'd like to try again."

He searched my eyes, asking for permission.

I forced myself not to stiffen and let my lips relax as I tilted my face toward him.

Was I doing this right? How did one kiss in their sixties? Tongue or no tongue?

Were my lips too dry? Should I moisturize them? I hadn't planned on being kissed.

But as soon as Joe's mouth connected with mine, the voices stopped. He knew the answers to all the questions.

It was the best kiss of my life.

# Chapter Sixteen

The Fourth of July rolled up on us before it seemed possible. Soon we'd be departing, going our separate way from Joe.

The three of us had settled into a routine of sorts. Periodically Kathleen would call a work day, and we'd clean and scour the RV, do the laundry, and make sure we had the right amount of everything we used consistently, like dish soap and toilet paper. Two or three times a week we'd pick a place in the park, drive to it, and spend time exploring. Other days we did what we felt like doing.

The days of choice were what allowed us to live together. All three of us had lived separately for a long time, although Kathleen had had her family, and I'd had Larry. Liz was used to her space and grew snappish if she didn't get it.

Joe and I spent more time together. Many evenings we went fishing, and took trips into the park to see things my sisters and I had missed, or revisited places we'd already seen. I was still frustrated by my lack of a good camera, but I hadn't made any move to change the situation, and Joe let it be. I refused his offer to go to church again, not finding the solace he obviously did. He told me I was bound and determined to be a heathen, and I agreed.

We didn't discuss the kiss.

Instead, we reverted to the safe spot of friendship. I, for one, tried to ignore the desire that had been awakened.

Impossible. Every time Joe was around, there was a need to get closer. Weirdly, I had the strangest desire to sniff his skin, like animals do when they meet and greet ... although the urge didn't extend to the intimacy animals seemed to need.

Thank god for small favors.

It was crazy-making. Trying to pretend everything was

normal, when all I wanted to do was touch him, hug him close, and taste him.

He seemed perfectly relaxed most of the time, but every once in a while I'd catch him staring at me with an intense look on his face. Almost always, he'd catch me looking and make a goofy face.

But I'd known what I'd seen.

He was as affected as I was.

And neither of us knew what to do about it, so we reverted to old ways and ignored the sands of time slipping through the hour glass.

I put on my make-up and costume and acted like none of it mattered.

My sisters and I intended to indulge in everything the small town of West Yellowstone had to offer for the nation's birthday, beginning with the Firefighter's BBQ. Joe said he'd meet us there.

"A hamburger and homemade root beer," Liz sighed. "It doesn't get much better than this."

"No, it doesn't," I agreed.

"Especially when it's made by a good-looking man," Kathleen said, eyeing the young man at the grill.

"Kathleen!" I exclaimed. "Michael is rolling in his grave."

"What?" she asked. "I'm supposed to give up living because he's dead?"

I felt my eyes widen as Kathleen studied the grill man. Then she turned back to me. "Don't worry. I'm not going to jump his bones. He's a little too young. But a girl has a right to look."

Who was this woman? I'd never known Kathleen—practical, down-to-earth Kathleen—to do or say anything remotely sexy.

And now she was mentally undressing the fireman flipping burgers.

I shook my head.

"Besides," Liz piped in. "Aren't you and Joe joined at the hip? You and he are off alone all the time. Kathleen and I wonder what's going on. You can't be spending all that time fishing."

"We're just friends. We aren't interested in each other that way," I said.

"Why the hell not?" Kathleen asked. "Besides, you're lying through your teeth. I've seen the way you look at him."

"The way she looks at who?" a masculine voice asked.

"Joe!" I said, blood rushing to my ears. Had he heard our discussion?

"We were just discussing whether your intentions toward my sister are honorable," Kathleen said.

"There is nothing going on between us," I protested. "You've been reading too many of Mom's old romances."

The others may have missed it, but I noticed the flash of disappointment that flitted across Joe's features.

"We're just friends," Joe announced with a forced smile. "Mind if I join you?"

"Sure," Kathleen said.

Joe set up his chair beside me, then asked, "Everyone got what they need? I'm going to go get some lunch."

"We're good," Liz said.

"How could you?" I asked as soon as he'd left. "Kathleen O'Sullivan, stay out of my business."

"Or what? You'll tell Mom?" Kathleen laughed. "I can't believe how much in denial you are. You've been in love with Joe your entire life. Even Mom and Dad knew. The only people who didn't have a clue were you two."

I looked at my watch. "It's almost time for pie. Hurry up and eat."

Liz checked her phone. "There's a whole half hour left, and it isn't that far."

"We don't want them to run out," I insisted. If I could only herd my sisters away from Joe, maybe my embarrassment would end.

But then he was back. "Say, did Di tell you about the parent who wanted his daughter to pet a bison calf?" he asked.

"She did," Liz said.

"People are idiots," Kathleen added.

"I've been working on this one," Joe said. "Listen up.

There once was a parent named Joe
Put his kid on a buffalo
A cowboy was born
When the kid grabbed a horn,
And, the beast raced across the plateau."

"Not bad," Liz said.

"Thank you." Joe beamed, but his gaze was on me.

"Don't give up your day job," I said.

"I already did," Joe said with a grin and plopped down beside me.

~ ~ ~

The afternoon sun intensified. I succumbed, and put on my hat, even though I hate wearing them. I'd found as I'd gotten older that hot sun could quickly dehydrate me and make me dizzy. Kathleen dug sunscreen out of her tote, and we slathered it on.

After securing our seats in the park near the venue for the buffalo chip chuck, Liz took out her pad and sketched while Kathleen and I reached for our books. Joe excused himself and wandered through the crowd, occasionally stopping to chat with strangers.

"He's someone who likes people," Kathleen observed.

"He can strike up a conversation with anyone, even people I know he disagrees with. And he listens. He's like a sponge absorbing the essence of the person he's talking with."

"Didn't you say he was writing a book?" she asked. "What's it about?"

"A mystery novel about suffragettes," I said.

"The mystery is why we're still fighting for our rights," Kathleen commented.

I nodded my agreement.

"They say a writer is always observing," Liz said. "Like other artists."

"That makes sense," I said. But I thought it was more

than that. Being interested in others was innate to who Joe was. His wife had been a very lucky person. Rare are the men who can simply listen without immediately trying to fix things.

"What's up with you two?" Kathleen asked.

Why wouldn't she let it go?

"We told you. Nothing. We're going in different directions when we leave here. The three of us are planning a year-long trip. He's headed back to Montana in the fall to move to Ennis. And even when we're done traveling, I'm probably moving back to the Bay Area."

"Why?" Kathleen asked.

"Because that's where I've lived all this time. I've got friends. There are things to do—museums and concerts and such."

"Uh-huh."

"What do you mean 'uh-huh'?"

"When was the last time you talked to a California friend? Or went to a museum or event? When you lived there, all you ever talked about was Larry, the house, business, and maybe your golf game."

I started to protest, then realized she was right. In spite of the access to 'culture,' my life had been pretty narrow.

"I'll do better next time," I said.

"I think you should stay," Liz said, finally looking up from her sketch pad. "We've missed you."

Kathleen nodded.

My throat tightened enough to cut off speech, and tears formed in my eyes. They wanted me here, back home in Montana.

"I bet Joe wouldn't mind either," Liz said softly.

For a second I felt like I was in my twenties again, with the world laid out before me in its endless possibilities.

But I wasn't in my twenties. I was in the fall of my life. Doors had shut behind me.

Still, my sisters wanted me home.

It would be nice to come back to the Big Sky.

"Thanks," I said.

My sisters nodded and went back to their tasks.

The book in my hand held no interest. My soul was filled with wonder. What would happen if I did pull up stakes and move?

Although Joe and I weren't a real possibility as anything other than friends, I'd have my sisters. I had already proven I could work from anywhere.

And there wasn't a better place to take pictures than Montana.

~ ~ ~

We spent the afternoon watching people pick up buffalo "chips" with rubber-gloved hands and tossing them as far as they could. Joe tried to get us to participate, but we were having none of it.

"I've picked up enough shit for a living," Kathleen protested. "I don't need to do it voluntarily."

He laughed, joined the line, and flung his chips a good distance. When the winners were announced, he was among them. He came back with his prize: a large bag of chocolate covered berries masquerading as bear poop, a certificate of achievement, and a T-shirt.

He'd also purchased shirts for the three of us. "I had to guess at sizes," he said.

"I'm thinking of boarding some horses when we get back home. The shirt will be good for mucking out stalls," Kathleen said. "Thanks."

"I think we should wear them when we're on the East Coast," Liz said. "Great conversation starters."

We laughed.

"Parade starts in an hour," Kathleen said. "Better get our spots."

The four of us folded up our chairs, stuffed them into their sleeves, and migrated to the next venue. Once there, Joe and I volunteered to round up some grub from the food trucks that lined the park.

On our way, we passed an open photography gallery and agreed to make a quick stop. The photographer had obviously spent a lot of time in the area, capturing details of animals, birds, fish, and even bugs that inhabited Yellowstone and Grand Teton National Parks. There were stunning pictures of aspens in full yellow surrounding the meandering oxbow of the Snake River.

I stood in front of a picture of a dark-colored wolf for a long time, recognizing the wildness in its eyes, so similar to the glimpse I'd had. It sent chills down my spine, but at the same time mesmerized me with its intensity.

"It's amazing, isn't it?" Joe asked.

I nodded.

"You need a camera," he said. "You don't have to take the same kind of picture. You need to take *your* pictures. And that will be good enough."

Dear sweet Joe. He was the only man I'd ever known who thought I'd ever be good enough at anything. Dad came close, but he was always more comfortable with Kathleen and even Liz than he was with me.

As we left the gallery, Joe took my hand and pulled me into the alcove of a closed shop. "We have to talk."

"About what?" I slid my hand from his.

"This." He cupped my face in his hands, then leaned down and kissed me.

It wasn't a long kiss, but it was enough for my libido to inform me it wanted more.

That wasn't going to do.

"There's nothing to discuss," I said.

"That's where you're wrong," he said. "There's a whole world of things to discuss."

He was right, of course. There were things we had to talk about. The problem was that I didn't want to talk about them. I didn't want to tell him how kissing him was everything I'd ever imagined it would be. And I definitely didn't want to risk his rejection one more time.

"I'm sorry, Joe. You're a nice man, a good friend. Let's just leave it that way without making it seem like anything more than it is."

I started back to where my sisters were waiting.

# Chapter Seventeen

I idly watched the house sparrows as they flitted around the campsite, searching for any possible crumb an inattentive human may have left. Their black chin spot made them easy to identify, and I'd seen them everywhere I'd ever been. They were cute until I'd realized they were an invasive species brought over from Europe in the mid-1800s. They were also lethal to native birds like purple martins or bluebirds when they wanted to take over the native birds' nesting sites.

Things were not always as easy as they seemed.

It would be easy to drift back into some kind of relationship with Joe. The barriers I'd thrown up to Kathleen were easily knocked down. Joe had waited decades to see me again; he'd last one more year. But I'd already spent more time than I wanted with a man. I was finally free. Why take it up again?

Men were projects, and I was done with working that hard for something I was no longer sure I wanted.

Except this man was an extremely good kisser.

As for coming back to Montana, was it really going to suit me after all the time I'd spent in the milder climate of California? Or was I like the house sparrows, no longer native?

I picked up my book, then put it down. Kathleen had gone off with some people she'd met at the park, and Liz was in her rent-a-studio. My work was done for the day, and truthfully, there wasn't much of it at the moment. I'd been deliberately cutting back as I drifted into semi-retirement.

But what was I going to do with myself with all the time I'd have, especially once this trip was over? Sit in front of the television, eating chips and flipping through different reality shows to see just how badly people could treat each other?

Adopt some grandchildren? Sign up for one of those pole dancing classes and become a stripper?

I snorted.

What if I made a second career out of photography? Tramping through the wilderness in search of an elusive bird or animal? All that hiking ... Then there was the software I'd need to manipulate the images.

God, I hated learning new software.

And I hated running through what-ifs.

Grabbing a walking stick, I took off toward one of the nearby trails.

It was a good day for a walk; clouds diminished the strength of the summer sun, and a slight breeze whispered through the nearby cottonwoods. Grass rippled and flowers were falling from bushes, leaving the hard nubs of nascent berries behind. Here and there birds and chipmunks skittered in the underbrush, while overhead birds flitted from branches. Occasionally, a squirrel scolded me from a branch above.

I breathed deeply, letting the peace of the earth quiet the questions I'd been using to torture myself. Instead of planning the future, or tormenting myself with the past, I let myself be present in the here and now.

It was glorious.

But my delicious walk was interrupted by acrimony ahead of me. I heard the man before I rounded the corner. He stood, large and imperious, leaning over a boy about eight or nine. The child's lower lip was twitching as he forced himself not to blubber.

"You're an idiot!" the man shouted. "I can't believe you're my son. What were you thinking?"

I stopped in the path as they were blocking my way.

"How many times have I told you not to flip your fishing pole up like that?" the man continued. "Now you've gone and snared a lure in the tree. Some cute little bird or squirrel is going to come along and get stuck on it. Then how will you feel? Why? Why?"

The kid was going to lose his battle with his lower lip.

While I sympathized with the birds and squirrels, what

this man was doing would scar his child. I knew, because I still carried the emotional wounds my ex-husband had inflicted.

And I'd been an adult.

"Can I be of any help?" I asked.

The man straightened and turned my way while the kid's eyes widened.

"Personal matter. None of your business."

I stood still.

"Did you hear me? Get moving, lady."

I wasn't used to confrontation. In fact I hated it with all my heart. It's why I'd caved to Larry time and time again. But I couldn't let him continue to berate that little boy.

"Other than the fact that you're in my way, I can't walk away and let you continue to abuse that child."

"He's my son, and he needs to be taught right from wrong. Keep moving." The man stepped off the path and pushed his son out of the way as well.

I stepped toward the boy as I took his father to task. "You ought to be ashamed of yourself! You're three times as big as he is and you're yelling." I spoke to the boy. "What happened?"

He pointed above him where the shiny spikes of a barbed hook glinted in the foliage.

"I was trying to cast like my dad," the boy whispered.

The man glanced up at the hook.

"Your dad must be a good fisherman."

"He's the best!" The boy smiled at his father, who was looking unsure of himself.

"He must be a good dad if you want to be like him."

"He is." The boy frowned, trying to reconcile his feelings about his dad with the yelling man in front of him."

I looked up at the hook. "It doesn't look that difficult to remove. I bet if you put your son on your shoulders he could get it down."

"I'm sure I could, Dad," the boy said eagerly.

The man glanced at me, then at his son. "Okay. Let's see. But be careful. It's sharp."

As I'd suspected, the hook wasn't hard to move.

After he put the boy down, the man looked at me. "Thanks," he said. "I was over the top. No excuse, but I'm a little stressed. My wife and I recently split. This is my first trip with my boy since. She didn't want him to come. If he got hurt ..." He pulled the boy close to him.

I nodded. "Have a good day, then." I looked at the boy. "And you mind your dad, you hear?"

"Yes! Yes, I will!"

I stepped off the trail and watched them walk hand in hand down the path.

"That was a good thing you did," said a voice behind me.

I whirled around.

A short, somewhat round man stood in front of me, a small-brimmed cloth hat adorned with hooks and flies on his head. His fisherman's vest sported more flies and pockets heavy with accoutrements, some of which slipped out of thread-webbed holes. His jowly chin displayed the short bristles of a man who hadn't shaved in a few days, but his smile was broad and his eyes kind.

"I hate hearing parents beat up on their kids," I said.

"So do I." He held out his hand. "Mason Bentley," he said. "From California. I've seen you at the RV park with your friends."

"Sisters," I clarified. "I'm Diane O'Sullivan." We shook.

"My wife and I take a trip to the Rocky Mountains every year," he said. "Her sister lives in St. George. She gets to visit her sister while I pretend to like my brother-in-law. Ah ... the things we do for love."

I grinned. His wife was a lucky woman.

He gestured toward the river. "My pole's over there. Mind if we go sit for a bit? Don't want to lose my pole if some rascal takes off with it."

"Or I can continue my walk," I said. "Leave you to it."

"Nah ... I'd enjoy the company. My own thoughts tend to be a bit boring if I sit with them too long."

I followed him back to the river. He insisted I take the small camp chair he'd brought while he stood.

"You did a good job getting him to realize what he was doing," Mason said. "I was a bit worried you weren't going to manage to talk him down, so I was coming to help you out. But you did just fine."

"Thanks," I said. "I have no idea why I did that. It's very unlike me."

"Non-confrontational?"

"As much as possible. Although I feel like I've done more of it since I've come back to Montana."

"Oh? Where were you before?" Mason pulled in his line and cast again, the line arcing back, then forward, before drifting to the surface of the water like a dragonfly settling down.

"You're very good," I said. "You must have been doing this a long time."

"Only since my wife died about ten years ago. That's when I finally figured out life wasn't as long as I'd always thought it was. I'd planned on having more time. Besides, I told myself, people were fighting for the job I had."

"What was that?" He must have remarried after his wife died.

"I was what they call a 'working actor.' Bit parts, walk-ons, touring shows if I had to do it. It sounds more glamourous than it is. After a while, hotel rooms, stages, and film lots all look alike." He swished his line. "But it was steady work, paid the bills, and even let me amass a retirement fund. We sent our one child to college."

"What did your wife do?"

"She was an agent. Worked just as hard as I did, if not harder. Suddenly, she dropped dead of an aneurysm. It took her before we had a chance to have the life we'd always planned. That's when I made my decision to start living the life I wanted, not the one I'd had."

"You didn't like being an actor?" I asked.

"I did, at first. But no one tells you it doesn't change if you don't become a top star. In my twenties being on the road and deprivation were an adventure. At forty, it got old." He shrugged. "But like I said, it gave me a comfortable living. But it wasn't the glamor people think of when they think of acting.

"I've seen you and that writer fellow together a lot,"

Mason continued. "Something there?"

"Joe? No, we're just old friends. We grew up together near Butte."

"I see." The line made another gentle tack to the right.

When people say they see something, it usually means they understand nothing at all.

"Like you, I had my life. I was married for a long time. I built my own business." I could feel the tension in my forearms building as I became more defensive about my past. "We weren't blessed with children, but then, not everyone is."

"I see I've hit a nerve," he said, reeling in the line and making another perfect cast. "When I met my second wife about five years ago, I knew, impossible as it seemed, it was love at first sight at the age of sixty. We had had very different lives. She'd married a Mormon like herself, had five kids, and did well in one of those multi-level marketing things. But her husband became more and more conservative, and went down the rabbit hole of conspiracy theories. Finally, she couldn't take it anymore. In spite of fierce opposition from church and family, she divorced him."

"Sounds tough."

Mason nodded. "But she was tougher. She re-established her own life and began to travel, something she'd always wanted to do. We met at a breakfast place in Sausalito, spent the day at Muir Woods, and haven't left each other since."

"Sounds like a romance novel," I said. Life wasn't like that for most people.

"It was, but that's not my point." He turned toward me, awkwardly bracing the rod against his foot and holding it with his right hand. "Life is too short not to be happy if you can. And finding happiness or love requires being open to possibilities, taking risks, being willing to confront your feelings and banish the ones that aren't working anymore."

He looked directly at me. "I have a deep feeling in my gut that you need to take a chance, Diane O'Sullivan."

I was gearing up to lecture him with a thousand reasons

why what he was suggesting was impossible when his rod bent, and he fumbled to hang on to it. I rushed over to help him as he lost his balance, seemed to stabilize, then stumbled again.

"Take this," he said, thrusting the pole at me right before he hit the ground on his hands and knees.

I gripped the rod tightly.

"The reel!" he yelled. "Don't let the line play out too much."

I put my hand on the reel and forced it to stop. He struggled to his feet, then took the rod.

By the time he'd played the fish into his net, had me take a picture, then released the trout back into the stream, the essence of my defense had gone down the river.

I waved good-bye and continued my walk, my mind slowly chewing over the arguments he'd made for love.

# Chapter Eighteen

I groaned as I lowered myself into the camp chair at our RV site.

"You sound like an old lady," Kathleen said as she sat down next to me.

"I *am* an old lady," I said. "And unlike you two, I've had a desk job for the past few decades."

"That's no excuse," Liz said, looking like she'd just stepped out of the shower instead of finishing a mile and a half hike that dared to go uphill. "No matter what you do for a living, exercise is a critical part of your well-being."

"Sadist," I muttered.

"And she's always spoken so well of you," Kathleen said. "How about I make a pitcher of cosmos. Would that make you stop moaning?"

"It would be a start." Everything about me ached. That was ridiculous. I'd been walking—a lot—since I'd returned to Montana.

But Liz's hike had a purpose. She was determined to see the Grand Prismatic Spring at the height of its color which meant hiking in the heat of the afternoon. And Liz didn't understand the concept of walking at a nice, leisurely pace.

"Oh, stop complaining," Liz said, flipping through her phone at the pictures she'd taken. "It was beautiful."

"It was." If I were truthful, I would have to admit that one of the reasons I was in a bit of a snit was that it *was* so beautiful. And I couldn't get the picture I imagined in my head. The phone didn't have the kind of resolution I needed to capture all the subtlety of color.

"Liz, I think you owe us something for going on this hike with you," I said as Kathleen returned with the cold pitcher and some glasses.

"How's that?" Liz asked.

"I want to see the pictures you create," I said, sitting up straight to look at her.

"Me, too," Kathleen said. "It's about time, Liz. I have no idea what you think you're protecting us from."

"We've both had sex," I pointed out.

"And at our age, discussion of bowel movements is almost mandatory," Kathleen added. "So is making it to a bathroom in time. You two don't know what you've missed not having kids. Those little buggers do a number on your body."

Liz looked down at her sketchpad.

"Maybe it's so abstract she doesn't think we'll recognize what we're seeing," I suggested.

"You two stop," Liz said. "I'll think about it, okay?"

"What if we return with the witch's broomstick? What then, oh great and powerful Oz?" Kathleen asked.

"I'll think about it. But I may have to return you both to Kansas."

"Toto too?" I asked.

"Toto too," she replied, attempting and failing to imitate the voice of Billie Burke who played the good witch.

"There is entirely too much levity at this site," Joe said as he ambled toward us, a beer in his hand.

Around us, other people were strolling with their dogs and drinks, smiling and chattering in small groups. RV cocktail hour had begun.

"Liz tried to kill us today," I told him, forcing myself to stay in my seat, despite the urge to greet him with a hug and kiss.

"May I?" he asked, gesturing toward the picnic table.

"Of course," Kathleen said. "I almost feel like you're one of us, you're here so often."

"Don't want to overstay my welcome."

"Never happen," Liz said. "Di enjoys you too much."

"And we enjoy watching Di with you," Kathleen added.

"Sisters," I said to Joe. "Ignore them."

"I'll try," Joe said, perching on the picnic bench. "But it's a little difficult. They are strong personalities."

"Overbearing," I said.

"Says the bossiest of all," Kathleen said.

"Pot," I shot back.

"Kettle."

"Stop it, you two," Liz said. "How was your day?" she asked Joe.

"Good," he said. "I got the writing done I've been trying to do for days. It's a particularly difficult section."

"What are you writing again?" Kathleen asked.

"A mystery set in Montana in the 1880s," he replied. "I need something to happen, and I kept running into time period problems. I needed to use things that didn't exist in that time period."

"Yeah, way back when we didn't carry phones in our pockets," Kathleen said.

"Exactly."

"Steampunk would be easier," Liz said.

"But not what I want to write," Joe said.

"Remember back when we were growing up, some places still had party lines?" I asked. "It was weird."

"They still had them in 2000," Joe said. "Most of them were connected to an individual line, so they weren't really the same thing."

"Why do you know that?" Kathleen asked.

"Because it was something I researched. In fact, a party line solved one of my key plot problems a while back."

"How did it do that?" Kathleen asked.

Joe grinned. "Now that would be telling. You'll just have to wait until I finish the book."

"I bet you don't know," Kathleen said.

"That may be true," Joe said. "But I'm not telling."

I smiled. This was good. Old friends, good sisters, for all the ribbing we gave each other, and a beautiful warm summer day. It didn't get much better than this.

Metal glinted on someone's hat, and I turned to look. Strolling down the road, holding hands with a lithe brunette walking a small dog, was Mason Bentley. She had to be six inches taller than he was and appeared about ten years younger, but they walked closely, and their heads often dipped toward each other.

"Do you know them?" Joe asked.

"I met him a few days ago by the river," I said. "Nice guy."

"Yeah, I've run into him a few times before. I don't know his name."

"He doesn't know yours either," I said. "Calls you that 'writer fellow.' His name's Mason Bentley."

"She's Naomi," Liz said. "She's taking watercolor lessons at the studio where I work."

"Well, I need to meet them too," Kathleen said and waved them over when they glanced our way. "Looks like we're having a party."

Mason and Naomi were all smiles, and the dog—a fluffy, white, wiggling mass—made an immediate beeline for Joe. As it perched its front paws on Joe's knee, Joe scratched around the dog's ears, making its rear end vibrate with ecstasy.

"That dog clearly likes you," I said.

"I like dogs. They know it."

"I haven't had a dog since I was a kid. My ex was allergic," I said. God, that man had limited me. Best not get involved with another one ... no matter how nice he was.

"Too bad," Joe said. "They're great companions, aren't you fellow." He put both hands on the dog's head, gently scratching down the neck and under the chin. The pup looked up at him with adoring eyes. "I'm thinking of getting one for myself once I get settled in the new place. What's his name?" he asked Naomi.

"Edsel," she said.

"Like the car?" I asked.

"Yep."

"Well, Edsel," I said. "You are certainly adorable."

Hearing his name, the dog dropped down and turned his attention to me. As he stretched up, I fondled his ears and chin, just as I'd seen Joe do. He was soft and responsive, a surging mass of love on four paws.

Joe leaned forward and scratched the dog's back. He was so close I could feel the heat from his body. He looked up at me, his eyes filled with an emotion I couldn't—or didn't want to—read.

Conversation flowed easily.

"Your painting is really lovely," Naomi said to Liz. "I caught a glimpse when I walked by the other day. Your door was ajar."

"What's it like?" Kathleen asked eagerly.

"You don't know?"

"She won't show us," Kathleen replied.

Naomi glanced over at Liz who shook her head.

"I'm afraid I'll have to honor the artist's wishes," Naomi replied.

Liz's shoulders relaxed.

"Not even a hint?" Kathleen pushed.

"I'm afraid not." Naomi tugged on the dog's leash. "C'mon pup. Dad and I still have to finish our rounds." The dog ran to her, and she scooped him up. "After bending over those pots for hours, I need to move."

Mason took her hand once again, and the couple walked back out to the pathway.

They'd barely left when our new neighbor ventured over. Several people had come and gone since Henry left. We'd been friendly to them all, but none had made a significant impression.

"Stuart Reeves," he said as he shook hands all around, his grip intended to dominate.

"You must be the lady in charge," he said to Kathleen, leaning on the picnic table.

"What makes you say that?" Kathleen asked.

"You have an aura about you that says leadership."

"You must be from California," Liz said. "No one else says 'aura.'"

"Guilty," Stuart said. "What's your occupation?" he asked Kathleen. "I mean, before you decided to take some time off and travel. You're far too young to have retired."

Joe and I glanced at each other, then leaned back to enjoy the show.

Kathleen leaned forward. "That's so nice of you to say. You asked my occupation?"

"I did."

"Shoveling shit and inseminating cows." Kathleen didn't even blink.

"Excuse me?"

"You heard me."

"I did, but what kind of job is that?"

"I was a rancher," Kathleen said.

He stared at her for a few moments, then said, "Oh. I get it. You were trying to make a joke."

She shook her head. "Just telling it like it is."

"Ha! Ha!" he said loudly.

Liz tried to cover her laugh with her hand, but bubbles of the sound escaped and tickled me like the effects of champagne. Joe shook his head.

"Now you ladies, be neighborly," Joe said. "What is it you do, Stuart?"

"I used to own a small company in the valley—Silicon Valley. We had some cutting edge AI technology, but I sold it to Google a while ago. Now I'm touring the country, trying to come up with ideas for my next start-up." He pointed to his rig. "Got myself a Living Vehicle Pro with all the upgrades. Even got a dishwasher. How's that, ladies?" Stuart beamed with achievement. All was good until he added, "I'm not sure you know what AI is ... it's a revolutionary new technology: artificial intelligence. It's going to change the world."

Kathleen gave him a sweet smile, then rose. "I'm a rancher, Mr. Reeves. Not stupid." She took his arm. "I trust you can find your way back to your Living Vehicle Pro. It's not very far." She gave him a little nudge in the right direction.

He glanced over his shoulder with a frown, then stalked off.

"What is it about that site?" Kathleen asked. "It seems to attract hopelessly uneducated men." She sat down and picked up her cosmo.

After a few moments of dissecting the annoying Stuart Reeves, Joe touched my arm. "I need to get back to my trailer. Would you walk with me for a bit?"

Kathleen had her eagle eye on us. "Don't let us stop you,"

she said.

I got up to go with Joe, but as we left, I looked back and stuck my tongue out at her. Immature, I know, but she was getting on my nerves!

Joe waited until we were out of Kathleen's direct line of sight before he stopped. "She can be a bit much, can't she?" he said with a grin.

"You don't have to tell me. I live with her." I was scowling until I looked up and saw the twinkle in his eye. Then I grinned. I couldn't help it. No matter how I was feeling, being with Joe made me happy.

"We do need to talk," he said.

"No, we don't," I protested, even though I knew he was right.

But I wasn't ready to explore whatever he had in mind.

"I'm leaving soon," he said. "And I'm not going without this resolved. You know I'm right."

"Can't we simply be friends?"

"I do believe that ship has sailed, as they say."

"But maybe it's gone in the wrong direction," I suggested.

"All the more reason for us to talk. Let's spend a day together—tomorrow maybe? Let's go into the park. We can have dinner at the Yellowstone Lodge. Then we can talk, far away from your sisters. My treat. Okay?"

I still hesitated. But this was Joe. We'd always been honest with each other, even as kids.

"Okay," I said. "Day after tomorrow. I've got a client call tomorrow."

"Sounds good." He looked around, then gave me a quick kiss. "Good night, Di."

"Good night."

Warmth flooded through me as he walked away. I'd always liked Joe.

*But where was that damn ship headed?*

# Chapter Nineteen

The day Joe and I picked to spend time in Yellowstone was one of those rare July days where the heat promised to stay reasonable, and a slight breeze kept bugs to a minimum. I didn't even have the excuse of rain to avoid the trip.

In my heart of hearts I didn't think there was a point to discussing anything. It was nice to know someone still liked me enough to kiss me. Larry hadn't done more than an obligatory peck for a very long time. Few people know what it does to the soul of a woman when the man she loves turns his back to her in bed. We have enough trouble trying to emerge from the invisible status society creates for us after our childbearing years are done.

Any ability I'd had to care for another human being, especially a man, had been starved of oxygen until it died. There was no resuscitating the victim.

But I waited patiently for Joe that morning, a tote bag filled with water shoes, a towel, sunscreen, insect spray, a book—okay, two books since I was almost finished with one—packages of snacks, extra water, a sun hat, a change of clothes in case I fell into the water, and a first aid kit.

Kathleen had helped me pack it.

She was always getting badges in Girl Scouts.

Sipping my coffee, I watched Joe put fishing gear in the back of his pickup, load up two coolers, and add a tote bag of his own. At one point he waved at me, his grin already wide in spite of the early hour.

I clutched my morning grumpiness as tightly as I did my coffee, needing one to dissipate the other.

Too soon, he pulled up to the RV and hopped out.

"Beautiful day!" he said.

"If you say so."

"I do." He took my tote. "You never did do well in the

morning. I remember that. I'll try to be gentle with you. But isn't it a great morning to be alive?"

I glared at him.

We got into the truck, and he drove south to the entrance to the park. Soft, new age music played through the speakers, the sort that was soothing to me for a while before it started to jangle my nerves with its repetitive calmness.

For now, it was doing its job.

About halfway to the first spot Joe had chosen, a place near where the Nez Pierce and Firehole Rivers met, he said, "Time's up. Grumps should be done."

I'd already been relaxed for several minutes. The beauty of the park sped up the process.

"Got me," I said. "Hard to be miserable with all this beauty."

"True. One of the reasons I'm moving to Ennis is to be closer to the park. I want to be able to make day trips when it's not peak tourist season. Or take the RV and stay a few days. Sometimes when I'm writing it's good to change the location."

"I don't know how you do it, put all those words on a blank page."

"Sometimes I'm not sure how the magic happens either," he said.

It was early enough that we were able to get a parking place not too far from the water. As we pulled the gear from the truck bed, anxiety began to tense my muscles. Although I'd been fishing with Joe in the river near the park, I'd never actually caught one. What if I did now? What if I made a fool of myself?

Joe chose spots for us. Mine was near a shaded pool where the water settled for a few moments before easing over some rocks to continue to cascade toward the Madison. A long time and ways from here, it might eventually exit the mouth of the Mississippi to end up in the Gulf of Mexico.

Or it might be gobbled up by thirsty cattle or corn on its way.

I got myself set up and cast the line, happy to see it float and settle like an elegant butterfly. My skills had definitely improved. Like the fly on the water currents, I let my mind drift, not really thinking. Images flowed in and out like an old photo album run through a projector: Liz artfully sneaking a fingerful of frosting off her birthday cake, Mom on her favorite horse, Dad's beaming smile at our father-daughter dance. The soundtrack was provided by the present: the gurgle of the stream, the rustle of leaves overhead, the chirps and caws of unseen birds.

Time passed in suspension.

I occasionally watched Joe, emotions I didn't want to identify coursing through my heart and mind. It was good to have him nearby, a solid anchor to make sure I didn't drift away with the current.

The sun was becoming hot on my back when something splashed into the water.

I turned quickly.

A bear had tumbled into the water about fifty yards upstream from me. I scrambled through my memory to remember how far bears were supposed to be away from us. I stood still, praying that the fish would pass on by my fly so the bear wouldn't notice me.

The shift of pebbles on the ground alerted me to Joe's presence.

"Are we safe?" I whispered. "Do you think the bear knows how far away he's supposed to stay?"

"I doubt it. But I think we're okay." He paused. "Or at least I am. I run faster than you do. He'll get you first."

"Don't even joke about this," I hissed.

"My bad," he said. "Let's keep an eye on him. I think if we stay still, we'll be fine." Joe studied the animal. "Of course, he might be smarter than the average bear."

"Joe!"

The bear was probably a young one, based on how he was behaving. He'd study the water, his big head weaving back and forth, his four legs squarely beneath him as the stream rushed by. Every once in a while he'd leap, splash down, then leap again, repeating the maneuver several times, but coming up empty. Then he'd growl his displeasure, move a foot one way or another, then do it again.

All of a sudden, he threw himself in the water and rolled onto his back. His paws flopped in the air as he gave himself a good bath, rolling back and forth.

"All hopes of him catching any fish are gone now," Joe whispered.

Just then, a hard tug came on my line, and my pole was almost pulled from my grasp.

"Not now!" I yelled as quietly as I could.

The movement attracted the attention of the bear, and he turned his head to look at us more carefully, but didn't relinquish his spot in the river.

I fought to hang onto the pole and fish.

"Let the line out," Joe whispered.

"Shouldn't we cut it and run?" I asked.

"He doesn't care about us. Let the line out."

I did as Joe suggested, and the fish took off downstream. The bear watched us, but didn't move in our direction.

"Now, stop the line and reel him in," Joe said.

"This is crazy!"

"Shh ..."

I reeled the line back in, the fish fighting me every inch of the way. When the tip of the rod was bent almost to the water, Joe told me to let the line out.

We repeated the exercise several times, the bear watching us like we were a National Geographic Special for wildlife. Finally, he tired of the game, flipped himself over, and climbed out of the stream before stalking off toward the nearest cluster of trees.

Seeing him wander off made me relax my grip on the line just as the fish made a last desperate attempt to escape. I windmilled my arms, the pole flailing wildly, as my feet slipped beneath me, but there was no stopping gravity.

Down I went.

The rod slipped from my grasp, and Joe dove after it, landing on his knees in the water as he managed to snag it. From that position he reeled in the fish while I watched, unsure if my limbs were still intact and not willing to find out.

Joe held up the fish briefly for me to see, then released it.

After staggering to his feet and placing the rod on the shore, he came to help me up.

"Are you okay?" he asked.

"Glad you finally got around to asking," I said.

"I didn't see any blood in the water, none of your bones were at funny angles, and you were conscious, so I figured there was no immediate emergency."

"Good for you," I said as he helped me up.

I looked down at my soaking clothes. I was going to have to tell Kathleen she'd been right about the change of outfit.

Bummer.

The sun was warm enough to get my clothes from soaking wet to merely damp in about a half hour. We continued to fish, and I was able to catch a few more before he suggested we stop. After packing up, we headed south to the next spot Joe had picked out, down by Lewis Falls.

The day went easily from then on out. We ate the picnic lunch he'd prepared, and took a nap on soft blankets before driving around the lake and fishing some more. Nothing major was discussed, and I was content.

~ ~ ~

"I met Patti my senior year in college," he said over elk steak and potatoes that night. "As soon as we met, I knew she was the right person for me. It took me a little while to convince her, but she came around. And, like I thought, it turned out pretty well. We had a ... um ... number of good years together."

Why the hesitation?

"I never thought I'd consider another relationship," he said. "We had a lot of common interests, but also enough to have separate lives so we didn't suffocate each other."

"Sounds ideal."

"It was, in many ways. Of course we had our ups and downs; all marriages do. But I believe it was one of the better marriages." His smile was just a little off. I'd known him too long not to miss it. There was something he was leaving out about their "wonderful" marriage.

We were quiet for a moment.

"Then you walked back into my life."

"And I'm about to walk back out," I said, trying to lighten the mood.

"Not before we talk about it," he said.

It was time to lay my cards on the table.

"I didn't have what you had, Joe," I said. "I thought Larry was a good man. In his own way, I suppose he was. But he was lazy. He'd been raised by a father who felt the world, and women, owed him a good life. So I worked all day to build my business and came home at night to clean the house and prepare his meals."

"I'm so sorry, Di," Joe said.

I shrugged. "It was what it was. And now it isn't."

"It's probably just as well you never had children," he said.

"I wanted them. Desperately." The last word came out in a whisper.

He let the silence build while he ate more of his dinner.

So did I. Telling anyone else that Larry had refused to admit he shot blanks or the blame he heaped on me seemed like the ultimate betrayal of our marriage vows. My Catholic upbringing had made me hang onto hope for wedded bliss for far too long.

We talked of casual subjects until it was time for coffee and dessert.

"I'm not sure what you're thinking," I said, tired of dancing around the subject. "But I'm not ready to involve myself in any other relationship—no matter how good the friendship."

The waiter served our coffee.

"Besides," I said. "My sisters and I have this trip planned."

"Where will you go when the trip is over?" he asked.

"I don't know yet."

"Ennis is a pretty place."

"Joe ..." I protested.

"I understand about disappointments," he said. "Believe me, I do. But I also trust in serendipity and second chances. Come back to Montana when you're done. I'll show you what's possible."

"I'll think about it," I said. "That's all I can promise."

# Chapter Twenty

"Let's sit on a bench and look at the lake for a bit before we go home," Joe suggested as we walked down the front steps of the old hotel. He took my hand. "Please? It's beautiful."

"Okay."

We walked across the roadway and down a short path to an empty bench. Without discussion, we sat close together, and I didn't protest when Joe put his arm around me. It felt natural.

I leaned into him.

We sat quietly and watched the light play across the lake's ripples. A pair of trumpeter swans descended to the water, their entry a bit ungainly. They swiftly transformed into the regal birds they were, their damp white feathers glistening in the end-of-day rays.

"I believe things occur for a reason," Joe said. "Call it serendipity, the Universe, or God, something or someone is put in your path to teach you if you allow it."

"And what do you have to teach me?" I asked.

"Possibilities."

"What do you mean by that?"

His hand clasped my shoulder. "I'm really sorry your marriage was so unfulfilling," he said.

"It's over now. No use dwelling on it," I said.

"If you're still using it to guide your future actions, then it isn't over yet."

"There's nothing wrong with using past experiences to guide future decisions," I replied, shifting away from him.

"That sounds a little too 'Dr. Phil' for my taste," Joe said with a laugh. "I'm not saying it's wrong, but I think it's a little simplistic. You told me you don't want another relationship because you had a bad one, right?"

"And because the odds aren't good of doing any better. You've seen the statistics. You know the divorce rate."

"So all men are off limits because Larry was a bad apple."

"Well ..." It didn't sound logical when Joe put it like that. I grinned up at him. "You're not the same. But I'm not ready to get back into the reality. You know: socks on the floor, cap off the toothpaste, toilet seat up, inability to cook anything beyond toast."

"Nice try, Di." Joe wasn't smiling. "What is it? Really."

I swallowed.

"I'm scared, Joe. I know who you used to be, but we were kids then. You seem solid now, but people get really good at hiding things as they get older."

"You mean I might be a big bad serial killer lying in wait for you to commit to me, then I'll take you off and torture you?"

I shook my head. "Of course not." I peered up at him from under my thinning lashes. "Are you?"

He roared with laughter.

"Di, I'm exactly what I seem to be. What you see is what you get. My warts are fully on display." He pushed a stray hair from my forehead. "And what I am is a man who's been in love with you my entire life."

He tilted my face toward him and kissed me. It wasn't a passionate kiss, more the dot at the end of his sentence.

I let out a breath, then turned away. I'd planned to make it perfectly clear that we were not a couple, had only ever been friends, and were not destined for the great happily-ever-after.

I was failing miserably.

We went back to looking at the lake while I tried to remember the good, solid reasons this was impossible.

"I'm thinking about staying for another week," Joe said. "Someone cancelled, so they have the room. My son might come down and join me for a bit, get some fishing in."

"He likes it as much as you do?" I asked.

"Let's say that for some strange reason he likes to spend time with his old man. He tolerates fishing because that's the way to do it. He's an avid hiker and cross-country skier."

"Dillon's a good place for him, then."

"Suits him. In the winter he plays bass for a string band."

"Violins?" I asked, trying to imagine Joe's son in a suit playing chamber music.

"Fiddles," he replied, and the image of blue jeans and flannel shirts clicked into place.

"It would be fun to hear them some time," I said.

"That could be arranged." He looked over at me. "If you decide to stick around, that is."

There was nothing to say.

"Well, we'd best be headed back before it gets too dark. Don't want to hit a bison on the road. If we time it right, we should hit the Upper Geyser Basin at just about sunset. I understand it's really beautiful."

"Sound nice."

As we drove south from the hotel along Yellowstone Lake, I told him about my one and only trip to Yosemite, hoping to stay away from uncomfortable topics.

"Some friends and I decided to go camping. Larry wasn't interested, which was fine with me," I began. "It had been a long while since I'd gone camping, and some of them had never been, so there was a lot of new equipment and new routines."

"Could be interesting," Joe said.

"That's one word. One guy brought along bear spray. We weren't planning on doing any back country hiking, but he insisted on carrying it anyway."

The accountant had never been in the woods before, thought a lot of himself, and figured going on the trip would be a great way to convince a young woman that he was date-worthy material. From the sparkling condition of his gear, and the well-used patina of hers, I'd figured he'd made a bad choice.

"We were hiking up to Vernal Falls when we ran into trouble. True to form, he had all his gear with him: carved and polished hiking stick, shiny hunting knife in a stiff leather sheaf, a Patagonia vest that still had its fluff. And the bear spray."

"Patti and I took a trip down there once and hiked that trail. It's pretty steep."

"Yep."

"Let me guess," Joe said. "New hiking boots."

"You got it. Pretty soon he was hurting. No one had a lot of sympathy because he'd already demonstrated what a blowhard he was. But the woman he was after took pity and stuck with him at the tail end of the group.

"All of a sudden we heard shouting. I turned back and saw her screaming at him. She flailed at her skin, coughed, and swiped at her eyes. A nearby ranger called it in, and she was whisked to emergency services."

"Was she okay?" Joe asked.

"Yes."

"So how did he manage to do that?"

"He was showing off, demonstrating how quickly he could unhook the spray and get a bear, proving she was safe with him. He stumbled."

"And she wasn't safe with him at all."

"Not a bit."

"People do the craziest things," Joe said.

"They do. I'm not sure what's more dangerous in a park—the animals or the people."

"Even toss-up, I'd say." Joe made the turn at West Thumb. "For the record, I've got bear spray. I've used it once in my lifetime, but it wasn't on a human."

"Good to know."

The silence settled in again as we started through the basin region. The colors on the horizon deepened as the sun slid down, and light angled over the valley before us. Steam pools sported stripes of colors, the mineral makeup of the water sharpening the hues. Steam drifted in the darkening air, providing an otherworldly sensation.

Joe pulled into a parking lot, and we got out. He took my hand as we walked to a sheltered spot that was free of people. Then he wrapped his arm around me and pulled me close.

Around us, steam clouds appeared as specters, hot

water gurgled, and mud plopped, providing sound effects suitable for *The Twilight Zone*. The smell was sulphur-acrid, unpleasant, but not overpowering.

But none of that compared to the feeling of being snuggled next to Joe, the heat from his body messing with the temperature of my own. In summer, coats didn't provide a protection against intimacy. His body contours were firm, especially compared to the over-softness of my own.

But my lack of physical fitness didn't keep my treacherous body from desire. The more we stood there, the hotter I became, and it wasn't from the geysers. All that heat was generated by desire, a rampant need for the man standing next to me.

That part of me was supposed to be dead. Larry had killed it years ago, hadn't he?

The bubbling stew rising to the earth's surface mocked me.

I'd buried my desires, unwilling to continue cutting myself on the sharp edges of Larry's disinterest. Joe appeared interested, but what was I supposed to do with *that*? It had been years since I'd even attempted intimacy, shutting it all away behind a closed door with five different kinds of locks.

But no matter how much I tried to box myself into the older-woman-done-with-juiciness image, it wasn't who I was. It had never been.

How had I wound up with someone like Larry?

I was saved from trying to answer that question by Joe.

"Amazing, isn't it? I never get tired of seeing God's glories."

"I wonder what He was thinking when He constructed this place."

Joe chuckled. "Maybe He was giving us a foretaste of what hell might be like, warning us to mind our Ps and Qs."

"What does that even mean?" Somewhere in the recesses of my memory, I knew the answer, but couldn't come up with it.

"Mind your please and thank yous," Joe replied. He pulled me close again, and we watched the sun sink lower.

His hand moved to my waist as I leaned into him. It was very close to my hip. Need arose within me. It would be so simple for him to shift down five inches. A small space between chaste and—what did they used to call it?—carnal knowledge.

Well, that was probably a bit much. It would only be a hand on a hip, not what was truly meant by the other term. Was that what I ultimately desired? To know Joe at that level?

Back in high school, when hormones raged, I wanted him to kiss me, and then go further. I wanted to let him explore my young body until I told him to stop. Because one thing I knew then about Joe was that he was safe. If I said stop, he would.

And now? The man hadn't changed. But he would let me take the lead ... which damned me. I no longer knew how. What did men want?

I turned to look up at him, but his hand remained stubbornly on my waist.

"It's beautiful," I said, then parted my lips.

That was the signal, right? It's what those young creatures with their plump lips, moist lipstick, and perfect teeth did in the movies, wasn't it? Did it still work when age thinned lips, teeth had always been crooked, and a woman couldn't remember where she'd put her lipstick?

Apparently, it still did because Joe's eyes looked directly into mine for a few seconds before giving me what I wanted.

I eagerly accepted his mouth on mine, leaning in as the kiss quickly became deeper than any we'd had before. Slowly, that hand finally drifted down and held my butt. Ever so slightly, I leaned forward, craving ... well ... something.

Was I replaying unrealistic sex scenes from novels? I don't know. But being close to Joe, kissing him, feeling his arms around me was nothing like they described.

It was better.

It was real.

# Chapter Twenty-One

We'd managed to untangle before things went too far. It was probably just as well. If the park frowned on people walking on the crust of the hot springs, what would they think of two old people having sex at its edges?

"We have things to talk about before ... well ... before we go any further," Joe said, his gaze averted.

It was the same damn argument we'd had in high school. This time I wasn't going to walk away without a fight.

"I was thinking more a hot and heavy short-term affair," I said, moving closer.

"You know I don't roll that way, Di."

Hadn't marriage changed him even a little bit? It wasn't like either of us had taken vows of chastity in the intervening years. It wasn't fair I had to have a do-over of prom night almost fifty years later!

He'd waited to ask me to prom, figuring I'd have lots of other—better—options.

Ha. The O'Sullivan sister everyone wanted was Liz, who looked more like an Irish fairie queen than her two older sisters. Kathleen and Michael were already an item, and everyone figured Joe and I were as well.

But we weren't. We were that worst of all teenage couplings: *just friends*.

An older or more cynical teen might have wondered if my friend was gay, but I was quite sure of Joe's sexual orientation, even if I never thought about it.

Finally, he asked. One of his sisters had pushed him into it, telling him he owed me for monopolizing all my time. The pictures my father took are still in a box somewhere: Joe looking stiff in an unfamiliar tux, and me beaming in a dress my mother had made for me. She was a skilled seamstress, so it was as good as anything the wealthier girls bought from one of the fancy stores in Butte.

We'd had a good time. Joe's sisters had taught him the basic rudiments of dance, so my toes stayed safe. It was only when he brought me home that trouble started.

I so wanted him to kiss me.

He'd finally made his move.

I eagerly accepted, years of pent-up desire driving me to behavior that wasn't at all ladylike. Teenage passion drove us beyond the kiss to hands fumbling over body parts before he held up his hands.

"Whoa," he said. "We're not ready for this. Well, *I'm* not ready."

I sat there and caught my breath while I tried not to cry from frustration and rejection.

"I'm sorry," he said. "It's not you." He caressed my cheek. "You're wonderful. But I want to wait. Let's see what happens. It's too soon. We're only eighteen. There's college. You might not feel the same later. If it's meant to be, we'll get there. But not now. You understand, Di."

But I didn't. No matter what he'd said, I felt unworthy.

I wouldn't talk to him for the rest of senior year. I hung out with other friends, or stayed home.

It was stupid. But I was a teenager. And teenagers do stupid really, really well.

He tried to get me to talk, but I was having none of it. Instead, I hugged my misery tight to my chest.

Exactly like I was doing now.

And it felt like the exact same damn choice.

Right now I wanted to be anywhere but here, standing at the edge of a boiling, steamy hell that reflected the emotions churning on my insides.

"Whatever you say, Joe," I told him before walking to the truck and climbing into the passenger side.

"Don't do this," he said when he got behind the wheel. "Not again. Don't shut me out."

"I'm not sure who is shutting who out here," I told him. I begged my adult self to take control from the wounded teenage angst driving me.

"I'm not. I swear to God, I'm not," he said. "Is it so wrong to want to take things slow?"

"There isn't a lot of time for slow at our age," I said. "I would think you would get that by now."

The pain I'd caused was reflected on his face.

Damn my uncontrolled words.

Finally, the adult took over.

"I'm sorry," I told him. "It was a lovely day. I'm sorry if I've ruined it."

He patted my hand. "It's okay. We're good. Although we could use a goofy bear about now."

I laughed.

As if on cue, a bison walked from a nearby copse and sauntered in front of us. He stopped when his massive head and shoulders were midway across the front of the truck and turned his beady eyes toward us.

We stayed perfectly still.

After a few agonizing seconds, he snorted, then continued on his way.

And so did we.

~ ~ ~

I didn't contact Joe at all the next day.

The more mature voice in my head pointed out that I was repeating my teenage behavior, but I ignored her. Instead, I threw myself into the logistics of our trip, checking and rechecking that I'd made the reservations I needed, especially in the more popular parks, calculating the distance between stops so that we could enjoy the drive without taxing ourselves, and making sure we had time to rest and recuperate at a park that had a laundry and a full-service grocery store nearby.

Once I'd triple-checked, I made sure my client work was caught up, then killed some time on Facebook. An advertisement for a camera caught my eye, and I clicked through to the item's page. I realized I had no idea what half of the terms on the page meant, so I went down the rabbit hole of research.

Before I knew it, an hour had passed.

I wasn't sure I was any clearer about all the functions of the camera, but I had an idea of the possible brands and models.

I could start with something basic, couldn't I?

*For what you use a camera for, a point and shoot is all you need.*

Larry's voice echoed in my brain, much louder than the protests of my tiny creative soul. I'd been to therapy before and after the divorce, and made progress, but I'd gotten tired of the process before the therapist thought I was ready.

I'd cancelled an appointment. Then another. Then the rest.

The world was geared toward the practical. Much like it had been at the end of the nineteenth century, workers worked and those who had money or were a little bit crazy did art.

I'd always felt Liz fell into the latter category.

She seemed to make money with it, enough to live on. Kathleen told me the ranch fund was actually greater than it had been when we inherited from our parents. Both Liz and I had put in money, while Kathleen had managed our property and business conservatively. The operation covered its expenses and made a small profit every year.

The manager she'd hired several years ago when Michael's health began to fail had been left in charge as we took our trip. Even though we'd sold the cattle, the fields of wheat and alfalfa needed tending. When we got back, we'd decide if we wanted to sell part of it, or get easements from something like the Nature Conservancy. One thing we were determined to do was keep it intact. It wasn't going to become another development of large look-alike houses stuck out like a treeless junk heap in the middle of the prairie.

I typed all the variations of Liz's name into the search engine.

There were a few items, but nothing I didn't already know, mostly local organizations she belonged to, or classes she taught locally. One connection was odd. She'd done some work with a birth mother support organization.

Probably taught a therapy class.

I clicked away and tried searching for artists from Montana. A half hour later, I'd turned up nothing.

With a sigh, I clicked off the computer, just as the third text message came in from Joe.

*You're obviously busy*, it said. *Can we plan something later this week?*

I ignored it and gathered my laundry. Undoing the sofa, I added the bedding. Liz and Kathleen had gone off to sightsee downtown, but I told them I was tired and wanted to stay home. Basket, soap, and quarters in hand, I trudged to the laundry room. Once I'd started my loads, I ignored the sign that told me not to leave my laundry and went back to the RV.

There, I got out the small vacuum we'd brought with us and tended to every aspect of that sofa. No crumb, dust mote, or spider was left undisturbed. Then a trip back to the laundry to move clothes from washer to dryer. Then getting out spray bottles and cleaning with fabric cleaner, polishing the fake wood in the areas surrounding my "bedroom," and rubbing the window and light fixtures until they gleamed.

The whoosh of the door made me look up. Kathleen and Liz walked in, packages in their arms.

"What are you doing?" Kathleen asked.

"Cleaning."

"Deep cleaning from the looks of it."

"So?" My sister brought annoyance to a new level. I was spoiling for a fight. Just let her keep pushing.

Kathleen shrugged.

"I'm going to make a super dinner tonight," Liz said, her voice overly cheerful. "I'm in the mood to get creative."

"Which means it will be amazing," Kathleen said. "Or not."

Liz playfully smacked our sister. "Just because one time I made something inedible ..."

"Totally inedible. And it wasn't only once."

"I only remember once."

"Let me remind you ..."

I let my sisters' chatter fade into the background as I

finished up my tasks, then left for the laundry. By the time I returned with folded clothes and clean bedding, Liz was hard at work in the kitchen.

"Let me help you with the bed," Kathleen said.

"Okay." Bedmaking was always easier with two.

As we snapped the fitted bottom into place and prepared the top sheet—hospital corners and all—Kathleen told me about the places they'd gone to during their excursion. "Did you know there's a camera shop on one of the side streets?" she asked.

"Yes," I said in a tone I hoped would end that particular topic.

"Not ready to get one yet, then?"

"I don't need one."

"So you say." We put the bed back together. She handed me the box that held all the little things I liked to have around me, mementos I'd picked up as a kid or after Larry and I had split.

There was nothing from my marriage.

"I remember you cleaning like this once before," Kathleen said.

"I'm sure I've cleaned like this before," I said. "Mom would never have let me get away with a messy room."

"Oh, don't get me wrong. Your side of our room was always neat." Kathleen sat on the couch. "But you only went in for sweeping under the bed or taking everything off the shelves and polishing when Mom made you. Except for that one other time."

I carefully arranged the pieces until I got to the pink-veined rock in the shape of a heart.

"The night after the prom," Kathleen said as I examined the rock Joe had found and given me.

How could I have forgotten where that came from? He'd given it to me the day of graduation. I'd stuffed it in the pocket of my dress where it nestled next to all the feelings I denied.

"So what's happened between you and Joe now?" she asked.

"What?" Then her words registered. "Nothing.

Nothing's wrong. I just needed a day to myself. Joe and I will do something later in the week. His son's coming, so he won't have much time." I carefully put the rock on the shelf.

"We never liked him," Kathleen said.

"Who? Joe? Everyone loved him."

"Not Joe. Larry. Dad knew he was lazy right from the beginning."

"Larry worked," I protested, flopping onto one of the easy chairs, my energy depleted.

"The bare minimum to keep his job."

"You don't know that."

"I do," Kathleen said.

"Dad grilled him every Christmas," Liz said from the kitchen. "As soon as you left, he and Mom would have a long talk on the porch. Kathleen and I took turns listening."

"How special," I said.

"We were worried about you," Kathleen said. "Larry made you sad. Everyone could see that. Being with Joe has brought back the sister we knew as a kid: happy and full of vitality."

"It was hard to see you so unhappy," Liz said.

"I was fine," I said.

Kathleen gave me "the look," the one that reminded me "fine" meant anything but.

"We love you," Kathleen said. "Whatever has happened between you and Joe, fix it."

"But nothing has happened."

"Maybe that's the problem," Liz said.

"Nothing's going to happen," I said. "Joe and I are friends, like we've always been. That's all."

"Then it's time for one of you to change it. Stop doing what you've always done, Di. It's only going to get you the same results. You deserve more. Believe in yourself. This time, reach for the moon."

Kathleen got up from her position.

"Need any help?" she asked Liz.

"Actually, I could. From both of you. This recipe is a lot harder than I thought it would be."

Kathleen looked over at me.

"Of course," I said. "What else are sisters for? All for one ..."

"And one for all," Kathleen said.

My heart filled with love for my family. It may not be everything I wanted, but for now, it was enough.

# Chapter Twenty-Two

Joe looked up from the book he was reading as I walked into his campsite late the following afternoon. "Are you done avoiding me?" he asked.

"I wasn't ... Okay, I was."

He gestured to the other chair. "Beer?"

"Sounds good."

He easily stood and went into his trailer, returning in a moment with two beers, caps already removed. The bottle was chilly, and I gratefully took a gulp. It had gotten hot, especially in the afternoon. The air was drying to the point where I could feel my skin on life support. In normal times, fire season would be right around the corner, but these were no longer normal times and the forests were already thick with flame and smoke.

"I can't change who I am at my core," Joe said, getting right into it. "After the prom, after the kiss, all I wanted to do was fix whatever had happened between us. But I couldn't figure out what had gone wrong. My dad had always taught me to do the honorable thing, and that meant waiting until everyone was sure. And I wasn't sure of anything. Man, I wasn't sure at all."

I stayed silent and sipped my beer.

"And then you wouldn't talk to me. How was I supposed to fix what was wrong if we couldn't talk about it? You broke my heart, Di. It took me a long time to get over that."

I took the hit. He was right. I'd been a coward, as much afraid of happiness as I was of anything else.

"I'm sorry, Joe. My only excuse is that I was immature."

"And now?"

"I'm here," I pointed out. "It took me a bit, but I'm here. I'm just not sure what I can tell you. My goal is to enjoy a year on the road with my sisters. After that?" I shrugged.

"That's anyone's guess." I leaned forward, my elbows on my knees. "Can't we let things be for now? You're leaving soon. Let's have some fun and not worry about being serious."

"As I said, I'm staying a little while longer," he said. "My son is arriving tomorrow. We're going fishing and sightseeing on Tuesday and Wednesday. I was thinking of going to Mammoth Springs on Thursday. Would you like to come with us?"

"That would be fun. Unless you think he'd rather have you to himself."

"Oh, he'll be tired of his old man by that time," Joe replied.

"Then, sure."

We discussed the details and finished our beers before I headed back to my temporary home, taking the long way around the park. I had thinking to do, and long ago I'd discovered my best thinking was done on my feet.

My parents had a marriage of equals. True, they each had their realms, and their traditions were old-fashioned, but I never doubted that Mom had her way as often as Dad did.

As teens, Joe and I had been equals, but his stance on slowing things down had messed me up a little. In the mid-seventies, the Sixties' creed of sex, drugs, and rock-'n'-roll had finally made it to Montana. Civil Rights weren't really a thing; the only substantial group of non-whites we had were Native Americans, and that was a whole different problem, one we still weren't addressing well. We may have elected the first female representative in the country, but women's rights were still mostly limited to traditional female occupations, getting married, and bearing children.

We were slow to change. Still are.

But the women's movement had made something come alive in me. I didn't want to wait, not for anything. I thought sex could be had without commitment, a few hours of pleasure with no strings attached. I didn't understand Joe's hesitation. Wasn't that what guys wanted?

When I married Larry, I discovered they actually wanted a whole lot more. I'd dabbled with sexual freedom in college and found it less satisfying than I thought it would be. I enjoyed myself, but something was missing. I got married to fill that unanswered need. To some extent, I'd been more interested in the fact that Larry was a man than who he actually was.

And I'd paid a heavy price for my inattention.

Here I was full circle.

Maybe Joe had been right all along.

~ ~ ~

The next morning I claimed the car for an afternoon exploration. I intended to go downtown and explore the shops and galleries on my own.

I'd spent an hour wandering and indulged in an espresso with biscotti before I finally succumbed and went into the camera shop. There were modern cameras as well as a display of antique models, including one with two lenses that I vaguely remembered my mother using occasionally.

Maybe my interest in photography was genetic.

She used to fuss at us for a long time before taking a picture. Film was expensive, and she was not a wasteful woman. Preferring black and white film, her images were sharp, with deep shadows providing contrast and drawing the eye to what she wanted the viewer to see.

As I stood there, I was stunned to realize Mom must have been a gifted, if untrained, photographer. Somewhere in my early teens, though, the camera had found its way onto the shelf and stayed there. I hadn't thought to ask why.

"Can I help you?" the woman behind the counter asked. Her coarse black hair, held back with a rainbow headband, was streaked with gray, and her face bore the lines of someone who spent a lot of time in the sun.

I liked her immediately.

"I'm thinking about getting a camera," I said. "I don't know anything about them, or how to use anything more than my phone, but ... I don't know ... I want to do *more*, whatever that means." I pointed to the old camera. "My mom had one of those."

"What kind of phone have you been using?"

I pulled my phone from my pocket and tried to ignore all the smudges on the surface.

"Got it," she said. "What kind of camera were you thinking about?"

"I don't know. That's the problem."

"What do you want to be able to do with it? Take some tourist pictures? Family? Action scenes? Animals and birds?"

The door opened.

"Let me take care of this customer, and I'll be right back with you. In the meantime, take a look at those photographs on the wall and let me know which one appeals to you."

I scanned the photos. The styles were quite different, from sharp abstract black and white photos of rock formations, to undulating grasses tickling the knees of a new-born elk calf. There was a traditional photo of Yellowstone Falls, and the wonder of a child as she watched an ant struggle to drag a bread crumb off to its lair.

It was the unusual shots that appealed to me, not the grandiose, recognizable photos, as wonderful as they were. Flowers, a bird resting on a branch, or a bubble in a mud pot right after it burst.

The woman came over to where I was standing as soon as the customer walked out the door.

"I'm Jane," she said.

"Nice to meet you. I'm Diane."

"So, Diane, what's the verdict?"

I pointed out what I liked and why.

She nodded.

"You're going to need a camera you can control," she said. "And you're going to need to learn a lot about basics and how the camera you get works. It will be an investment of time and money. What I would advise is to do some research on the internet to learn about the different kinds of cameras."

"I've been doing that and all I do is go down rabbit holes where things don't make sense."

Jane smiled. "I get that. I'm going to give you some sites

to use that I think are best for understanding the differences. I'll also put down some brands and models that will give you what you're looking for, depending on how much you want to spend."

"Thank you," I said. "I'd really appreciate that."

"Just remember," she said when she gave me the list. "It takes 10,000 hours to have a new skill become part of who you are. Be patient with yourself. Make mistakes and forgive yourself for them." She laughed. "At least we have digital now. It's not nearly so expensive to take bad pictures."

"Thanks," I said again.

When I left the store, I was exhilarated with possibilities.

I could do this. I knew I could.

# Chapter Twenty-Three

"This is my son, Joe," Joe told me when I arrived at his site prior to our excursion to Mammoth Springs.

"You can call me Bug," the young man said as he shook my hand.

"Bug?"

"Mom used to say I was cuter than a bug's ear—not that anyone could ever tell me what a bug's ear looked like. I'm not sure they even have ears. Anyway, it got shortened to Bug. It stuck. A lot less confusing than having two Joes in the same house."

"I bet."

"Dad said the two of you used to be friends in high school."

"That's true," I said.

"You'll have to tell me all the things he wouldn't want me to know," Bug said with a grin.

"I've sworn her to secrecy," Joe said.

"But I can be bought," I said.

"Good to know."

As we piled into the car, Bug gave me the front seat beside Joe. My trepidation lightened. It was going to be a good day.

As we traveled into the park, Joe caught me up on the adventures he and his son had had over the last few days. I told them about a hike my sisters and I had taken on the North Rim Trail by the Grand Canyon of the Yellowstone. I had to admit all the walking Liz insisted on doing was becoming easier.

"Did Dad force you to listen to his limericks in high school?" Bug asked.

I groaned. "All the time. It was his favorite way to get out of a lesson. I don't know how he comes up with them."

"And they're so *bad*."

"There was a young lad from Butte ..." Joe began.

"No!" Bug and I said at the same time.

Joe laughed but didn't continue.

As we drove through the Norris Geyser Basin area, Bug commented on the heavy sulphur smell. "It's pretty overpowering at times," he said. "I'd rather muck out stalls than smell that all day."

"Do you muck out stalls often?" I asked, expecting a negative reply.

"Every day. We've got a small ranchette outside Dillon. My wife runs it while I'm teaching, and always makes sure to leave the ugliest chores for me."

I glanced at Joe. He hadn't mentioned his son was married.

"With the new baby, I don't mind. She's got enough on her hands," Bug added.

I arched an eyebrow.

"Yes," Joe said. "I'm a grandfather. I tried to get Bug to name him Joe IV, but he was having none of it."

"You hadn't mentioned it," I said.

"Didn't get a chance."

"Dad neglected to tell us having a baby is so much work. Do you have any kids?" he asked me.

"Uh, no. I wasn't able to have any."

"I'm so sorry," Bug said. "That's tough. A friend of mine went through rounds and rounds of fertility treatments before she gave up and adopted."

"How is she doing with that?"

"She's happy and fulfilled," Bug said. "She says she should have quit a long time before she did. She's taken in a couple of at-risk kids—older ones—and says it's hard work, and there are some tough days but overall, she feels she's doing something really positive."

"And her husband is on board with that?"

"One hundred percent," Bug said. "They've built a nice family."

Lucky woman.

"How did the semester go?" Joe asked his son. "We've

been so busy I forgot to ask."

"It was long," Bug said. "Kids seem less and less prepared for college every year. Sure, they can read at a basic sixth-grade level, as long as the text isn't very challenging, but interpreting what they're reading is a lost art. And trying to get them to express themselves on paper? They never met a meme they didn't like. It's all declarative sentences without anything substantial to back it up."

"Sounds deadly," I commented.

"Some days," Bug admitted. "But then that gem comes along: a finely crafted paper that makes me look at things in a way I never did before. That makes it all worthwhile." He smiled, an exact replica of his father's expression. "I love my job. I'm making a difference, no matter how small, and it allows me to lead the life I want to have: a slow, sustainable existence."

I could picture his ranchette with its small herd grazing in the cool mountain air, a dog with a tail that almost wagged itself off when he came home, and great aromas in the kitchen where his wife played with their new child.

Had I not been so impatient, it might have been the life I could have had with Joe.

But it was the road not taken. No use wallowing in remorse.

I'd made my choices and lived my life. There wasn't going to be a do-over. Once Joe left to travel on to wherever he was going, my life would be my own to create.

~ ~ ~

Parking was difficult to find at Mammoth. Summer was in full swing and with it the hordes of tourists that made the trek to the large parks of the Rocky Mountains. Their campsites, RVs, and hotel rooms were well-equipped, but they had the perspective that came from a carefully constructed living environment.

We dodged large families with five or six children, inevitably one in a large stroller, or even two in a double stroller that took up the entire path. Twenty-somethings threw Frisbees to each other without regard to anyone else. And determined elders used their motorized devices to mow down whoever was in their way.

Amid all this chaos, a few determined elk tried to graze, while a bison stood at the edge of the official buildings like a statue.

"I thought we'd do the Wraith Falls Trail, come back and have lunch, then do as much of the Mammoth Springs Trail as we feel up to doing," Joe said. "There are a lot of staircases involved in that one, and I'm not all that into stairs on a hot day with lots of people."

"I agree with you there," I said.

"I'm hoping to come back again in the fall with my family," Bug said as we headed to the trailhead. "In my mind I've always thought it was a long way from Dillon, but four hours isn't bad, especially once you get that place in Ennis, Dad."

"You're welcome anytime," Joe said.

We ambled through the sagebrush, marshland, and small pine and fir trees to get to the falls. While the trail was more crowded than I would have liked, the view was definitely worth the walk. It was easy to see how the falls got their name. Shimmering water spilled over ripples of rock. There was still a steady flow for mid-July, but there were already spots where the water no longer flowed. The water was a thin layer, looking ghostlike in its whiteness.

I took a photo with my phone, then tried to imagine what types of pictures I wanted to take if I had a better camera. A fern clung to a piece of rock at the edge of the falls. It would be nice to zoom in on that. Momentarily, a bit of light caught the falls just right, producing a momentary rainbow. Catching it would require quick reactions. No time to fiddle with settings.

"What are you thinking about?" Joe asked.

I told him about the trip to the camera store, Jane's questions, and my assignment.

"I'm glad you're moving forward with this," he said. "I think photography will suit you, and fulfill something inside you that's been missing all these years."

"You mean something other than true love and children of my own?" I snarked at him.

"I'm sorry you didn't experience that through your life," he said. "And no, photography won't replace that but if I'm right, it will help ease the pain you feel."

"That and God. That your prescription doctor?" Why was I being so testy? It was a nice day, and Joe hadn't done anything wrong.

"It'll do for a start," he said, not engaging in the barbs I was sending his way. "Just be patient, Di. Give it a chance and enjoy the journey."

I pulled out my phone and snapped a picture of him, the wispy falls behind him.

If nothing else, at least I'd have a memory.

~ ~ ~

Lunch was casual dining at the Mammoth Terrace Grill. I'd hoped our walk back would dispel my crankiness, but it didn't seem to be working. Fortunately, Joe and his son had no problems holding a lively conversation so my reticence wasn't noticed.

My old friend had done a good job raising Bug. It was obvious there was a lot of love between them. Not everyone got to experience that.

Then I realized the problem. I was jealous. Not jealous of Bug, but of Joe and the relationship he had with his son. I'd missed the entire experience.

Well, put a nail in the coffin of my relationship with Joe. How could we have anything more than a friendship if I was going to be pissed off that he had children and I didn't?

I buried the remains of my chicken sandwich in its wrapper and stood. "I'm going out front for a bit. I'll wait for you there."

"Everything okay?" Joe asked.

"Sure."

I walked outside and looked up at that big beautiful blue sky, the roof of my childhood. I'd spent hours lying on my back looking up at that sky, imagining what I would be when

I grew up. In my teenage years, I'd looked up and planned my wedding to some nameless man, figuring the job thing would sort itself out. Trying to raise children and hold down a job seemed like an impossibility to me.

Now over half my life was lived and I have no recollection of the decisions I made—other than choosing Larry—that brought me to this moment. What was it someone had said? Life is what happens when you're making other plans?

That suited my life to a tee.

I brought my attention to what was in front of me. The bison hadn't moved far from his spot by the building. A few more elk had started to graze at the edges of the green lawn. One good-sized bull elk, not too old by the size of his antlers, had taken up his position where the Frisbee players had been.

Out of the corner of my eye, I spotted them: Two parents tugging kids that were five or six toward the big bull.

"Come now. We can pet the pretty elk," the mom said in accented English.

What was it with these people and petting wild animals?

I made a beeline toward them to give them a piece of my mind. It would be a better use of my negative energy than snarling at Joe.

"Hey!" I shouted when I was in earshot.

The elk's head lifted; the people paid me no mind.

"You can't pet the elk!" I shouted.

Other people began to look at me.

The elk snorted, but then swiveled his head to peer at the small group heading toward him.

I started to run and wave my arms.

"Stop! No petting! No petting!"

Where was a damn ranger when you needed one?

I was getting closer to an elk than I'd ever been in my life, and I did not like it. Not one bit.

He snorted and turned back to me, following my path as I reached a point where I could intercept the family. I held up my hand in the universal sign for stop.

They halted.

Calling them idiots wasn't likely to get their cooperation, much as I wanted to do just that.

"Did you read the rules?"

"Rules?" the mom asked.

I pointed to a nearby sign.

"Oh," she said with a laugh. "Don't feed them. We have no food." She smiled brightly.

"Twenty-five yards," I said. "The rule says you can't get within twenty-five yards of an elk. Or a bison," I added for good measure.

She turned to her husband, and there was a rapid exchange in a language I didn't understand.

"Yards, like meters."

"Yeah, sort of. Twenty-five. No closer."

She looked at the elk. "We're too close. No petting?"

I expelled a sigh of relief.

"No, no petting."

"Okay." Beyond her a ranger was walking toward us.

Then one of the kids yelled and pointed behind me.

I turned around.

The elk was on the move. Not with an ambling gait, but more deliberate steps.

"Let's get out of here. Now," I said, and started them moving away from the beast.

They moved rapidly, but when I glanced over my shoulder, the animal had picked up speed.

"You go that way; I'll go this way," I said. "Maybe he'll follow me." I pushed them in the direction of the ranger who was on his walkie talkie.

I headed toward the restaurant.

The small family started to run and for a moment the elk hesitated. Then he made his choice.

I started to run.

People pointed and screamed and dashed away from me. I kept hoping they'd divert the animal's attention, but apparently once he made up his mind, he was fixated.

Typical male.

I started to pant. I was getting used to walking, but I hadn't run since who knew when.

Hooves thumped behind me.

A pain pierced my side.

I wasn't going to make it.

I veered toward a tree. Maybe if I got behind it, he'd go right past.

My breath ran out. I twirled around.

The elk stopped, seemingly confused by my stance.

Then he lowered his head, the spines of his rack pointed directly at me.

I backed away.

There was a motion to my right, and then Joe was by my side.

The elk pawed the ground.

"Stop!" Joe yelled.

The elk looked up.

"We're people!" he yelled.

# Chapter Twenty-Four

Once the elk, seemingly baffled by Joe's assertion, had turned his back on us and trotted away, we had to deal with the ranger.

The small family stood in a cluster, heads slightly bowed, as the ranger handed them a ticket and pointed to the administration building. Then the ranger, bristling with authority, marched in our direction.

"You do know the rules," he said. "And yet you disobeyed them. I'm giving you a ticket."

"Wait a minute," Joe said. "Shouldn't she get a warning first?"

The ranger drew himself up to his five foot eight stance and squared his shoulders. "We're getting tough with people like you. You come here, disturb the animals while they're eating, and try to cook chickens—chickens!—in the hot springs. We can't allow it. Not in the least." He whipped back the cover of the black book he carried. "Name."

"I was trying to get those people to stay back," I explained. "That was the only reason I was that close ..." I peered at the name badge on his chest. "... Duane." I deliberately used his first name. This pompous young ass didn't need my respect.

"Your reason is irrelevant," Duane replied. He pointed his pen at my chest and punctuated each word with it. "You. Were. Too. Close." He poised the pen over the pad. "Name."

"You're out of line," Joe said. "People do this all the time. You warn them. Move them. Sometimes animals take things into their own ... uh ... hooves. But I've never seen anyone get a ticket. Unless they do something like pick up a calf or something like that."

Duane yanked a brochure from his back pocket. Tapping the last line with his pen he said, "New policy. 'Offenders may be ticketed.' There in black and white."

"Actually, that's blue," I said helpfully.

Duane glared and thrust the brochure at Joe who took it.

"Name," Duane repeated.

The small family came up to us.

"Thank you so much," the father said. "My children, my wife, could have been hurt very bad. We are so happy you have helped."

The wife nodded. "So happy." She pushed her children forward. "What do you say?"

"Thank you," the two small children chorused, and my anger melted. They'd made a mistake, one that almost cost them their lives. And unlike the man who'd been determined to get to the bison in Lamar Valley, they were contrite.

"You need to go over there to pay your fine," Duane said, again pointing to the administration building. "I have to finish with this lady."

"You are writing her a ticket?" the father said.

"Yes. She was too close. Just like you," Duane admonished the man with his pen.

I was going to yank that pen from his hand and stick it in his ear pretty soon.

"No," the man said. "The lady came too close to save us. We were wrong. She was not. No ticket for her."

Duane looked up at the tourist. "It's not for you to say. I'm the ranger here. Go pay your ticket." He was sounding irritated.

"It would have been a lot more paperwork if they'd been gored," Joe said. "And on your watch too." He moved to one side of the ranger, glancing at the father.

"She saved our lives. No ticket." The father moved to the other side of Duane.

The ranger glanced from one man to the other.

The lady and her two children arranged themselves next to me.

"No ticket," the mother said firmly.

Duane looked around, his mouth firm with determination.

"No ticket," a soft voice said.

He looked at the little girl beside me, and his shoulders dropped. After putting his pen in his shirt pocket, he closed the cover of the ticket book, then stuffed it in a back pocket. With a sigh, he extricated himself from our little group. Two steps away he turned back. "Stay away from the animals!"

"We will," Joe said with a friendly wave. Then Joe turned to the group.

"There once was a woman named Di
Who made a park ranger cry.
She acted illicit
But tore up his ticket
And bid the poor ranger goodbye."

The family looked bewildered as he took a bow.

"And that's what you've been thinking about this whole time?" I asked.

"Not entirely. It kind of went on in the background."

I shook my head as Bug came up to us.

"What's going on?" Bug asked.

"Nothing important," I said. "Where were you?"

"Using the facilities," he said. He looked at his father, then at the small family. "Nice to meet you?" he said to them.

They nodded.

"Your mother saved our lives," the father said.

"She's not my mother," Bug said with a frown.

"Okay. But she saved our lives." The father took my hands. "We will forever owe you. You come to our country, and you see us. Okay." It was a statement, not a question.

He handed me a business card, then held out his hand to his children. As they walked away, the small girl turned and waved at me.

I waved back, the ache in my heart making itself known.

"Well, that was interesting," Joe said as we walked toward the Mammoth Springs Trail.

"You can only say that because you didn't have an eight-hundred pound beast with pointy things chasing after you," I replied.

"What happened?" Bug asked again.

Joe told him.

"Wow, that was dangerous," Bug said to me.

I shrugged. "All in a day's work."

Bug laughed, but I could see the concern in his eyes. The echo of his voice when he declared me "not my mother" rang in my memory. Joe may have been set to move on, but I wasn't sure Bug was on board.

~ ~ ~

The Mammoth Springs Trail had been strenuous at times, but worth it. Any conflict between Bug and me eased as we examined the colors and structures of the travertine terraces. Like everything else depending on rocks and geology, the history at the surface could be older than the ground surrounding it. The water of the hot springs, which is acidic, gathers limestone as it rises from deep beneath the earth's surface. Air causes a chemical change which causes the limestone to be deposited, creating the amazing terraces.

The effect was captivating, and I snapped as many photos as I could, mentally noting what I couldn't do with this camera for my next discussion with Jane.

After we climbed the steep stairs to the top of the Main Terrace, we stood and panted for a while. The view before us was otherworldly, like much of the hot springs areas in the park.

"Anyone got a chicken?" I asked. "I'm feeling hungry."

"What?" Bug asked as Joe laughed.

"Apparently," Joe said, "people want to see how a chicken cooks in a hot spring."

Bug shook his head. "People are nuts."

"Yep," we agreed and headed back to the main parking lot where we'd left Joe's vehicle. As we passed the hotel, Joe peeled off. "Need to use the facilities," he said, tossing Bug his keys. "Why don't you open the truck and let it de-steam."

"Sure, Dad."

As we walked back to the lot, careful to avoid any animal larger than a chipmunk, the tension ramped up again.

"So you knew my dad in high school," Bug said as we stood by the open truck doors. "What was he like?"

"Not much different from how he is now: a nice guy with a tendency to spout bad limericks," I said, not wanting to get into this too deeply. "We were friends then, just like we are now."

"Are you sure that's all you are?" Bug asked, a slight edge to his voice.

"Of course."

"I've seen how you look at each other when the other one isn't looking," Bug stated flatly.

I shrugged. "There may have been something a long time ago. It's leftover feelings. Things didn't work out then, and we've both had different lives. You're living proof of that." I pasted a grin on my face.

"My mom was wonderful. They loved each other very much. We had a great family. He was devastated when she died. It was only two years ago."

"I'm so sorry for your loss," I said. "It's got to be hard to lose a mom when you're so young. I was in my late thirties when mine died. It was still hard, but at least I had time with her."

*But not enough.* I suspect it never would have been enough.

Bug stroked his chin in a gesture reminiscent of Joe when he was trying to find the right way to say something.

"I overheard my parents talking about you once ... at least I'm pretty sure it was you."

"Oh?"

"Dad was reminiscing about how you two used to take long hikes. He thought you were a forever person, but then you dumped him after the prom."

"That was me. I was young and stupid. I've already apologized to your dad, and he's accepted it." I could feel an edge creeping into my voice. This kid had no business discussing my relationship with Joe, even if he was his father.

"But you hurt him," Bug said.

"I did."

"I don't want you doing it again," he said. "I don't want my dad hurt." His right hand closed into a fist, but then he released it.

"I won't. Like I said. Just friends. Once he leaves here, we'll exchange Christmas cards and that will be it."

"Promise?"

I tried to think of an answer that didn't commit me to anything.

"Ready to go?" Joe asked.

"I sure am," I said, turning toward him.

"Good, 'cuz I'm starving again. Anyone up for a cup of coffee and a slice of huckleberry pie when we get back to town?"

"Sounds good to me," Bug said.

"Sure," I said, trouble rumbling in my belly. I did *not* want a pie. Not in a diner, not in a café. I did not want pie.

No way.

# Chapter Twenty-Five

"Where's Joe?" Kathleen asked as we had a second cup of coffee on the couch while Liz took her shower.

"Spending time with his son. Then he says he needs to catch up on his writing."

"Still friends?"

"Of course. We're going to church tomorrow."

"Twice in a month?" Kathleen asked. "Has anyone been warned?"

"Ha."

"And when we get back to Montana in a year?" Kathleen asked. "Will Joe be waiting for you?"

"No," I said quickly. "I'm sure some other woman will snatch him up and treat him the way he deserves."

"And you wouldn't?"

I idly watched the neighbors undo their hookups and pull in their sliders as I sipped my coffee. Life on the road had a different quality to it than life in the Bay Area, or even small town Montana. People were much more self-contained. When they were ready, they moved on, and no one questioned why. Idiosyncrasies were on full display. In some places, so were politics, but more and more RV parks were banning political signs or flags.

I was grateful. I wanted to get to know people without being subjected to their ideology first.

"Di?" Kathleen asked.

"I don't know," I said. "I'm damaged, I think."

"Damaged like a cow-kicked-the-irrigation-pipe damaged? Or something else."

"Something else." I stared at the local news rag I'd intended to peruse before Kathleen embarked on this in-depth conversation. It was the first time I'd considered the possibility that thirty years with a man who picked at everything I did had left some lasting wounds that weren't easily scarred over.

"Want to talk about it?" Kathleen said.

"No." I wasn't ready to yank my guts out of my body in front of anybody, least of all my somewhat critical sister.

"Message received," Kathleen said. She picked up the cozy mystery she'd been reading.

We were silent for a few moments as we read. The local tabloid was a mixture of old-fashioned news like a fiftieth wedding anniversary celebration and a farmer's report that aliens had made a shape of the president's head in his alfalfa field.

"I knew it was the president," the farmer had explained. "It's got those big ears, you know the way he does."

The world had gotten stranger since I was a kid. Back then the mysteries were far simpler: Who really killed Jack Kennedy? Why did Nikita Khrushchev bang his shoe on a desk?

"Marriage isn't always easy," Kathleen said, putting down her book.

"I *know* that."

"Michael and I were so young when we got married. We had no clue what we were doing."

"Age has nothing to do with it," I said. "None of us really know what we're doing."

"All I knew was I loved Michael and thought he'd be a good father for our kids."

"That's way ahead of some people. I think some people get married just to legitimize the wild sex they're having." I picked up my coffee. "And then it gets weird. I had a friend— I had to cover my ears when she told me some of the things she and her boyfriend were doing."

"Eww."

"Exactly. Why don't some people realize there are things a person doesn't really need to hear?"

"Like what?" Kathleen leaned closer.

"You don't want to know."

"I kinda do. My experience was ... um ... limited."

"Missionary all the way?"

"A little better than that," Kathleen said and shook her head. "But not much. It fizzled out once the kids were teens. My doctor kept asking me how my sex life was—why do they get to ask that? I told her it was about as to be expected." She leaned toward me. "So what did they do? Was it like that fifty shades book?"

"I think there was a little of that too. But the worst was she said they had another woman with them."

"In bed?" Kathleen's mouth stayed open.

"Yep."

"Gross. Why would they *do* that?"

I shrugged my shoulders. Late at night when my mind wouldn't turn off, I sometimes tried to figure out how that would work, but my mind didn't twist in that direction.

"So they got married," I said.

"And?"

"It stopped. All of it. He told her she was now his wife, and wives didn't do that kind of thing."

"He didn't happen to mention this beforehand?"

"Nope. Told her he hadn't realized how he'd feel."

"What did she do?"

"She stayed with him and adjusted," I said. "She realized she was getting a little old for all the cavorting, that he was a good man, and she wouldn't do much better."

Silence punctuated my statement. Then Kathleen said quietly, "That seems sad."

"Mmm."

"It's like she gave up part of who she was for him."

I nodded. Kathleen put into words the thought I'd had at the time. Although I didn't understand the sexual gymnastics, and wasn't entirely sure I approved, it was her life, and they'd been consenting adults.

"So you and Joe ..." Kathleen began. "Doing the horizontal mambo yet?"

"Kathleen!" I smacked her with my newspaper.

The sliding door opened, and Liz stepped out. She looked at me, then at Kathleen.

"Did I miss something?"

Kathleen and I looked at each other.

"No," my sister said. "I was trying to get Di to tell me just how far she'd gone with Joe."

"Oooh," Liz said, plopping down into an armchair.

"I'm still waiting," Kathleen said.

"And you're going to wait a long time. Nothing's happening. We're just friends. I've been telling you guys that forever."

"You weren't just friends on prom night," Liz said. "I saw you. Kissing."

"Were you watching?" Little ants crawled up my arms.

"Of course," Liz said. "I watched both of you."

"You did?"

"How else was I going to know what to do when I got a boy of my own?"

"I'm creeped out," Kathleen said. "It was half a century ago, and I'm *still* creeped out."

"Well, that was the only kiss," I told Liz. "And it was a mistake."

"Is that why you didn't talk to him for the rest of the year?" Liz asked.

"You didn't?" Kathleen asked.

I shook my head, then glared at Liz. "None of your business then, and none of it now."

"No, but you were so moody back then. And now you are too. You need to admit you love him and make it happen."

"And you need to mind your own business." I could feel myself getting hot under the collar.

"Enough," Kathleen said. "Di is right. It's her business."

"Just trying to be helpful," Liz said.

"You're not," Kathleen and I said in chorus.

I got up and got more coffee. "Now, can I sit here and read in peace, maybe watch a news channel to see if we're going to get blown up anytime soon?"

"Sure," Kathleen said, settling back down with her book. "Sounds like a perfect plan for a Saturday morning."

"I think so, too." Liz got a cup of coffee, then settled in her arm chair.

As I read through the news of the local cattleman's

association meeting, questions about my sisters lingered in my mind. Were Kathleen's problems with Michael only run-of-the-mill? Or was there something more? Occasionally, something she'd said had caught my attention, leading me to believe there had been more trouble than she let on.

And Liz? I didn't know much about her life. I'd gone to college by the time she hit her junior and senior years in high school. She'd gone to art school near Portland, but her life had been busy. Email and texting didn't exist back then, so communication was limited to when we all met at the ranch house for holidays and summers. I seemed to remember someone in her college years, but she'd been alone ever since.

At least that's what she told us.

For a family I thought I knew, there were a lot of secrets.

~ ~ ~

Mid-afternoon, I received a text from Joe.

"I know it's short notice, but early dinner? Burger and beer?"

"Sure," I typed back. He asked me to bring along some water shoes.

Water shoes? Why water shoes? We couldn't go fishing at night. There were critters. Big ones. Un-cute ones.

But I'd bring the shoes anyway.

I went back to writing up notes about what I wanted in a camera. I did a little more research online to try to understand the terms that photographers used for what I wanted to do. Although I was focused on the details, my subconscious whirled with the question Kathleen had posited: If I asked him, would Joe be waiting for me when we got done with our road trip? Or was I right that some other woman, someone smarter than me, who knew a good thing when she saw it, would have snatched him up like a prize bull?

Wow. I hadn't thought in ranch and Montana terms for a long time. My colleagues in the San Francisco accounting world didn't know what a prize bull was.

They were better off. Bulls were ornery creatures.

I was distracting myself. I needed to concentrate.

"Joe's leaving Monday, right?" Kathleen asked as she emerged from the bedroom where she'd been watching an old movie and knitting.

"Yes."

"We need to throw a going-away party," she said.

"Who will come besides us?"

"There are a number of people who've been here the same length of time we have. They all know Joe. They'd come. Your problem is that you're so focused on Joe you haven't seen anyone else."

It was true. I didn't know many of the park residents except to say hello. Vestiges of my Bay Area existence. I'd had a lot of surface friendships, but rarely took time to stop and pass the time of day like I had when I was growing up.

Like Kathleen still did.

"I think Joe would like that," I said.

"Good. Then I'll invite people. Pot luck. Bring your own meat and drinks. Easy peasy."

"I take it you've done this before," I said.

"With food prices the way they are, and beef prices cut to the minimum, it's the only way to party these days. The only variation is if someone butchers one of their cows. Then they supply the meat, but everything else stays the same."

"And you think it will fly here?"

"I'll call it an authentic Western experience. They'll love it."

I laughed.

"Let me know what I can do."

"Your job is to get Joe here at the appointed time. No wandering off to the park."

"Got it. We're going out for a burger tonight. I'll figure out his plans for tomorrow."

"Dinner again?" Kathleen deliberately arched an eyebrow.

"Just friends," I said. "Especially now that I know Liz is on spy duty."

"If you say so."

# Chapter Twenty-Six

After our burgers had been served, and we dispensed with any small talk we had left, I decided to take the plunge.

"I'm sorry I did what I did after prom—freezing you out," I said.

I'd expected "No problem." Not what I got.

"Yeah. It was pretty devastating." He picked up his burger, then put it back down on his plate. Leaning on his elbows and interweaving his fingers, he stared at me, his sky blue eyes clear and focused. Around us, the bar noise faded into the background.

"It took me a long time to figure out why it happened. I was doing what I'd been taught. I even asked my mom why you would stop talking to me."

"What did she say?"

"She said I hadn't been clear. For years I'd been acting like our friendship was no big deal, when everyone else in my family could see it was. I mean, Di, I was so focused on you. All I could do was think about you: the things you said, how you looked in a dress, maybe what was under that dress."

"Joe Kelly!"

"What? I was human. I was a teenage boy. What else was I going to think about?"

"You were always going on about books you were reading. I didn't think you considered much else."

"Well, I did. I considered you." His smile had a wickedness to it.

"I never knew."

"And that, Mom explained, was the problem. I never admitted my feelings to myself, much less to you. Then all of a sudden, when we were in the car, I wanted to kiss you. I *needed* to kiss you. It must have been confusing."

"*I* wasn't confused," I said. "I knew what I wanted."

"You knew what your hormones wanted," he said. "My dad had had multiple conversations about girls, sex, and a guy's responsibility to stop. I thought it would be easy. Right up to the point when I had to tell you no."

"Things in the abstract can be much more difficult in reality," I said.

"Yes," he agreed.

We had been teens. It couldn't have been love back then. But why did I feel drawn to him so strongly even now? Back then I'd had a hazy idea of what love was and absolutely no idea what a marriage entailed. But somehow, I thought, if I'd waited, if I'd had even an ounce more of maturity, we might have made it.

We ate quietly for a few moments, both of us unsure, I thought, as to how to take the conversation forward. I didn't really want to talk about Larry, but in fairness I needed to lay it out on the table.

"Larry and I met through friends. They thought we'd be perfect together. He oversaw several auto parts stores, part of the corporate headquarters, not really getting his hands dirty. After we met, he hired me to oversee the bookkeeping staff, make sure taxes were done, that kind of thing. We spent more and more time together, one thing led to another, and we got married."

"Did you love him?" Joe asked.

"I thought I did. I mean, he was good-looking in an alpha male kind of way. He went to the gym and took care of himself. He had good teeth, nice clothes, and a recently purchased car. He even had retirement savings."

"Be still my beating heart," Joe said, putting his hand on his chest.

"Oh, shut up," I said and laughed.

The waitress came by, and we ordered another round.

The interruption, as well as the laughter, lightened my mood. Life with Larry had been miserable, but it was over, and by some miracle I was sitting here with my high school best friend.

"What went wrong?" Joe asked.

"He was all glitter and no substance. I'd thought he was going places, but he'd already reached his limit. In fact, toward the end of our marriage, they were easing him out of the company. I couldn't do anything right, but his expectations of what I earned and how I kept house became more demanding."

Joe nodded, but remained quiet.

Did I dare tell him the truth about children?

The waitress brought our beer.

"We tried for kids. I got tested. He got tested. We were both told we were fine, that it should be no problem having kids. At least that's what I thought. That's what Larry told me."

Joe cocked his head.

"We kept trying, but it killed our sex life. Fights escalated. Finally, he demanded we stop trying so hard. I was worn out, so I agreed." The wave of never having children of my own rolled over me again.

"I hate Mother's Day," I said.

"Sounds reasonable."

I gave him a weak smile. My hands steepled, and I looked around the tavern to settle my emotions. It was typical for Montana: lots of beer signs and kitsch, including the famous Clydesdales, a few deer heads and one good-sized elk, and a tanned mountain lion skin. A small stage at one end would give a spot for a band on the weekends. Chalkboards announced daily specials and upcoming events.

"I was going through some papers," I began, laying my hands back down on the table. "About ten years after we stopped trying. We were moving to a smaller house, closer to my business office. I was trying to go through things ... downsize ... you know ..."

He nodded, then put his hand over mine.

I stared at it for a moment, but let it be.

After chewing on my lower lip for a few moments, I continued. "I came across an envelope with our names on it. I didn't remember seeing it before, so I opened it."

The stark white envelope hadn't been sealed. Even as I'd

held it in my hand, I'd known it was bad news. My finger had easily flipped the flap up, and the paper slid out. I unfolded it and read it, but the words and numbers didn't make sense. It had taken several minutes before the meaning became clear.

"It was a report from the doctor. One Larry had hid from me. It had a bunch of scientific jargon, but the end result was Larry's sperm count was so low that it would be nearly impossible for us to conceive in a natural way."

I fought for breath as the pain squeezed my lungs.

"I'm so sorry, Di."

"It was cruel."

"It was."

The warmth of Joe's hand was a comfort. I concentrated on that.

My breathing slowly regulated. I looked up into Joe's concerned face and kind eyes. He'd been my rock in high school. Even with a good group of kids, high school is emotionally fraught. Feelings get hurt, allegiances change, and no one is quite sure who they are from one day to the next. Back in the seventies, when we were in high school, there had been whispers of girls who liked girls, or the shy boy who never asked anyone out, but discussion of anything other than normal sexuality didn't happen. Nerds were picked on by jocks, and fights erupted because someone looked at someone else's "girl."

And the word "dis" hadn't even been invented.

The Vietnam War had ended, but we'd exited the conflict in shame. Soldiers came home to a country that didn't know what to do with them. Carter was a president who couldn't pull off homey sweaters and fireside chats the way that Mr. Rogers or Franklin Roosevelt had done.

But no matter what the country was doing, or how cliques changed, Joe had been there, steady and friendly. He'd been as truthful as a teenager was capable of being.

He'd always been my friend.

"I wasn't sure what to do," I continued, looking down at the table. "Did I even want a child with this man anymore, assuming I wasn't too old to have that miracle occur? What was the use of confronting him? He'd have some excuse, or make it my fault, like he'd been doing for years."

Which, of course, was exactly what Larry had done. It was the kind of man he was.

"When I finally confronted him," I said. "He yelled at me for going through his papers. I told him the envelope was stuck in with our medical records. It had my name on it!"

I sucked in air.

"Then he told me he'd never seen it." My short laugh held only bitterness. "When that didn't fly, he finally told me when he found out about the test results, he'd felt a sense of relief. He'd never wanted children. That's what he told me. He'd never wanted them."

I was deflated, just as I'd been when Larry made the statement the first time.

Joe didn't speak, instead holding my hand steadily.

"The marriage never really recovered from that," I said. "Although it limped along for another fifteen years. I'd meant my vows when I said them. Besides, it was too late for me to have children with someone else. I finally divorced him two years ago. My finances took a hit because I had to pay him off, but it was worth every penny." I straightened up and looked Joe in the eye. "It's over. It's in the past. Yes, it's part of who I am. I doubt I'll ever trust any man totally again, but that's no problem. I'm happy being single." I withdrew my hand from his.

"I can understand why you feel that way," he said. "But you trusted me a long time ago. Surely, you could learn to do so again."

Could I? I wasn't sure. What I'd said was true. I wasn't sure I could trust any man. I barely trusted my sisters. I shook my head, then tried to lighten the mood.

"We could always have a romp in the hay now and again—no strings attached. All you have to do is bend your rules a little."

Joe shook his head. "Not in my wheelhouse. Sorry."

My hurt teenage self reared its head again. Did he think I was too old for sex? Not pretty enough? Too overweight? My skin and hair no longer bright enough to attract a man?

But I bit back my words. They were cruel, not only to Joe, but to me.

He was consistent; I had to give him that.

But he must have known what I was thinking.

"Don't get me wrong," he said. "I find you attractive. But I want the whole package, not just part of it." He finished the last of his burger.

"What does that mean? The whole package?"

"It means more than the sex part. It has to mean love and commitment to each other. For life. Or else it doesn't mean anything at all."

There was almost bitterness in his voice. Until I knew what that was about, I was unsure about anything. It all seemed so big. I was nowhere near ready for a lifetime commitment. Not yet.

"Unfortunately, I'm not sure that's in *my* wheelhouse," I said softly. I looked at the half-eaten mess on my plate. "I'm not hungry anymore," I said.

"Then I'll get the check. I'm paying, remember. I asked you out."

"Yes. Thank you. I'm going to the ladies' room. I'll be right back."

I could feel his gaze on me as I walked to the back of the bar. Once I closed the door behind me, I stared into the mirror. My face, in spite of the makeup I'd slathered on before I left, looked as gray as my hair. Telling the story had devastated me all over again. I don't think I'd ever really get over the pain of that moment, no matter how many hours of therapy I had.

Our parents had taught us how to be part of a family. Having kids had seemed a natural extension of that. The day—the moment—I learned that wasn't going to happen, I became unmoored from what I thought was a fundamental truth: I was destined to be a mother.

My therapist told me I needed to shape a new vision of my future. She'd said it would take time, but I would get there. Instead of moving forward, though, the universe had decided to throw me a curve ball.

*Hey, wouldn't you like to go back to what might have*

*been? Here's a taste! Look! The man even has kids you could pretend were yours!*

Right. One of those kids had already told me politely to get lost.

I ran some color over my lips and glared at the face in the mirror while mentally reciting the mantras my therapist had given me: *I am not a victim. I am in control of my own life.*

My head held high, I left the room and joined Joe by the front door.

"How do you feel about fishing?" he asked as we walked toward his car.

"You're obsessed," I said. "Besides, it's late."

"It's July. The sun doesn't set until nine p.m. Plenty of daylight. And you brought your shoes."

"I'm wearing jeans," I pointed out.

"They dry."

"I don't have equipment."

"Back of the truck."

I almost reverted to "I don't wanna," but remembered time with Joe was running out. "All right."

He laughed. "I'm not going to drown you. You don't have to sound so miserable about it."

"But you want me to get w-e-t ..." I moaned as I got into the truck. Memories returned. Whenever I used to get into a funk—which happened often enough, I was a teenage girl after all—I'd whine to Joe.

"You won't melt," he said.

"But I will," I protested. "My great-great-aunt on my mother's side was the Wicked Witch of the East."

"I thought it was the West." He put the truck in gear.

"Well, her too. She's the one who got smashed by the house. The family was devastated," I moaned.

"There aren't any houses floating around. No tornadoes predicted."

"But she *melted*."

"You said she was smashed by a house."

"That was the other one," I said.

"The other other one?"

"The East witch."

"Eastwick? I remember there were witches there. That was a movie." Joe had a big grin on his face as he showed his senior pass to the park attendant at the booth.

"They didn't live in Eastwick," I protested. "They lived in Oz. The West witch melted. The East witch got smashed by a house."

"Which witch was your relation?"

"Both of them. They were sisters."

"So your choices of death are smashed by a house or melting? I'd go with the house myself. Faster."

The absurdity of the conversation made me chuckle. The chuckle turned to laughter, and soon there were tears running down my face. I playfully punched Joe in the arm.

"You are soooo bad!"

He grinned, looking pleased with himself. "Just doing my job, ma'am."

It was as if we were back to our teenage years when he'd use words and jokes to tease me out of whatever was bothering me. Later we'd talk about it, after the laughter and exercise had taken the edge off, and I was able to think rationally instead of with my hormones.

A few miles in, he pulled off into a broad spot where there was a path to the river. Trees lined one side, but on the other, green meadows stretched far to another patch of forest. There were shapes at the edges of the trees.

"Elk," Joe said quietly as we got to the river bank.

I nodded.

The air had a slight breeze which provided welcome relief from the lingering heat of the day. We appeared to be alone—tourists congregated in more populated places, enjoying a late dinner or drinks.

Joe suggested places for us to fish so we were far enough apart from each other to avoid catching each other instead of fish. I reluctantly stepped into the water, but as soon as it hit my ankles I was once again surprised by its warmth. Rivers around Butte could get cold enough to freeze off body parts ... at least that's how they felt.

I made my cast, pleased that it was beginning to

resemble something graceful. Idly, I watched the lure, but also let my gaze wander to the wildlife moving away from the edges of the forest, feeling safer in the fading light. The sky was putting on a show; its blue deepening and starting to be edged with a soft pink.

I was grateful for the less than vibrant colors. Sunsets and sunrises during fire season took on a brilliant red due to the smoke in the air. Beautiful to look at, but not safe to breathe for very long. The birds chirped good night to each other, reminding their world about territories and calling out to stay safe from things that came out in the nighttime.

There was a breeze, enough to cause the grass tips to whisper secrets to each other, like the secret I'd finally given up to Joe.

The words faded as I fished. Nature cocooned my soul and made me feel safe. I wasn't thinking with my mind, but at a deeper level. Sharing with my oldest friend had released the tight grip the events had on me even more than talking to my therapist. He'd known me before life had beaten me into a shape I'd no longer recognized.

I'd been naïve. We all were. For all the wildness of the Last Best Place, it was a haven for dreamers. My plan had been to go to Montana State and figure out what I wanted to be when I grew up. I knew I wanted to do something with the arts.

I'd even toyed with the idea of photography. The memory had been buried under piles of life's debris. I'd planned to have a small studio, doing graduation and wedding shots to make a living, then going off to the wilderness whenever I could to take pictures.

My father had insisted on something a little more practical, and since he was footing the bill, I went along. After things ended with Joe, the light had gone out of the arts for me.

He apparently hadn't had that problem. He'd gone on with life just as if kissing me hadn't mattered.

I jerked the line enough to pull it out of the water and splashed it back into the river.

Joe turned. "Everything okay?"

"Yeah."

We went back to fishing.

I tried to recapture the zen feeling I'd had earlier, but once I'd let a thought into my brain, it multiplied. It pinged from one topic to another. Thoughts permutated from benign to hostile and then took prisoners. Every time I tried to interject a more peaceful topic—Look! There's an elk! Getting closer!—the thought-monster twisted it into danger.

*What are you doing in the wilderness? Don't you want your nice, warm, Bay Area condo? With your cappuccino maker?*

*Your sisters are going to make you crazy after a few months. You know they will. They've always done that. Remember what a slob Liz can be? And how controlling Kathleen is?*

*And Joe? Joe? Really? Don't you remember how he dismissed you when you threw yourself at him in high school? You made a fool of yourself then! And you're doing it again!*

It was worse than gnats. Buzzing thoughts swirled around my brain, leaving pinpricks of pain and itching.

"Di!" Joe yelled.

"What?" I snapped back.

"You've got a fish. You're about to ..."

The pole almost jerked out of my hand, but I gripped it tight. I was going to get that fish!

My arms went into their familiar seesawing motion before I landed on my butt in the river.

*Not this time, buster.*

I sat up and reeled the fish in until I felt I had control of the situation. As I let him run a bit, I somehow staggered to my feet, then began the dance with the fish. Out and back, out and back, each time a little closer.

I could see him! He was right there! A little more?

"How's the fishing?" somebody called from the bank.

Instinctively, I turned toward him.

And lost my footing.

Down I went again.

At that moment, my line went slack. The fish was gone.

I leaned back in the water and groaned. Then I looked over at the figure standing on the bank.

"Fishing's fine," I told him.

"Oh. Sorry." He had the good sense to disappear.

"You okay?" Joe asked, standing over me.

I groaned again as I tried to find my footing. "Getting too old for this," I said, accepting the hand he extended. "Good thing I have enough padding to cushion my fall."

When I finally stood, we were inches apart in the streaming water. His face was in the shadow, pinks and blues arcing across the sky behind him.

It would be natural to kiss him.

"It's getting late," I said instead. "I'm tired. Let's head back."

"Sure thing," he said.

We gathered up our gear and left, weary and quiet during the ride home.

# Chapter Twenty-Seven

When Joe picked me up for church the next morning, Kathleen informed him he was expected for cocktails in the afternoon.

"Was she always this bossy?" he asked on the way.

"Yep."

"I'd forgotten that."

"So did I, but I was reminded a few days after my return."

"I still have a bunch of things to do so I can be ready to leave in the morning, but I should be able to be done by the time the queen has commanded."

"How early are you going?"

"As soon as I get up. I love traveling first thing in the morning. Everything feels fresh."

"That's not a possibility with us," I said. "Getting three people dressed and fed takes a lot longer than a solo trip."

"You're going to Jackson next, aren't you?"

"Yes. The Tetons. I'm looking forward to it."

Joe pulled into the church parking lot. He greeted a few people on the way to the church while I smiled politely at strangers. One woman, a pretty brunette about a decade younger than I latched onto his arm, ignoring my existence.

"Joe, I hear you're leaving us," she said.

"Tomorrow," he said, trying to disentangle.

"It was so nice to meet you here. Imagine, we don't live that far from each other, and we had to be down here to discover each other."

Joe maneuvered her around to face me. "And here's another local person, Diane O'Sullivan. She and I were close friends in high school."

"Nice to meet you, Diane. Charlotte Quinn." We shook hands. "Do you still live near Butte?"

"Right now I'm on a year-long road trip with my sisters."

"Oh, what fun!" Charlotte laughed. "We'd have to rent three RVs to do that," she said. "There are nine in my family. *All* girls. Can you imagine?"

"No," I said.

"And when you're done with your road trip?" she asked.

"I'm not sure about where I'm going to settle." I decided to ease the poor woman's mind. "I spent most of my adult life in the San Francisco Bay Area. I'm seriously thinking of returning there. Can't beat the weather."

"I've been to San Francisco a few times. All those hills! But you're right. The weather is lovely."

"I'm trying to convince her to come home," Joe said.

"Come back to all our snow? She'd be out of her mind." Her laugh sounded like a bunch of kindergartners hitting their triangles at the same time.

She seemed like a nice woman. She would be perfect for Joe.

I took a step toward him.

"It was nice catching up," Joe said to Charlotte, placing his hand on the small of my back to guide me toward the church.

Ordinarily, I hate that kind of gesture but right now, it was perfect.

This Sunday was one of those endless days of Pentecost. What had they called it when I was a kid?

Ordinary time was what the few nuns attached to the parish called it. Nothing special going on. Kind of like most of life. Once the big milestones of life—first day of school, becoming a teenager, the coveted driver's license, college, wedding, babies—had passed, it was all ordinary time.

Ordinary time is where one lived one's life.

Automatically, I followed the service ritual that had been ingrained into my body at an early age: standing, sitting, kneeling, singing, listening, responding. A few things had changed since I'd lapsed, but the rustling around me always cued me that a change was coming.

The routine of Mass, enlarged, had been similar to the routine of my life: get up, eat, work, eat, work, head home to the second shift, eat, settle onto the couch with Larry to watch television. Sex punctuated the end of the week.

And so my life had passed.

Damn! *Sorry, God.* I hadn't really been living.

At least this trip would throw a curve in the road.

Then I'd have to grab my life with both hands and make something of it before it was too late.

I glanced at Joe next to me. Where did he fit in?

And my brain was off. What if this? What if that? Every once in a while, I tried yanking my brain back to what was going on in reality, but it was too familiar and my mind felt it had permission to play. Shuffling feet was my only clue the service had ended.

"Thanks for coming with me," Joe said as we sidled out of the pew. "I hope you got something from it."

I nodded. I hoped he didn't quiz me on the sermon. I had no idea what the jocular priest had said, but from the chuckles, the congregants had enjoyed it.

As we walked down the aisles, a toned and fit woman with blonde styled hair said, "Now don't run off, Joe. We've gotten some goodies for a good-bye party for you." She leaned in. "I baked the cake myself."

"We'll be sure to stop by," Joe said.

The woman flicked a glance at me, then turned to continue down the aisle.

"Another member of your fan club?" I asked.

"As soon as someone found out I was a widower, the competition began," he said. "I understand it's worse in assisted living places. The ratio is so bad there, that women read the obits to find out who's come on the market. At least here there are only two or three." He put his arm around me and said, "They're going to be disappointed."

I couldn't help myself. My shoulders went back with a little boost of confidence.

What was it about winning the guy, even for a moment, that felt so damn good?

*Sorry, God.*

I really had to stop swearing in church.

"Back again, Diane," the priest said. "It's good to see

you. Will you be leaving town with our friend, Joe?"

"Oh, we're not traveling together," I said. "I'm with my sisters. We'll be heading out next week. And going in different directions. Joe's going to South Dakota, and we're going to Jackson."

I slammed my lips shut.

"I see," the priest said, glancing between us. "And will you be going to church in Jackson?"

"Maybe." I shrugged my shoulders to let the father know my return wasn't guaranteed.

"I will pray for it," he said.

The few people behind us stirred.

"I'll see you at coffee hour," he said, and we continued down the steps.

Coffee hour had been set up outside, in a small grove of aspens. People crowded around the urns, and the blonde stood smiling by her cake. Other goodies filled in around it, most covered by some type of lid to keep away the bees who were having trouble distinguishing between natural and refined sugar.

On our way to the urn, Charlotte snagged us.

"I wanted to make sure you had my contact information," she said to Joe, holding out her phone.

"Yes, you made sure I had it as soon as you learned I lived near Butte. But like I said to you then, I'll be moving to Ennis not too long after I return, so there may not be an opportunity to get together."

"Oh, pooh. Ennis isn't *that* far from Butte."

I plucked two mugs from the table as Charlotte continued to chatter at Joe. This would be over soon. Sooner if I could speed it along.

I shouldn't care how long it took to go from Butte to Ennis.

The priest waved his arms for attention, and everyone stilled. "Normally, we don't say a lot—other than prayers— for people who are leaving the congregation. There are just too many people coming and going around here."

Chuckles.

"But Joe has made his presence known in the few short

weeks he's been here, and some of the ..." He cleared his throat. "... ladies wanted to give him a send-off."

"I baked a cake," the blonde pointed out.

"Yes. And we know from experience, they are very good cakes. So everyone have a piece." He raised his coffee cup. "Safe travels, Joe. May the good Lord bring you safely back to see us some day."

"Here, here," the crowd murmured and drank from their cups.

The blonde escorted Joe to the snacks table. "Now you get to cut the cake," she said, handing him a cake knife.

The message on top of the cake said, "Come back soon!!" Joe dutifully cut.

She took the knife from him, her fingers lingering on his hand as she did, and deftly cut him a corner piece. "You know," she said, as she handed him the piece. "Ennis isn't that far from here. I'd be happy to drive over. You *do* have my info, don't you?"

I almost spat out my coffee trying to hold in the laughter that bubbled up.

"Don't forget to take a brownie," Charlotte said. "I know chocolate is your favorite." She plopped a good-sized piece on his plate, almost tipping it to the ground.

Putting my coffee on a nearby table, I pulled out my phone and took a few candids.

"Um ... thanks," he said, trying to balance it all, but finally putting the plate back on the table. He picked up another plate and the cake knife the blonde had put down, and sliced both the cake and brownie in half, placing them on the other plate. "I can't possibly eat all these sweets," he said. "You don't mind if I share them with my friend, do you?"

All three turned to me, and I snapped a photo of Joe's smiling face caught between twin pairs of dagger-like glare.

"You are evil," he said as he held out the cake plate.

I slipped the phone back in my purse. "Can't possibly be," I said as I took his offering. "We're on holy ground."

"Somehow I don't think that's stopping you in the least," he said.

Out of the corner of my eye I saw the two women hissing at each other, then looking at me.

Trouble in paradise.

"I think you better get me out of here before they start assembling wood and a stake," I said.

He laughed.

"Eat your cake. Father Tim will protect us."

"I think he's having too much fun watching." I nodded my head to where the priest stood with a few other men, his gaze on the group by the snack table.

Father Tim glanced at us, then marched to the women, picked up a plate, and held it out. Immediately, all attention went to the priest who was gesturing wildly as he talked.

The blonde grabbed for the plate, missed, grabbed again, and snagged it.

The group around the priest chuckled.

"Now," Joe said.

We put our plates and cups down and walked toward the parking lot. Just before we left the grove, Joe turned back and waved.

"Thanks for everything!" he yelled.

Father Tim waved. "Safe travels! See you soon!"

With a final wave, we made our escape.

# Chapter Twenty-Eight

"Church still standing?" Kathleen asked as I entered the trailer.

"Appears to be," I said, dropping my bag on the couch. "But Joe was lucky to escape with his life."

"Why?"

I told my sister about the antics of the two would-be suitors for Joe.

She laughed. "If I ever get like that, put me out to pasture," she said.

"You'd marry again?" I asked.

"If the right guy came along, I might consider it."

I stared at her, stunned. I'd always thought Michael was the be-all and end-all for Kathleen.

"Why not? I'm not dead yet."

"I guess that's what a good marriage will give you," I said. "Hope for the future."

"We had our ups and downs. Especially at the end."

"Illness can be hard."

"Yep." Her response didn't quite have the finality it should.

"Was there something else?"

"What?" she asked. "No. No. Nothing else." She picked up her knitting again and her fingers flew as yarn moved from one needle to the next.

I let it drop.

"What time's the barbecue?" I asked.

"I told people drinks would start at four. I told Joe that, too. He said he should be finished prepping and dumping by then, but he wanted to get a shower in before he came over."

"It's a hot one. Good thing the awning and trees provide enough shade."

"It'll be hot no matter what site you're at. There won't be

that many people, at least as far as I know."

"You don't know who's coming?" I asked, visions of running out of food filling my mind.

"It will be enough no matter who shows up. Everyone brings a dish, their grilling choice, their drinks, and their chairs. The more people, the more choices for sides. Expandable party. Just like Mom and Dad used to have."

I smiled remembering the spring and fall gatherings, as well as parties in the neighborhood for the significant holidays. The person with the biggest house or well-appointed barn held the Christmas gathering. Everyone was invited as long as they contributed something. Some people could only afford a bag of apples for bobbing, but they were welcomed with the same grace as those who provided a fully-cooked elk roast.

At least that's how it had been when we were growing up. Liz had confessed it was changing now. People with expensive "second homes" were a lot more cliquish.

"Joe will like a pot luck," I said.

"Still haven't made up your mind about Joe? And what you're going to do when this trip is over?"

"Not really. At least not to the point I want to talk about it," I said. "Can we drop it?"

"Sure," Kathleen said, focusing back on the growing garment in front of her.

"I'm going to change," I said as I walked to the bathroom area, sliding the door closed behind me. Peeking into the back bedroom, I saw it was empty, so didn't bother with that door.

Alone at last.

I stripped down to my underwear, then caught a glimpse of myself in the mirror.

Time hadn't done me any favors.

While I didn't have the stretch marks common to pregnancy, my skin no longer had the taut firmness of youth. Even with underpants, I could see my rear end sagging. A sedentary job hadn't help keep it firm. With my bra on, I couldn't tell how far down my breasts had gone, but perky no longer described them.

It had been a long time since I'd made love with anyone.

How had I thought having sex with Joe would be a good idea?

Because I hadn't been thinking at all; I'd only been driven by desire. I didn't intend a long, drawn-out, slip each piece of clothing off process. Just a quick slam-bam-thank-you-ma'am would be dandy, thank you.

But did it actually work that way for men at this age? Didn't they need a lot more foreplay to ... er ... function? How long did one of those little blue pills take to work? And how long did they last?

It would be terribly uncomfortable for a man to still be erect when I was long satisfied.

Ugh. This golden age living was for the birds, as my aunt used to say.

Vaguely, I recalled a story an older friend had told me about a new lover who used some kind of pump to help out in that department.

But there was something ...

I pulled on my shorts, my mind still wrestling with the image of plastic tubes and a hand pump. Or did one use batteries?

Sex was a lot of work at our age.

It was when I was buttoning my blouse that I remembered the rest of the story.

Apparently, the poor man came to bed, only to have things fizzle out quickly. Back to the bathroom. Another attempt that met with failure. Then a third trip to the bathroom.

What had the poor woman done with herself while she was waiting?

The third attempt hadn't been any better.

She called it a night, and they went to sleep.

Was that why Joe wanted to take it slow? To prepare me for the agony before the ecstasy?

Could I come out and ask him?

Right. I could just imagine how that conversation would go.

*"Joe, do you have ED?"*

*"Why, Di, how kind of you to ask. Yes, in spite of keeping fit, life has been limp in that area. But it's no big deal. I have my trusty pump."*

*"Pump?"*

*"Don't worry. You'll get used to it. Sex will be great. All I need is a little time, and I'll be ready to romp!"*

Just like me to finally hook up with my high school boyfriend only to find out it wasn't going to be like high school at all.

~ ~ ~

I had to hand it to my sisters. They knew how to pull a party together, even amid a group of relative strangers. Somehow they'd gotten some extra tables, and one of the more long-term residents had wheeled over a good sized grill. I'd made a store run and stacks of paper plates, napkins, cutlery, and red Solo cups were arrayed at the beginning of what would be the sides table. Ice-filled coolers waited for bottles and cans.

A pitcher of G and T was sequestered in the RV for our use.

The grill owner, a tech mogul from Silicon Valley, and his wife, a friendly woman I'd met a few times while walking around the park, were the first to arrive. She'd brought a large green salad that just begged me to eat healthy.

After my mirror inspection, it might not be a bad idea.

Mason and Naomi arrived next with a large container of potato salad.

So much for diets.

Their dog, Edsel, was all energy, and quickly reintroduced himself to people.

Slowly people trickled in, all of us knowing each other on some level or another. A few had brought small gifts, gaily wrapped boxes, and a couple of bags that clearly contained wine.

Joe had made a lot of friends in a short amount of time.

Even in high school, he'd known practically everyone, able to easily move from one group to another, no matter how dissimilar they were.

Soon everyone was there except for the guest of honor.

"Go fetch him, Di," Kathleen ordered.

Sometimes she acted more like the oldest sister than I did.

I obediently walked to Joe's trailer and knocked on the door.

Only a towel was wrapped around his waist when he answered.

He didn't look like a man who might have ED.

Heat rushed to the juncture between my legs, an unusual feeling. It had been a *very* long time since I'd felt that.

I looked away.

"Um ... we're waiting for you," I said.

"I know. Just give me a minute."

Thankfully, the door closed.

I sat down at the picnic table as all the chairs had been stowed somewhere. The entire site was spick and span, the only things remaining were the electric and water. Even his truck had been backed into position to easily hook up.

A wave of sadness washed over me. He was really leaving.

A crow landed on the fire ring and eyed me, as if asking, "What are you going to do about it?"

"I haven't the faintest idea," I told him.

He cawed at me and flew off.

"Sorry," Joe said as he emerged from the trailer, thankfully with clothes on. "I had an inspiration for a problem with my book. I've been wrestling with it for days, so I had to get it down. I got involved, and well, time got away from me."

"It's your party," I said with a shrug of what I hoped was nonchalance.

"Yes." He glanced at our space. "And I can see it's already started. Shall we go?"

A cheer went up when we arrived at the party. Someone handed Joe a beer while I went inside to retrieve a G and T. I'd always been a rip-off-the-Band-Aid kind of person. I'd rather say goodbye and have it over and done with.

This send-off was going to make for a long afternoon.

The Silicon Valley exec was in his element as he flipped burgers and grilled hot dogs. Some folks had brought chicken and steaks. There was a lot of exclamations about the sides, which now included beans, coleslaw, a variety of pasta dishes, and another green salad. Brownies, cookies, and a few loaves of sweet breads finished off our choices. Large bowls of a variety of chips sat on the picnic table.

It was quite the party.

I pulled my chair to the edge and people-watched for a while, before taking out my phone to snap a few candid shots. I wasn't sure how they would turn out, but I'd started playing with Photoshop so I might be able to pull something from them.

Joe had a big grin while he talked with some of the men I didn't know well. Edsel had been unleashed and made the rounds, putting his small paws on knees until he was properly greeted. People had earnest conversations. A young girl had wandered in from somewhere and was helping herself to the chips.

No one cared. It was a beautiful day in one of the most amazing places on earth. We had food and good company. Someone had set up their phone with a set of speakers. Country music provided a party beat.

"Having fun?" Mason settled himself next to me.

"Sure," I replied.

"You like photography?"

"Very much."

"But you don't have a camera."

"I'm close." I'd never gotten back to Jane. I'd invented a thousand excuses and then "forgot."

"You should do it for yourself. Something to keep you occupied after he leaves."

"I'll be just fine after he goes," I said. "We're simply friends."

Mason nodded and took a sip of his drink, something clear and bubbly in a red cup.

"Edsel's having a great time," I said.

"He always does. I think he has more fun than us mere humans. Something about no shame in asking for what he wants."

"How is the fishing going?" I asked, putting down my phone and picking up my drink. A nice buzz about now would help me through the day.

"About the same as normal. It's a good way to spend time by myself, contemplating what life is all about."

"And, what is it all about?" I asked.

"The hokey-pokey, of course," he replied with a grin.

"You're bad."

"You don't expect someone to reveal their innermost thoughts on the meaning of life at a party, do you?"

"I don't know. I've often heard long discourses on that very subject at parties."

"And how much of that philosophy held water after the person sobered up?"

"Exactly." I grinned. Mason was easy to be around. No wonder his wife had snapped him up.

Did *she* have to deal with ED?

I pushed the thought from my head.

"Remember what I said about life being too short," he said.

"I do."

"So what are you going to do about that young man over there?"

"Young?"

"It's all perspective, my dear. From my ancient perspective of seventy-nine, you are both young. You just don't know it."

My eyebrows shot up. "Seventy-nine?"

"Every bit of it. Sometimes my body reminds me more than other times."

"You don't look it."

"Thank you. But enough about me." He reached down to lift his dog into his lap. "Where are you gals off to next?"

I told him about our plans to go to Jackson, then on to Moab to see the big parks there. We were quickly engaged in a discussion about the "must-see" portions of that vast landscape.

"While I envy those who have the energy to hike to the Delicate Arch, I found it amazing to stand at ground level, too. A nice camera with a good lens would allow you to capture the arch, as well as all the minute hikers arrayed beside it."

I vowed to myself that tomorrow, no matter what, I'd get to the camera store and buy one.

Maybe it would replace the ache I already knew I was going to have in my heart after Joe left.

~ ~ ~

About an hour later, someone herded Joe over to the gifts. He talked about every gift and thanked the person, allowing everyone a moment in the spotlight. The small plaque given to him by Mason and Naomi made everyone laugh. When Joe read it aloud, Mason gave me a big wink.

"If the trailer is rockin'
"Don't come knockin'"

I had to laugh. For someone close to being an octogenarian, he was as full of life as anyone else I knew.

While I had successfully avoided Joe for most of the party, part of my attempt to keep him in the friend zone, he was equally determined to spend the remainder of it by my side.

"Have you been avoiding me?" he asked. "Every time I turned around, you were talking to another guy."

"Jealous?" I teased.

"You bet." He looped his arm around my waist.

"No need," I said, extricating myself. "They're all taken, and from what I saw at church this morning, you won't be on the market long." I put my fist on my hip, and considered him, tapping my finger on my lips. "Who will it be? The blonde or the brunette? Our audience can't wait to find out. Don't keep us waiting."

He laughed. "It will be the former redhead if she gives

me a chance."

I touched my gray hair. "I was thinking purple for a change."

"Don't you dare," he said. "Just be who you are."

If only *I* knew who I was. The brazen hussy who wanted to take him to bed, ED be damned, or an old high school friend?

"What is it you want, Joe?" I whispered so only he could hear.

"You used to be an English teacher, didn't you?" one of the guys said to Joe, interrupting us.

"Yes."

"I need you to settle an argument between me and my wife. She's over here."

As he was pulled away, Joe looked over his shoulder and mouthed, "Later."

"You know," Liz said, coming up next to me and refilling my glass with the last of the G and T from the pitcher. "One of the things that I was worried about when we planned this trip was meeting all these new people."

"Why?" I asked. "You go to New York at least once a year—although you've never told us the reason. There are lots of people in New York."

"That was different," she said. "I never really interacted with strangers. Everything I needed was taken care of."

My curiosity ramped up. "And what did you do while you were there?"

"Took care of business," she said. Her attention was focused on the people around us. "But these people are really nice. They help each other out."

"Some of them are a bit long-winded," I pointed out.

She laughed. "They don't have anything else to do but talk."

The truth of the statement startled me. Liz and I had things to do while we were on the road, although my few remaining clients didn't keep me too occupied. While I was comfortable enough talking about business, or meeting strangers during an event, talking to a lot of people sapped my energy.

I didn't see myself taking up crafts the way that Kathleen was doing. Maybe I could volunteer at something once I decided where to settle.

"It's been a good send-off for Joe," Liz said. "Will you miss him?"

"Yes," I replied.

"Me too. He's a good guy."

My shoulders relaxed. I'd been prepared for a grilling like Kathleen always gave me, and Liz's gentle acceptance of my answer was a relief.

"I've really enjoyed Yellowstone," she continued. "I know I drove you nuts with the mud pots."

"They're stinky," I said.

"Very stinky." She laughed. "But fascinating. I've been inspired." She sipped her drink. "More than that. There's so much power rumbling beneath the surface. It may look like a tranquil place, at least when there aren't lots of tourists around, but the steam vents and geysers made me aware of how much energy is underground, building up, and waiting for the perfect moment to come together and blast out of there."

"I hope we'll be far away when it does."

She shook her head. "Montana will be obliterated."

"Aren't you full of good cheer."

She laughed again. "I don't want it to happen, but it will be spectacular when it does."

"You think Yellowstone will explode again?"

"There's no doubt. The question is when." She put her hand on my arm. "I didn't mean to worry you. I'm sure we're perfectly safe. It's just the way my mind works."

"Your paintings must be very wild," I said.

"Some are."

As tempted as I was to push to see if I could get more information from her about her art, I gave her the same respect she'd given me, and let it be.

A couple who'd been talking to Joe picked up their almost empty bowl from the side table, stopped to chat with Kathleen for a few moments, then waved and started back to their RV. Soon others repeated the sequence as the party began to break up. Liz and I rejoined the main group to say goodbye to those who'd be on their way the next day, including Mason and Naomi.

"We're headed up to Glacier," Naomi said, her eyes sparkling as she stood next to her husband. "It's one of our favorite places, although it's a shame it's so crowded now. My dad would take us up there as kids in the 1980s. It was wonderful back then. We'd camp by Lake MacDonald and explore as much as we wanted, like a personal playground."

"But I still know the best places to fish," Mason said. "Places most people don't know about."

Naomi laughed. "I'm definitely a fishing widow. But I've recently taken up watercolor painting, as you know." She gestured to Liz. "Glacier is full of colors and shapes."

"Yes," Liz said. "I spend time there as much as I can. Even in winter, I'll go up for inspiration. It's amazing how many different colors can be found in snow."

"Brr. Too cold for me," Naomi said. "I turn into a homebody in winter. Thick soups and round loaves of bread."

"I'm coming to your house next winter," I kidded.

"You should," Naomi said. "And bring Joe. We'd love to see you. Mason, give her our contact information."

"Yes, dear." Mason and I exchanged phone numbers.

"Well, we need to be going," Naomi said. "Still lots to do so we can get an early start."

Once the last people left, the grill man dragging his grill behind him, we cleaned up. Joe was still there to lend a hand. Once the bulk of it was done, Kathleen turned to me. "Now get out of here. We've got this. I'm sure there's things to be said between you."

"I ..."

"Scat." Kathleen made shooing motions.

"Kathleen wants us to leave," I told Joe.

"Her wish is my command," he said. He walked over to my sisters and hugged them both before returning to me.

I half expected him to reach for my hand, but he didn't. He'd gotten my message earlier.

Just friends.

"Beer, water?" he asked. "I've got club soda."

"Sounds wonderful. I need to take the edge off these G and Ts."

He was quickly back with two chilled cans and a brown bag. We settled on opposite sides of the picnic table.

"I wanted to give this to you," he said, handing me the bag.

I peeked inside, then pulled out a print I recognized.

"You admired that when we had dinner at the Faithful Lodge," he said.

"I remember."

"Keep it to remember Yellowstone."

"I will. Thank you, Joe. This is sweet." I looked over at him, unsure what to do next. I was so damn bad at relationships.

"You asked me what I wanted," he said.

"Yes." I tried to think of the best way to begin. "You told me earlier that you want something long term, but I'm not sure what that means, or what you expect of me ... or anyone else."

"I had a good marriage," he said. "I hate the fact that you didn't, but it can't take away from what I had."

"Of course not."

"I think that makes me a little more predisposed to want a second chance." He sipped from his can. "I know I never forgot you, but I never dreamed you'd walk back into my life." He grinned. "And definitely not in a West Yellowstone RV Park."

"Hard to believe. Coincidences happen."

"Good coincidences happen," he said. "Getting to know you—a little—over these last few weeks has been amazing. You're exactly how I'd imagined you'd be when you grew up."

"A little too round and opinionated?"

"You were always opinionated—although I don't think you can hold a candle to Kathleen. As for the other, I wish there wasn't so much emphasis on women's bodies. It's amazing you all stay sane with the pressure media, parents, and the health industry puts on how many ounces you weigh. Put it out of your head."

"I don't think Bug likes me," I said. If Joe wasn't buying the 'I'm too old' excuse for not getting together, I needed to find a new one.

Joe shrugged. "Bug doesn't like change of any kind. And he's a little protective of me. He ... well ... he saw how the ... how Patti's ... how her cancer exhausted me. He'll come around."

I'd never heard Joe stammer like that. I gave him a sharp look, but he was staring toward the river. Suddenly, I had a very strong feeling he wasn't being totally honest with me.

He sighed, then turned back to me. He sat forward, his elbows on the picnic table. "What I want is a chance to get to know you even better, and for you to see me in my natural habitat." Another grin. "I want to kiss you, and yes, eventually make love with you, but not until we're sure about what we want from each other. And, when the time is right, if we both agree it's what we want, I'd like a lifetime commitment."

I was doing okay up until the last sentence. When he said that, it felt like an iron cage wrapped around my chest and squeezed. I wasn't sure I would ever be able to commit to anyone again. I wasn't sure I would be able to trust anyone that much.

And if we got close, and it didn't work out? One of us would be devastated. I didn't want that for me, and I certainly didn't want it for him.

"I'm sorry, Joe," I said, putting the can down on the picnic table. "I'm not looking for a permanent relationship right now. I just got my freedom back. I need time to find out who I am."

He nodded and leaned back. "Understandable. Well, if you ever decide to give it a try, you know where I am."

"Oh, you'll be taken by then." I put a leg over the picnic bench and twisted to get out.

"I don't think so," he said, getting up as well. "I'm not willing to settle for second best."

"I'm sure you won't have to. It was good to see you

again." I stood awkwardly, not knowing the proper exit strategy. I tentatively held out a hand.

He chuckled, took my hand, and pulled me in for a hug. "Take care of yourself, Di. And buy the damn camera." He kissed my cheek and released me.

With a half-hearted wave, I turned to walk back to our rig, forcing myself not to swipe at the tears forming in my eyes.

# Chapter Twenty-Nine

My sisters were smart enough to leave me alone for the rest of the night. I let them know I wanted the car the next morning, and they agreed with no protest.

To my amazement, I slept in the next morning. It was as if my mind refused to wake up and face the fact that Joe was going. No, far better to ignore the whole thing.

When I finally did wake up, I resolved to put all thoughts of Joe aside, just like I had after the aborted prom kiss: steel locks snapped shut on memories. I picked up my notes about the camera.

He'd been right about one thing. It was time to buy something for myself before too many opportunities slipped away.

Taking my notes and coffee outside, I found myself staring at Joe's empty site. No doubt it would be filled with someone else soon, Joe's presence erased like it had never been.

If only he were so easily erased from my memory.

A woman with three labs on leashes walked by. They were happy, bouncy, eager dogs; one yellow, one brown, one black. She herded them into her spot where her husband waited to great them. They were soon slobbering all over him.

Their trailer was half the size of our rig.

Next to catch my eye was a woman holding a small dog with white fur in her arms, while two brown versions trotted behind her. All four had matching topknots tied with identical ribbons.

It might be nice to have a dog when I got settled again.

Or maybe a cat would suit me better.

I had no idea.

With a sigh, I picked up the notes and started reading,

my analytical mind sorting and categorizing the research I'd done on cameras and what they could do. I was still coming to grips with some of the arcane terminology that seemed to matter when capturing a good photo. Why did a lower f-stop allow more light into the camera? If film didn't exist anymore, why did cameras track ISO? Jane had assured me I'd understand all of this in time. I needed to be patient with myself.

Then I took out my phone and scrolled through the photos I had taken, seeing what I'd attempted. There were pictures of the mud pots where I'd tried—and failed—to get a photo of a chocolate bubble popping. And a couple of attempted action shots of my sisters. And Joe.

I scrolled quickly past them.

So, action shots were important to me. That meant a camera that was able to take photos of action.

Most of my shots of flowers and foliage were a little bit blurry. I had no idea what that meant, so I wrote down, "blurry flowers." Jane would figure it out.

Broad scenery photos were important, as was the ability to have strong light and shadow—contrast.

By the time I finished reviewing my notes and photos, I felt comfortable enough to go to the store and let Jane know what I wanted. Then find out if it was something I could afford.

Why not? I wasn't doing anything else with my money. We'd used our combined incomes from the year's take on the ranch to buy the RV, so there wasn't any expense there. My income from the few clients I had covered my living expenses.

It was, as they said, a no brainer.

Why couldn't love be as easily analyzed and dealt with?

I sipped my coffee and stared at Joe's space, which the park personnel were inspecting. Everything must have been in order because it didn't take long.

My chest ached. I was already missing him.

*Change your focus!*

I finished my coffee.

~ ~ ~

"It looks like you took my assignment seriously," Jane said with a smile. "I bet you turned your homework in on time, too."

I blushed. I'd been a model student, even if I never achieved straight As.

"Based on what you've told me, I'm going to recommend this camera body and lens to begin with. She pulled a camera out from under the counter. "It's a Nikon, one of the newer models. It will take lots of different kinds of lenses, including some of those huge ones you'll see people toting around in Yellowstone."

I nodded. I'd seen the two-foot-long monstrosities propped on tripods. The photographs must be amazing, but I wasn't ready to lug around the weight.

"Try it out," Jane suggested, handing me the camera. "I've set it to automatic, so you don't have to worry about settings. The camera does the work for you. As you become more comfortable, you'll be able to switch to manual settings so you're the one in control."

If only life came with automatic and manual settings.

"Take it outside," Jane encouraged me.

"Really?"

"Sure."

I'd forgotten how trusting people could be.

I walked outside and tried a close-up of the pink and purple petunias hanging from a basket. Then I took a shot of a young boy running down the sidewalk on the opposite side of the street. A crow balanced on a street sign gave me a chance at wildlife of a sort.

After a few more shots, I brought the camera back to Jane.

She punched a few buttons, then turned the camera so I could see the small screen. Then she flipped through the photos. "You have a good eye."

"Thanks," I said, a bit in awe of the pictures I'd taken. Even on a tiny screen, they approximated what I'd seen in my mind's eye.

"So how much is it?" I asked.

She told me.

I held in my gasp. I'd expected something around the figure she'd quoted, but to hear it said out loud made it real.

The last time I'd spent that kind of money on a splurge, I'd bought a new stove. Somehow the sheer size of it had made the price palatable. Besides, stoves were practical.

Jane put down the camera.

"I have some others I can show you that are less pricy, but for what you want to do, this is the right choice."

The postwoman came in and handed Jane a stack of mail and had her sign for a box.

I stared at the camera.

*"Buy the damn camera."*

"Well?" Jane asked.

"I'll take it," I said. Then I repeated more firmly. "Yes, I'll take it."

Jane held up a finger. "I have one more thing for you to consider."

"What's that?"

"A person I know recently bought a professional lens for that camera body," she said. "He's given me the old one to sell on consignment. It's a really good price. I think you should consider it for the type of photography you are looking to do. Let me get it."

She disappeared into the back.

I was already spending too much.

It was a bargain.

I didn't deserve it.

Joe would encourage me to get it.

Larry would tell me I was wasting my time.

My mom would have simply smiled.

All these voices in my head. Which one was actually mine?

Jane came out with a box. She undid the wrapping, then swiftly changed lenses. "Go back outside," she said.

The camera was off balance from the heavier lens, and it took a few moments for me to adjust to it. Focusing was easy—once I remembered to take off the lens cap.

I zoomed in on a rounded-bellied older man in shorts and a short-sleeved shirt licking an ice cream cone. The expression on his face was like a young boy on a summer day. I focused in on the expression and clicked.

One of the crows took off from a nearby roof, and I tried to get him in flight. Checking the photo like Jane had showed me, I was disappointed in the black blur.

Another thing to learn how to do.

But that was what the camera would give me: an opportunity to keep learning. Like a body, the mind was a use it or lose it proposition.

"I'll take it," I told Jane when I walked back into the store.

"Good. You will make good use of it. I can tell."

I ignored the momentary panic when I handed over my credit card.

"Call or email me if you have any questions or problems," Jane said as she handed me the bag.

"Thanks for everything," I replied.

"Just take wonderful pictures and enjoy yourself. That will be thanks enough."

I walked out of the store, my nerves racing with conflicting emotions: joy, fear, and anticipation.

~ ~ ~

A new family was setting up in Joe's site when I walked past toward the river to take some pictures with the new camera. I'd gone back to the original lens, figuring I needed to understand that before graduating to the longer lens.

How I wanted to show Joe what I'd gotten! He would have appreciated it, asked me questions, encouraged me to explore. My sisters had been encouraging, but I missed his unbridled enthusiasm for life.

I would find joy without him. In spite of his protestations, I was sure he would be involved with someone after we got back from our trip. I tried to imagine him with either of the women from church who'd been eager to latch onto him.

Who would land him?

A tall Amazon with medals in fly fishing? A widowed stay-at-home mom with talent in the kitchen? A retired teacher who could discuss plot points? Or a woman who oozed sex simply by walking? Those winter nights in Ennis could get cold.

I walked the path by the river, my feet taking me to our favorite fishing spot. I stood there for a moment before taking a picture.

I crouched down and got a shot of the water tumbling over the rocks. Although these didn't have the bright reds and greens of the rocks at the bottom of Lake MacDonald in Glacier, they were pretty in their muted yellows, browns, and umbers.

Pulling out the crib sheet I'd made before I left, I played with the settings on the camera, taking a picture after each adjustment. I made notes on the paper of what I'd done. It was analytical, painstaking, and it forced my mind away from the subject it most wanted to contemplate: Joe.

Eventually, I stood. My sudden appearance startled a buck across the river and he stared at me. Slowly, not wanting to scare him away, I raised my camera and took a shot. He graced me by staying still for a few more before the noise of someone coming up the trail scared him away.

"Ah, so you bought the camera," Mason said as he came into view.

"Yes." I smiled at him. "Yes, I did."

"Joe will be happy for you," Mason said. "Have you told him yet?"

"Um. He left early this morning."

Mason laughed. "I knew that. But I'm told there are these marvelous new inventions called phones. You do have his number, don't you?"

"Yes. Of course." Joe had insisted on exchanging them when we first got together.

"There you go!"

No way was I contacting Joe. My lower lip pushed slightly out, just as it had when I was a kid getting worked up to tell my mom I wasn't going to do what she wanted.

Mason laughed.

"Or not. It's your life." He touched his hat. "I'm going fishing. Have a nice day." He continued down the path.

I sat down on a nearby boulder and stared at the river. We'd had a lot of fun at this spot, even if I had fallen into the water.

So many new experiences in a short amount of time: being with my sisters all the time, RV life, fishing, the camera. I was overwhelmed. That was all that was wrong with me.

I couldn't be missing Joe, could I?

Ridiculous.

He hadn't even been gone a day.

# Chapter Thirty

I went back for thirds at dinner time.

Kathleen raised an eyebrow, but fortunately didn't say anything. I would have jumped her like a pissed-off teen girl fighting for her last ounce of respect.

I was hungry from all the walking around I'd done with my new camera today, I told myself.

Toward the end, I'd gotten overwhelmed by all the information and sat down on a grassy spot near the river. I'd laid back and stared at the sky overhead. So vast. Was there a heaven above? Or only more vastness of space going on for an infinity we humans couldn't quite grasp, a place from which not even the Starship Enterprise could return.

"How is your new camera?" Liz asked.

"It's great. It will be even better when I understand it."

"Give yourself time. You just got it. Every time I get a new brush, or kind of paint, or even a new brand of canvas, I have to learn about it, internalize the effect it has on my work."

"That's far too mystical for Di," Kathleen said. "She's pragmatic to the core. Also impatient."

"Well, I'm smart enough. A camera should be easy to understand."

"Then you should have stuck with your phone. You can't have it both ways, Di. It's easy and limited, or complicated and flexible."

She was right. All my life, I'd been frustrated by things that refused to come quickly to me. Those things were rare, and my modus operandi was to either find a way around them or abandon them altogether.

I was not giving up on this camera.

"I'll figure it out," I said, filling my mouth with the chicken casserole Liz had put together. I chewed and swallowed, chewed and swallowed, while Liz and Kathleen discussed the things that needed to be done before the next leg of the journey.

"Let's do one more visit to Old Faithful tomorrow," Kathleen suggested. "It will give you something else to capture with your new camera."

"It will also get your mind off Joe," Liz said.

"Joe who?" I said with a forced smile. "This is so good, Liz. You should make it more often." I went to take another bite, but my plate was empty.

Fourths were too much even for me, although I was sure I would be able to finish them.

It would be fun to try out the camera on the moving geyser.

"Sounds like a plan," I said, picking up the dishes and carrying them to the sink. "Thanks for thinking of it." I turned to face them, and my throat choked up. "I love you guys," I squeezed out.

"We love you, too," Liz said.

My sisters got up and put their arms around me. We hugged for a few moments, and when we released, a little of the ache in my heart had diminished.

Suddenly, there was a sting on my butt.

Kathleen stood there, a smug look on her face, a towel in her hand.

I grabbed another one and swatted back.

Liz yanked one from the cupboard.

Soon we were all squealing, as our towels hit targets, but I'd swear I'd taken the most hits.

I opened up the door and ran out.

Kathleen was on my heels.

I ran from her and dodged around the back of the RV.

A sting made me turn.

Liz stood there, triumphant.

"Why you ..." I chased her back around where Kathleen waited.

My sister smirked and struck.

I ran back around.

Liz met me.

I could hear Kathleen panting behind me.

I darted to a chair and threw myself down. "Uncle!" I cried. "Uncle!"

They laughed.

"Just like we used to do with Mama," Liz said.

"Man, she had a wicked aim," Kathleen said.

"You two don't do so badly," I said.

"You'll get back in practice," Kathleen said. "We'll make sure of that. After all, what are sisters for?"

~ ~ ~

We packed a picnic lunch and headed for Old Faithful mid-morning. The line to get in was longer than it had been when we'd first arrived in June, and the license plates indicated a great many different states, as well as Canadian provinces.

The ride to the geyser was slower, too, as we had to navigate around the cars parked haphazardly as people leapt out to see the wildlife, some for the first time in their lives. While many were intent on selfies proving they'd been to the grandest park in the United States, one young couple stood there, a toddler by their side. All three faces were filled with wonder.

Life was good.

We snagged one of the last spots in the Old Faithful parking lot.

As we maneuvered through the crowds to the viewing area, Kathleen said, "I think I'm going to be ready to leave here. There are getting to be too many people."

"Jackson and Moab are going to be crowded too," Liz pointed out. "It's summertime. Kids are out of school. Parents take vacations."

"It wasn't like this when we were growing up," I said.

"Not at all," Kathleen agreed.

"How did you live in California?" Liz asked. "There are so many people there."

"I guess I got used to it," I said. "The first few years were hard, but then it seems normal. I expect crowds like this.

Yellowstone is nature's Disneyland."

"Well, I wish they'd go back there," Kathleen said. "And give us our parks back. Glacier is just as bad."

"Aren't you turning into a grumpy old person," Liz said.

"Humph."

"Come on, grumpy," I said. "Let's go see one of the most amazing things on the planet: water shooting out of the ground on a more or less regular schedule."

Liz laughed, and we made our way forward to a decent spot on one of the benches surrounding the geyser. Once we settled down, I took out my camera and fiddled with it, taking shots of people, as well as the geysers I could see in the distance. The longer lens would be ideal for some of these shots, but I knew as soon as I put it on, Old Not-So-Faithful would erupt.

A small child, about four or five, bounced in front of her parents in the front row. She asked her mom a question, then peered over at the bubbling hole. She took a step in that direction, but her father quickly took her hand and went with her as close as he could go. He hoisted her up on his shoulders so she could get the best look she could before returning to their seats.

My chest ached.

"I'm sorry you were never able to have children," Liz said. "It must have been hard. I know you always wanted them."

"So did you."

Liz shrugged. "It wasn't meant to be."

"How come you never got married?" I asked.

"Never found the right man," she said. "I'm extremely picky." She grinned, but there was a sadness in her eyes.

"You could have adopted," Liz said.

"Larry was opposed to the idea. He said if we didn't have kids of our own, that's the way the dice rolled, and we needed to accept it."

"But what about what *you* wanted?" Liz asked. "He never really listened to you. It was always lots of nods with one eye on the ballgame."

"You didn't like him," I said.

"Not for a moment."

What had my sisters seen that I hadn't?

"Why didn't you or Kathleen say anything?" I asked.

"You wouldn't have listened," she said.

"Probably not," I agreed. I took a few more pictures while Kathleen and Liz chatted.

They hadn't liked Larry, but they appeared to like Joe. Well, why not? Joe was one of us, a kid raised in the open landscape of the fourth largest state in the country. Larry had been a Californian all his life, the son of an aerospace worker from LA. Sun, sand, and satisfaction had shaped his life.

But Joe was someone we understood. He had the same values of hard work and devotion to family. In a place where Mother Nature liked to toy with us every chance she got, we relied on our siblings and parents, and helped a neighbor out when he or she needed it.

It made us conservative in the old-fashioned sense of the word: conserving resources, not only money, but the land and wildlife around us. We were sustainable before it became a buzz word.

If I'd had the courage to talk to Joe after prom, my whole life might have been different. His sperm count was obviously just fine.

*Shoulda, coulda, woulda.*

The geyser began to spout.

I picked up my camera and concentrated. All around me people talked animatedly. The little girl was transfixed.

*Snap.*

I could always be a substitute grandmother.

The eruption became higher.

More snaps.

Finally, the water soared into the air, glinting with sunlight and spray. I took as many pictures as I could, periodically changing settings, trying to remember what I did so I could see what worked best. When I had enough, I put the camera down and stared, trying to fix the image in my mind's eye. While there was a chance I may come back to this spot, I would never be here in this exact same moment, sitting next to my travelers through this life: my sisters.

A few minutes later, the geyser subsided. People stayed where they were, hoping for an encore, but the ranger began to move us along to prepare for the next group. I'd been right in my Disneyland analogy.

"Let's get away from these crowds to find a picnic area," I suggested.

"I'd like that," Liz said.

We decided to take the road toward West Thumb. The first few spots were crowded, but as we moved up the mountain pass, there were fewer cars. We stopped near De Lacy Creek where there were several free tables.

Once again we had a small feast laid out: green salad, a selection of olives, tomatoes and mozzarella, sandwiches of turkey and cheese, bristling with sprouts and oozing with avocado. Different flavors of ice tea gave us choices to drink, and I spied a container of cookies at the bottom of the basket.

We were halfway through the meal when Kathleen asked, "So what are you going to do about Joe?"

"I told you," I said. "It's over and done with. No problem. Move it along." I picked up a sandwich and took a bite.

"It's your fourth sandwich," she pointed out.

"They're small."

"You're an emotional eater. Always have been. The last time you broke up with Joe, you gained ten pounds."

"I did ..." The protest died on my lips. Actually, it had been more like fifteen.

I dropped the sandwich on my plate.

"It doesn't have to be over," Liz said. "Let him know you made a mistake."

"I can't."

"Why not?" Kathleen asked.

"Because I need time for *me*, that's why!" I picked up the sandwich and took another bite. Glaring at them, I chewed and swallowed.

"You were right, okay? Larry was an ass. It was his fault we never had children. He hid the lab results from me. If I'd known, we could have ..." I lost my grip and started to sob. It was all too much.

The few other picnickers stopped talking.

Great. I'd embarrassed us. I got up from the table and fled down a nearby path.

My sisters had the good sense to leave me alone.

It took a while, but my steps slowed. A rustling in some nearby bushes reminded me I was not alone.

Oh well, if a bear wanted to eat me, it was the perfect ending to my life.

I leaned against a tree.

After learning of Larry's betrayal, I'd made it a point not to get too close to anyone, male or female. But my sisters were wise to me. They'd known me too long.

And they were right.

Like he'd been decades ago, Joe could be the right man for me. The only way to find out would be to take the risk and let him know how I felt.

But where would I find the courage to bare my heart?

# Chapter Thirty-One

Even though the sun was shining when I woke the next morning, the world felt gray. I was stuck. There didn't seem to be a good path forward. I wished Joe had never shown up. Then I could have concentrated on the trip in front of me.

I should do that anyway.

I pushed off the sheet that was crumpled and damp from my wretched night's sleep. My dreams were a mixture of past scenes of my life with Larry and memories of walks with Joe, with intervals that seemed to come from a consciousness well beyond any I knew. Spiders turned into beautiful women; evil men turned into snakes, but I flew above it all with my huge wings. I was supposed to be going somewhere, but I'd forgotten where that was.

Swinging my legs to the floor, I headed to the bathroom, but one of my sisters had beat me to it. I stood at the sink and washed my face, then cursed myself for running water when I had to pee.

Kathleen staggered out of the toilet room a few moments later and crossed to the sink mumbling, "Morning."

"Yep," I said and scurried to the room she'd left.

Much relieved, I plodded to the kitchen area for my coffee, which was already brewed. Kathleen and I sat scrolling through our phones, our silence interrupted by a chuckle now and then, or the muttering of "idiot," when reading about some bone-headed antic or statement by a politician.

"We need to get ready to move tomorrow," Kathleen said when she was able to string several words together.

"Can you still access the app I sent you?" I asked.

"The list thingamajig?"

"Yes, that one." We'd made a list of things to do before

leaving the RV park, at least as many as we could figure out. "We'll need to add everything we've forgotten."

"It's going to come in handy," Kathleen admitted. "There are too many little things that are easy to forget."

That gave me an idea.

Later, after we'd breakfasted and gotten ready for the day, we started on the chores. Liz made a last run to the store, Kathleen assembled the things she'd need to do a final dump and put the hoses away, and I—somewhat graciously—agreed to do a last load of combined laundry.

There's nothing like watching clothes go around and around in a washer to get your mind to go into all the places you've been avoiding.

I'd been so sure watching Joe drive off into the sunrise was the right thing to do for both of us, but the ache in my heart wouldn't go away. I hadn't heard from him, but he'd told me it was up to me to contact him.

Grabbing an out-of-date flyer from the community bulletin board, I drew a line vertically down the back. One side I titled pros. The other side was cons.

Pros
Joe is a nice guy.
He had a successful marriage.

Of course, the second could be a con too. I'd failed at my marriage. He'd expect something I wasn't sure I was able to give. I copied it into the cons column and added, "Patti's ghost."

It was impossible to compete with a ghost. Anyone who'd ever read Daphne du Maurier's *Rebecca* knew that.

Another pro: He likes me.

I smiled.

But liking someone was no guarantee of anything.

Cons
He had a successful marriage.
He lives in Montana.

I wasn't sure Montana was the best place for me. I hadn't lived there for most of my adult life. The pace and values were totally different from the bustle of the Bay Area. I was used to the climate and the pace of California. I'd miss it when winter had its icy talons dug in deep in Montana land.

I got up and moved the clothes to the dryer.

Another con: I haven't learned how to be me first.

Since the divorce I'd been "not married," but I'd begun to figure out that wasn't all there was. I needed to rediscover who *I* was, without a man to orbit around, either positively or negatively. It was true I'd have the year to travel with my sisters, but would that be enough?

I wrote down a few more cons, but couldn't come up with any more pros.

There was my answer, in black and ... er ... green.

The data on the paper was depressing. It may list all the facts, but it didn't make me feel any better about my decision. There had to be more pros about Joe than I was remembering.

But what did it say about me that I couldn't remember. I stuffed the paper in my back pocket.

The clothes tumbled.

A fishing pole of my own. That would be nice. It had been fun fishing with Joe. Maybe if I practiced, he'd be impressed the next time I saw him. The times we'd spent together, lines floating in the water, sun overhead, had been peaceful, content.

Conversations over dinner. He was a smart, well-read man. He had his novel to give him purpose. Would photography provide me the same kind of fulfillment?

Kissing Joe had been magic.

Why was I willing to give that up? It wasn't that he never wanted to make love, it was that he wanted to take it slow and steady. I had been the one in a rush, afraid the opportunity would disappear if I didn't snatch it up right then.

The clothes slowed and tumbled to the bottom of the massive dryer. I pulled them out and started folding.

~ ~ ~

Once I got back with the clothes, we ate lunch: sandwiches Liz had picked up in town. Then we went back to stowing things we'd strewn about and strapping things in. By late afternoon, we were ready to go to town for cocktails followed by dinner at Firehole BBQ Co., a place we'd gone to once before and deemed worthy of a return visit, no matter how messy.

"I'm looking forward to getting to the East Coast," Liz said as we settled in with our ribs and sides of coleslaw, beans, and macaroni and cheese. "Especially the Hudson River Valley. There was a group of artists there in the mid-1800s. Their paintings are so moody, it's wonderful."

"Are you going to drag us to lots of museums?" Kathleen asked with a groan.

"As long as you can put up with it. And then a little bit more." Liz's eyes sparkled. "Art is good for the soul. Besides it will give you inspiration for your weaving."

"I don't need inspiration. I need to learn to weave faster."

"What you need is patience," I said. "The same thing you're always telling me about my photography. Look in the mirror and say the same thing."

"You're right about that," Kathleen said, waving a barbeque bit speared by a fork in my direction. "Weaving sometimes feels more tedious than driving that damn combine harvester up and down the field."

"Really?" I asked. "That would drive me nuts."

"I've got a radio blasting, sun in the sky, and the land all around me," Kathleen said. "It's being free and in control at the same time. Harvesting wheat I planted on land we own? There's no greater satisfaction."

"I thought Michael did most of the planting?"

She looked at her fork and plopped the meat in her mouth.

Whenever I brought up Michael, she changed the subject or gave me some kind of generalization.

"Was there something wrong between you and Michael?" I asked gently.

"You mean other than being married too long and his illness?"

I nodded.

"Nope. Nothing to speak about. Just the normal stuff." She turned to Liz. "This coleslaw is so good. What do you think they put in it?"

"I'm not sure." Liz dug her fork into the slaw and chewed, her brows pulling close together as she concentrated. "Almost tastes like pickles. You know, instead of vinegar. What do you think?"

"Me?" I asked. "I've got no sense of taste. You guys know that. If you blindfold me, I can't even tell a white wine from a red one."

"That's no big deal. It's only those wine snobs from California who care," Kathleen commented.

I laughed. "You're right. There's always one person trying to prove their chops by announcing the varietal, region it came from, and the year. It's nice to be back among mere mortals."

"We have both kinds," Liz said with a grin. "Red and white."

"I'd rather have a beer," Kathleen announced. "There's a few microbreweries in Butte that Michael and I tried before ..."

And we were back to that topic. I opened my mouth, but Liz shook her head. She knew something I didn't.

"Well, if we're going to put up with hoity-toity art museums," Kathleen said. "I'm going to drag us to some honky-tonk bars in Texas. I can't wait."

I let the topic of Michael go and joined the lively discussion of music.

My sisters were great human beings. I'd be fine.

~ ~ ~

As we reached our RV, I noticed there were some papers and an envelope jammed into the gap by the door.

"Probably just our bill," Kathleen said, grabbing the stack before unlocking the door and climbing up the steps.

She tossed the papers on the counter and kicked off her shoes.

After ditching mine, I grabbed a glass in the kitchen and poured some water.

"This is for you," Liz said and handed me a thick envelope.

I stared the neatly printed address and Montana return address. I knew that handwriting.

"Are you going to open it?" Kathleen asked.

"Not now," I said and put the envelope on the desk.

We agreed on a new comedy to stream, and I got it going while Liz made some tea. Soon we were settled down, watching Jane Fonda, Candice Bergen, and Diane Keaton do and say everything we wanted to but didn't have the courage to pull off.

All the while, the envelope on the desk beat like the telltale heart of Poe's dark fiction. And just like the organ in the story, it seemed to grow louder and louder as time went on.

It was long after the movie ended, and my sisters had gone to bed that I forced myself to open the envelope.

Dear Di,

I know I said I wouldn't contact you, but I found as soon as I got on the road, that was going to be impossible.

I care about you too much. Until I saw you again, I hadn't realized how much I'd buried it all my life. I loved Patti, but you were my first love. Nothing compares to that. And to get a second chance at that?

A miracle.

I can't wait a whole year to see you again, but I don't want to dishonor your trip with your sisters either.

Can you spare some time for us? To talk more and figure out where we go from here?

I'm here in the Black Hills for only a week, but then I'm spending three weeks in the Badlands. I know, prairie in the summer. Insane!

But I know I can get some quality writing done there. The national park is vast, but not home. I think you could find some good uses for your new camera. (You did buy one didn't you?)

The park has small cabins. I'd love to rent one for you.

Will you come? For a little while?

Please?

Joe

I reread it three times. And I was no clearer on what to do than I was before I opened the envelope.

# Chapter Thirty-Two

We arrived at the RV park near Jackson Hole, Wyoming four hours after leaving West Yellowstone. Driving the RV along winding mountain roads took a lot longer than navigating the same distance in a car. Sometimes the road would angle in such a way that I could see a long line of cars following us like ducklings. Whenever we hit a straight-away with a dotted line, several would zoom past.

A lot of them regarded double yellow lines as a suggestion.

"Idiots," Kathleen would mutter every time a near miss would occur.

The terror of the road kept me from focusing on Joe's letter.

Kathleen parked without incident. This time there was a man in a cart to guide us and instruct Kathleen on the hookups.

She took that guidance as well as possible, and the man escaped.

It took another hour or so to set everything up.

We were settling down in our chairs with cocktails and books when the inquisition began.

"What's in the letter?" Kathleen asked.

"I don't want to discuss it."

"It's from Joe, isn't it?" Liz asked leaning forward.

I pretended to read my book.

"Oh! I knew it!" Liz said, clapping her hands together.

"I didn't say it was from Joe," I said.

"That's how I knew it was," Liz replied.

I shook my head and read the same sentence over again.

"You need to put the poor man out of his misery," Kathleen said.

"And you need to mind your own business."

I spotted a friendly wave from the road and propelled myself out of my chair. The wave belonged to a couple we'd met at the previous stop. They'd left a week before us. It was easy to drag them from their nightly rounds walking their dogs, cocktails in hand.

"What have you seen? What should we do?" Liz asked them.

"The Teton Mountains are amazing. But I'm sure you saw that on the way down," the woman said.

"We went through Idaho," Kathleen said. "I didn't want to try to thread the rig through animals and tourists."

"Good idea," the man said. "I wish we'd done that."

"You're going to love painting them," the woman said to Liz. "The light and shadow change all the time. If you get there early, it's quieter."

"Summer and tourists. Can't avoid them," the man added.

"And go to the museum," the woman said. "They've got a great exhibit."

"What about Jackson itself?" I asked. I had memories of a small town with a big square in the middle. Most memorable were the arches of elk antlers on the corners. I had been charmed by the town, always vowing to come back.

"Have you been here before?" she asked.

I nodded.

"It's changed. It used to be fairly quiet, a place you could find some nice things, or enjoy window shopping if it was too much for your pocketbook. It's much more ... I don't know ... commercial now. It's more a place to quickly pick up your souvenir saying you've been to Jackson Hole. Lots of bars and music. I mean, that was always there, but ..."

"They've taken a step down," her husband said. "More neon, less class."

"They even rebuilt and moved the arches."

"They had to do that, dear. They were falling apart."

"I suppose. It's always hard when my memories don't match reality anymore."

That was the truest thing I'd heard in a long time.

Except for Joe. The exterior had changed, yes, but the

interior was the same solid person I remembered.

~ ~ ~

The next morning, I took the car and went into the park with my camera. This time I'd decided to practice with the long lens, hoping my early rise would allow me to see some birds and animals. Looking at the park-provided map, I drove to the oxbow bend of the Snake River and hiked closer to it.

Then I waited.

Soon my ears became accustomed to the rhythm of the sounds. Birds, already awake for hours, chattered at each other to defend territory or argue over who saw an insect first. Overhead, ospreys and eagles swooped low over the river, searching for breakfast.

A few other humans were scattered about, but six a.m. was too early for most.

I tried taking pictures of the birds flying overhead, but realized it was going to take a lot of practice for me to get a still shot in the air. I did better when they landed on a limb of a tree.

A fisherman walked close to water's edge and cast in his line. It wasn't the elegance of fly fishing, but he made a good focal point for a picture of the river.

As I waited for something to happen, my subconscious focused on what to do about the letter.

What would my sisters think if I abandoned them for a man, no matter how short the time away?

How would I even get there? I couldn't take the car, Liz and Kathleen needed that.

*Impossible.*

I tried to capture another eagle scanning the river.

*Better.*

A longing in my heart told me I'd better figure out a way to get to South Dakota.

Why did he have to choose the Badlands which so richly deserved their name? Couldn't he have picked somewhere else? Like a hot springs with a lovely inn? Someplace where

I could get pampered while he scribbled?

Somewhere more conducive to a seduction. Because that might be what it would take.

The eagle flew by again, but I wasn't ready for the shot.

People down river from me stirred and a shape emerged from the bushes. That big rack could only belong to one animal—a moose.

I extended my lens and took a shot.

It was still far away, but I had my first moose picture.

The eagle came by again, but this time there was a second one right on his tail.

A third watched from shore.

The next time around the bird swooped and snatched up a wriggling fish.

Immediately, the second eagle was on him, talons out, beak wide.

They struggled in the air, close to the river, their huge wings almost touching.

The third eagle dive-bombed them. Soon it was a whirr of feathers, beaks, and talons, with screams that made me think someone was being murdered. The fish was torn in two, and the second eagle took off with its portion. The first eagle finally pulled free of its rival and flew off.

The third eagle went back to its position on the bank as the moose came plodding up the river.

Joe was like that plodding moose, just putting one foot in front of the other to go in what he thought was the right direction. I'd been like that forlorn eagle on the other side of the river, going after the things I wanted, but failing.

Or maybe I wasn't being clear enough to either myself or Joe. Would I be satisfied with a fling? Would finally having sex with Joe complete whatever we had between us? Would a long weekend in bed be enough for me to move on from a multiple-decade fantasy?

Two ospreys cruised above me, working in tandem. They mated for life, a life that included responsibilities, but also the soaring freedom of the sky.

It had taken me a long time to get up the courage to leave Larry and stand on my own two feet. As non-existent as the relationship had become, it hadn't felt right to give up. Married for life. Wasn't that what the church had taught us over and over? And the magazines we were addicted to as teens showed us how to attract a man and make them the center of our existence.

Who was I if I wasn't in a relationship?

Much as I was being blasé about a slam-bam-thank-you-ma'am event, I wasn't sure I could really see myself doing that again. I was hungrier for more than I had been in my twenties.

I looked up at the osprey again.

I'd fought for that freedom. Would it be possible to fall in love and still figure out who I was on my own?

I snapped a few more pictures, then turned to go. In front of me the morning sky highlighted the crags and fissures of the Grand Teton Mountains. Their outlines were crisp against the sky, and from this distance it was possible to frame them even with the long lens.

Such majesty in this country. How had I lived so long away from it? Whether I was with Joe or not, I needed to do some serious thinking about coming home.

~ ~ ~

"She'll go to her grave with the secret," Kathleen said to Liz as we ate lunch.

"Too bad. We might help her with whatever is bothering her," Liz said.

"She never was good at taking advice."

"But she's older and wiser now."

"She's right here," I pointed out. "And I wouldn't be dissing me about secrets. It seems to me the two of you have some things you are keeping to yourselves."

"I'm an open book," Kathleen protested.

Liz glanced at her, a frown on her face.

"What? We've never seen your paintings," she pointed out to Liz.

"I don't want you to," Liz said, her voice tense.

"Oh, for god's sake," I said. "Go back to picking on me. I

don't want you two squabbling."

My sisters stared at me.

"Well, I don't. Besides, you're right. I need to make a decision, and I'm failing at deciding anything at all." I retrieved the envelope and my pros and cons list from the desk and placed them on the table.

"What's that?" Liz asked, pointing to the list.

I told her.

"A list to decide whether or not you like a man?" Kathleen asked. "Is that how they do it in California?"

"No," I said. "I told you. I don't know how to make the right choice. The last time I did, I wound up with Larry."

"She's right," Liz said. "She needs serious help."

"Let me look at that." Kathleen grabbed the list and studied it. "That's it? You're right. It's pitiful."

"You got a better idea?"

"There's always daisies. You know ... he loves me, he loves me not. It makes about as much sense as this." Kathleen tossed the list back down on the table.

"Of course she loves him," Liz said.

"That was never in doubt," Kathleen said.

"I do?" I'd never wanted to put a label on my feelings for Joe.

"Yes!" they both said.

"I can't believe she doesn't know," Liz said.

"Me either."

My sisters continued to discuss my relationship with Joe while I sat there and turned the idea over and over in my brain.

"What did the letter say?"

"He wants me to come visit," I said. "But I can't do that and leave you two alone with the trailer. This is supposed to be our trip. No men involved."

"Honey, at our stage of life, if a man comes knocking, and we're interested, I say go for it," Kathleen said. "I'm certainly going to do it."

"You just buried your husband!" I exclaimed.

"Means he's good and dead," she answered. "But I'm still on the right side of the grass. Definitely not dead yet.

This girl still has a lot of life left in her. So do you."

"One mistake doesn't mean you have to punish yourself for the rest of your life," Liz said, her face soft, and her eyes a little out of focus ... wistful.

Her secrets went well beyond what she was painting.

As for Kathleen, her relationship with Michael at the end must have been very difficult for her to be so eager to move on.

I didn't know my sisters at all.

"So you think I should go."

"You *need* to go," Liz said.

Kathleen nodded her head.

"But how do I get there?"

"Rent a car," they said at once.

~ ~ ~

Renting a car proved to be a lot more difficult than I'd anticipated. It seemed that rental car places had decreased their stock during the pandemic. Now that people were back on the road, the fight for rental cars was fierce.

My sisters convinced me to use ranch funds to buy a used car.

"We're going to need two," Kathleen said. "Liz wants to do more painting, and now that you have that camera, you're going to want to get out as well."

"But what about you?" I asked.

"I'll be happy to see your backsides so I can have some peace and quiet," she said.

Liz packed me supplies for a two-day trip. I'd spend a night in Casper to break up the almost nine-hour drive. While I was tempted to make it a three-day drive, there was far too much open space in Wyoming to find accommodations.

With my route locked into my phone, a playlist set up for the long drive, coffee and water in their appropriate holders, and a quick text to Joe, I set off for the Badlands to see if what I felt for Joe really was love.

# Chapter Thirty-Three

Wyoming is lonely country, especially if driving alone in a small car. Semis roar bay, slow for the upgrades, then roar by again, on their way to somewhere else to make a delivery or greet loved ones. Wind howls across the treeless ground, which itself isn't the least bit level. Instead, it contains small ridges, water-blasted fissures, and cliffs gouged by huge machines to extract the minerals that lay below the surface.

Mud-covered trucks zoom by, occasionally pulling horse trailers. The sleeker, newer trucks pull RVs that are barely held on the road during a sudden wind blast. The rest of us dodge the traffic and focus on where we're going, not where we are.

In between moments of panic when a wind-pushed vehicle strayed into my lane or a semi cut too close after passing, there was way too much time to think.

It was great that Joe wanted to see me to talk about our future, and polite that he'd found separate accommodations. But he hadn't said he loved me.

Maybe he'd reconsidered and decided all he need was a few nights of wild sex.

But why the separate accommodations then?

Was I being too pushy about sex? Did Joe think less of me? Did he consider me a "brazen hussy," a term my mother occasionally used about a woman in town who took too much interest in other women's husbands?

"Nympho" was the term Larry had used about me.

My chest twisted when I remembered that. Just like all the other name-calling he'd done, that one pierced my soul. I'd bought into it, quietly crying out my shame in our marriage bed after he'd turned his back on me.

I couldn't go through that again.

A black pickup came within inches of my front bumper

when he pulled into my lane.

"Idiot!" I yelled and raised my fist for good measure.

He gave me the middle finger and zipped into the fast lane, causing the driver of a passenger car going the eighty mile an hour speed limit to stomp on his brakes and land on his horn.

People had gone insane and dropped all pretense of manners.

I took a couple of deep breaths. Road rage was a thing. And these people had guns.

Time to go back to pretending I was a harmless little old lady.

~ ~ ~

Hotel rooms can be depressing in the best of circumstances, but the chain hotel in Casper didn't reach that threshold. Once I let my sisters know I'd made the first stop, I ate my dinner in the hotel dining room before returning to my space. Surfing through the dozen channels gave me few options for entertainment, so I settled on a rerun of a movie I vaguely remembered.

I should let Joe know I stopped at a hotel for the night.

My fingers were poised above my phone, but I had no idea what tone to use.

Serious?

Fun-loving?

Flirty?

No, strike the last one. Ironically, sex was going to be the most serious discussion of all.

In the end, I decided on neutral.

*I'll be there tomorrow*, I texted.

*I can't wait to see you*, he replied quickly. *Where are you?*

*Casper.*

*Long drive.*

*Yes.*

The three little dots indicating typing appeared, disappeared, and re-appeared again.

*Drive safe*, he wrote.

Then nothing.

What was I expecting? A declaration of undying love over a text message? We weren't teens anymore.

I tried watching the movie I'd found, but I couldn't get into it. Flipping through the channels, I came upon some viewing options, so I scrolled through those.

Adult movies.

I sat up.

I'd never watched one, always too afraid someone would find out.

If I watched one now, someone could find out I'd done it, but why would they? It was relatively anonymous. And what harm could it do? I might learn some things. Old dogs and new tricks.

My heart pounding, I charged a movie called *Guilty Pleasure*.

After a few moments, I almost turned it off, the acting was so bad and the script only a vehicle to get to nudity.

But then they started doing things.

And my eyes popped wide open.

How did they get into those positions? And did it really fit ... um ...

I covered my eyes with my fingers, then opened them and peered through.

Apparently, it did.

That night I had erotic dreams. I must have tried to get into some of the positions I'd seen because muscles I didn't remember I had were aching when I woke up.

~ ~ ~

I'd been on the road an hour the next day when the skies opened up, cutting visibility on the interstate and increasing the terror of driving. Every time a semi went by, I was blind for a few moments. I drove the next half hour with my heart in my throat, gratefully exiting the highway and heading north when I reached the small town of Lusk.

The rain didn't stop, but its pace slowed, and I felt more

comfortable navigating. The going was slower than I'd anticipated, because I drove more cautiously. Maybe I was a little old lady after all.

The scenery, if there was any, was lost to me. All I could concentrate on was the road in front of me: wet black tar, faded yellow line, slap of the wipers as they smacked down to the bottom of the windshield. Another hour went by before I turned east into South Dakota and began to climb the hills.

In spite of the miserable driving, I couldn't turn off my mind. The anticipation of seeing Joe grew with each passing mile. The whole situation was complicated, but one thing stood out: I'd always felt a closeness with Joe I'd never felt with anyone else. Maybe he was right about first loves. The bonds we formed as teens, our shared experiences, would connect us for the rest of our lives.

How we kept that connection alive was going to be the thing that mattered. We could go back to being old friends who'd lost touch, get a more active friendship, or move on to something more. It was the shape of that something more we needed to determine.

But I'd committed to a year-long trip with my sisters, and I was determined to complete it. It was the chance of a lifetime. There was so much of this country I'd never seen, and I wanted a sampling.

What if Joe tagged along with us?

I dismissed that thought as soon as it arose. Having Joe around permanently would upend the delicate balance we'd achieved. For the first time since we were kids, none of us had significant others. As far as I knew, Liz never had been involved with anyone for long.

Spending the next year with me on the road and Joe back in Ennis or wherever didn't bode well for a renewed relationship with him. Whether or not Joe succumbed to a church lady or some other desperate widow, it was a recipe for growing apart, not coming together.

Maybe it was all an illusion. If it was, why was I making this trip?

Because I was a stubborn old fool who believed in

second chances.

I pulled over at the first restaurant of any kind I'd seen in a while. I'd expected a Mexican place, but was surprised to discover it was Asian Indian.

Staring at the menu, I tried to decipher the unfamiliar listings. I'd been to a few Indian restaurants in California, but usually with a group. Someone always took charge of ordering a series of dishes we passed around.

"Can I help you?" a woman about my age asked.

"That would be nice. I didn't expect to find this kind of restaurant out here in the middle of nowhere."

The woman laughed. "There are more and more of us. There are many Indian truckers; it's a good job for us. They are looking for familiar food, so we provide it."

"How interesting!" I said. "But this seems so far away from anything. Don't you get lonely?"

"We have brought many cousins, nieces, and nephews with us," she said. "There are many things truckers need besides food. And with the internet, a few of my family work offsite for big companies, but prefer to live near us. Most of our children and their families are here, too."

"That's amazing."

"Let me help you decide what to eat," she said.

We chatted about the weather as she helped me choose dishes with names I couldn't pronounce. The food came out quickly, and I devoted my time to tasting the incredible spices and textures. When I was close to done, the woman came back, and I invited her to sit as there were few other guests in the restaurant.

"Would you mind if I took some pictures before I left?" I asked. I'd already taken a few of the food to send my sisters.

"Not at all," she replied. "In fact, if they turn out well, I'd love to see them. Perhaps we will be able to use them for our website."

"Sure. May I take one of you right now?"

A few poses later, I hoped I got what I saw in the restaurant owner: beauty and inner wisdom.

"How long have you been married?" I asked.

"Over thirty-five years," she said.

"Wow."

"It was an arranged marriage," she continued. "They aren't so common anymore, but they were when I was young, especially in small villages. I was lucky. My parents chose a compassionate and handsome young man for me."

"And you are still together."

"Yes."

"Happy?" I asked.

"Very happy," she said.

"How did you manage that?"

"I take it you are not married."

"No." I shifted my gaze to the silver bracelets on her arm.

"We were awkward at first, especially ... well, you know."

I nodded, although I couldn't imagine my first time being with a man my parents had chosen for me. Although she probably knew him better than I knew my first sexual partner—a college buddy after a long night of drinking.

"But we both had the same goals, and more importantly the same values. We respected and loved our families, were willing to work hard, and had a dream of emigrating to America."

"And you made it come true."

"With hard work, yes. Along the way, we learned to trust each other and to care for each other. I believe we also realized how important it was to be honest with ourselves and admit our own flaws. We discovered how to talk things through, even difficult things we would not like to reveal to each other. He was, and still is, a loving man."

"And you love him."

"I have learned to do so. It has been a great gift in my life."

A man pulled open the front door, and the woman's face lit up. He may no longer be young, but he was still a good-looking man. He leaned down and kissed her cheek.

"You have been chatting to our guest?"

"Yes. Telling her how we got here."

"Ah, good." He smiled at me. "It is a good story, is it not?"

"The best kind of story," I said.
A love story.

# Chapter Thirty-Four

The story made driving the next few hours tolerable. I couldn't imagine being party to an arranged marriage, but maybe older people who had a more clear-eyed vision of what people became were better judges of the perfect match.

That conversation would not have gone well for me.

"Diane, we've been talking to Sam's parents. The four of us agree the two of you would be great partners," my father might intone.

"We've agreed you two should marry," Sam's father would announce at a formal meeting between the two families.

My mouth would drop open in shock.

"Flies," my mother would say, a warning to shut my mouth before a fly got in.

"I'm not doing it," I'd announce.

"It's really for the best," my father would say, his tone getting that I'm-not-taking-any-flack-from-you-young-lady edge.

"Diane's got a boyfriend," Kathleen would taunt in a voice only I could hear.

"We know better about these things," my mother would explain.

"Adults don't know anything! I don't love Sam! I'll never love him!" I'd jump to my feet.

"And who do you love?" Sam's mom would say.

That was the question, wasn't it? Did I love Joe? Did I love him enough to give up some of my freedom? To adjust to living with another human being again?

Once I'd left Larry, I told everyone I knew that I was never living with another man again. They are simply too much work!

As nice as Joe was, he probably still left socks on the

floor, the toilet seat up, and the cap off the toothpaste. Unless Patti had trained him really, really well.

The wheels on my car slipped as the car started to hydroplane. Damn it!

Automatically, I turned into the skid. The car corrected itself, and I slowed down. A few yards up there was a pull-out with a trash can.

I drove in, stopped the car, and took my hands off the wheel.

My body shook as the adrenaline worked its way through.

*That was close.*

No more thinking about alternate realities.

I checked the weather app on my phone. Rain for the rest of the trip. Maybe I should turn this into a three day trip. Checking the map, I decided to see if there were accommodations at Hot Springs.

Apparently, not many people stopped in Hot Springs in late July, because I was able to find a room. When the desk clerk suggested a mineral springs spa add-on, I decided to go for it.

Pampering myself sounded good, and the price was right.

With a deep breath, I pulled back on the road, maintaining a slower speed than I'd been doing previously. In a few hours, I'd checked in and sent messages to Joe and my sisters, telling them of my delay and assuring them everything was okay.

Then I indulged myself.

The spa was an easy walk from the hotel. For over an hour, I let myself be ministered to, first with a soak in a hot springs pool, followed by a short massage with fragrant oils. I floated back down the sidewalk to my room where I instantly fell asleep.

Just before seven, I woke and got dressed for dinner.

The hotel shop had a selection of best sellers, and I picked up a thriller before taking myself to an upscale restaurant where I indulged in a beautifully prepared trout with rice and vegetables as a side, accompanied by a fine wine, and followed by a rich chocolate dessert.

A perfectly balanced dinner.

Even the television cooperated when I got back to my room. A rom com relaxed me enough to fall into a dreamless sleep.

The next morning I was ready to tackle the world.

Well, if not the world, then I was ready to hit the road.

Better yet ... the sun shone.

~ ~ ~

The Badlands were as stark as I thought they'd be. Driving down from the rich greenery of the Black Hills, the high plains stretched before me, miles and miles of parched prairie. In some ways it reminded me of Eastern Montana. Familiar, yet totally new.

As I approached the RV park where Joe was staying, I could feel the effects of my blissful evening wear off. These next few days would determine the direction of my life for the foreseeable future.

No pressure.

The conversation with the Indian woman replayed in my head. Would I have the courage to say what needed to be said out loud? I was so unpracticed at telling the truth, the real truth, to a man. In business I'd learned to play to their egos to achieve success. In my marriage I'd avoided any topic that would give Larry a chance to inflict more verbal pain.

Time to suit up and show up.

Joe was a good man. I had to trust he'd tamed his ego enough to hear the truth.

After stopping in the office, I was directed to the cabin I was to occupy.

I spotted Joe's RV, but went to my cabin, willing embrace my solitude for as long as I could.

It was not to be.

I'd barely had time to use the bathroom before there was a pounding on my door.

"You made it!" Joe exclaimed as he pulled me into his

arms. "I'm so glad you're here safe and sound."

"Me too. But if you don't stop squeezing, I'm not sure I will be."

"Oh. Sorry." He released me.

We stood there staring at each other. I wasn't sure what to do next, and it didn't appear he did either.

When I couldn't bear the posture any longer, I moved in to give him a kiss—just a quick peck on the lips. At the same time, he moved in to kiss my cheek.

Bam! Our noses collided.

"Ow!" I said, rubbing.

"Sorry," he said again. "I don't mean to hurt you. Really. Let me try that again." He dipped in and kissed my cheek.

Just like you would an old friend.

This was not what I wanted at all. When he lifted his head, he spotted my camera.

"You got it!" he exclaimed.

"I did. And I love it. I'm only sorry I waited so long."

"But you have it now. Do you want to use it? It's still early enough, we could go for a short hike. Or there's a local bar down the way that has a pool table, if you like that. Tomorrow night they'll have music."

I held up my hand.

"First," I said. "I want to take a nap. Then a shower. Then I'll let you know. Okay?"

"Okay, I guess." He frowned a bit as I maneuvered him out the door. "See you later?"

"Yep."

I closed the door.

~ ~ ~

When I woke an hour later, I was groggy, unsure of where I was. Living in the RV had lulled me into a safe sense that I knew where everything was. This was the third time in as many days that I'd slept in a strange bed, and it took me a moment to figure out where the bathroom was.

After splashing some water on my face, I took a quick shower, then changed into shorts and a t-shirt. Time to get this show on the road.

Joe spotted me coming toward his RV spot, and closed the book he'd been reading. His smile was cautious.

"Feeling better?" he asked.

"Yes," I said. "Long drives aren't as easy as they used to be."

"Nothing is as easy as it used to be."

Including us.

He cleared his throat. "Something to drink? I got some gin and tonic for you. Or I have beer." He gestured to his cooler.

"Beer, if you don't mind."

"Here you go." He handed me a beer and gestured toward the empty chair. "How was your trip? I didn't get a chance to ask you ... before."

"It was longer than I anticipated. Rain really messes everything up."

"I thought you were used to it after all those rainy winters in California."

"I've driven a lot less over the last few years. My business office was close to home. By the time the pandemic arrived, I was down to a few employees. I let the office go, and then the remaining employees."

Joe nodded.

"I needed a change, especially after Larry and I split." I considered the feeling I'd had at the time. "Bookkeeping felt like it no longer fit my life." I shrugged. Examining all the changes I'd made in California would be a good task for the drive back to my sisters.

"I had a good time last night." I went on to tell him about my meal and spa treatment. I left out my experiment with adult movies. *No one* was ever going to hear about that!

"I'm not sure I can give you as good a culinary experience here as you had there," Joe said. "But I did lay in some ingredients to make up my special chili. Tonight I thought I'd throw some burgers on the grill."

"That would be great," I said, then added, "You mentioned some small hikes earlier."

"Yes." He looked at the sky. "It's probably a little late now, but maybe tomorrow we can get up early and do the

Cliff Shelf Trail. I did it the other evening. There's a small pond there. I'm not sure how it made it in all this heat—the ranger said it's there later than it's ever been. Anyway, it attracts the animals at morning and dusk. I thought you could bring your camera."

"That would be fun."

"How is that going, by the way?"

I told him of my experiments as he prepped the grill for burgers.

"But I was really happy with the photos I took of the couple at the restaurant." I'd surprised myself with how well they came out. I'd always been shy about taking pictures of people, feeling like I was invading their lives. But with the permission of the couple, I'd been free to express the beauty of their love shining through their eyes.

"They had an arranged marriage," I told Joe.

"Really! I didn't think that happened anymore. Were they happy?"

"Very. She told me they'd learned to trust each other, and they became friends. Finally, they learned to love each other."

Joe turned his attention back to the grill, and I let the silence be.

Could I find that kind of love with Joe? Although we'd known each other once, we were strangers now. I stared at my old friend, and my body twitched with awareness. Over time, if we worked at it, I believed we could find happiness far beyond what I thought I'd had with Larry.

I was willing to do the work. Was Joe?

"I picked up some salad and dressing," he said, totally unaware of my deep thoughts. "One of those pre-made things. I don't have the patience to cut everything up anymore."

"Lucky for me, Liz loves to cut up things into little pieces. She's quite vicious about it, actually."

He laughed. "I can see that. She's always been a bit of a wild person."

"You'd never tell by looking at her," I said. "But if we ever got together, we'd probably have to stick to pre-cut things. I'm lazy in the kitchen. At least that's what Larry always said."

"From everything I've heard, Larry is an asshole."

"Joe!"

"Well, it's the truth." He pointed the spatula at me. "If we ever get together—which I hope we will—we'll share kitchen tasks."

"Maybe we can cook naked," I suggested with a grin. "Except for aprons."

He reddened. "We'll see," he mumbled. "I'll go get the fixings."

While my parents put their love on display with frequent kisses, hugs, and words of love, Joe's parents had been more of the keep-it-behind-the-bedroom-door type. It wasn't going to be easy to get him to be more openly affectionate, even if it was just the two of us.

But I couldn't hide my desire to explore the juicier side of life. Not any longer. I'd been hiding who I was for way too long. If Joe couldn't accept that, I was going to have to walk away.

Although it made me sad in a way, I also felt liberated.

"Can I help you?" I asked as Joe came out of his trailer with condiments and the salad.

"I've got it," he said. "Burgers should be about done. We can eat at the picnic table."

We spent a few moments prepping our burgers before Joe said a quick grace. Then we dug in. It was silent for a while as we ate.

"What have you been doing with yourself?" I asked.

"I'm making great progress on my book," he said, then grinned. "Best of all, an agent got back to me. He wants to see more of the manuscript!"

"That's great! Did you send it?"

"I have to finish it first."

"Details, details." I laughed. I was happy for Joe.

We managed to find enough small talk to make it through dinner. It was only after the dishes were done, and we walked to a nearby river that I felt it was time to start talking about what really mattered between us.

# Chapter Thirty-Five

Two bullfrogs competed by the river as I gathered my thoughts.

*Jug-a-rum. Jug-a-rum.*

Not a bad idea.

"Joe," I said when we reached the parched stream. "We need to talk."

"Yes," he said. "Isn't that why you're here?"

I wanted to blurt out: I'm here for a night of wild passionate sex! It's been way too long!

But I was kinder than that ... at the moment.

"We're going to be on the road until next May," I said. "I'm not giving that up."

"I don't expect you to."

"But that's a whole year away from each other. How can we find out if we're compatible at all, if there is something worth building on, if we never see each other?"

"We can keep in touch."

I shook my head. "It's got to be more than that, or all we'll be is strangers with common memories."

"We can talk on the phone every night," he suggested.

Maybe we could learn how to do great phone sex.

"I'm not sure that's enough."

"And I'm not sure what you're looking for." His fists flexed in frustration.

I wasn't sure how to tell him what I needed.

Larry had been great at grand gestures that ultimately meant nothing.

Joe was honest to the core, but probably didn't have a florist on speed dial.

"I'm not either," I said truthfully. "I love old romantic classics. They're full of great moments. Maybe that's what I need. Things like Lancelot laying his sword at the

Guinevere's feet."

"She was a married woman."

"Oh, yeah. Ilsa and Rick from Casablanca?"

"She left," Joe deadpanned.

"Rhett and Scarlett?"

"*He* left."

"How about Romeo and Juliet?" I asked.

He frowned. "They committed mutual suicide. I'm not up for that."

"Maybe not, then." We walked on. My mood was lighter, but the original question hadn't been answered.

"It doesn't have to be a whole year," he said. "I'd love to see New England in the fall. I can see Tess at MIT, then catch up with you in the Hudson River Valley. Kathleen said Liz is determined to go there."

"She's insistent."

"I could meet up with you there, and we could run off and see the foliage while your sister paints."

*Separate rooms?* I wanted to ask. But we weren't there yet.

"That could be fun."

"Where are you spending Christmas?" he asked.

"Nashville," I said. "Kathleen's kids are coming. Patrick is home on leave. Megan and her husband are happy to leave Hardin in the winter."

"I get that one," he said. "Tess is going to Dillon and staying with Bug and his family. We're celebrating there. That's important to me."

"And you should be with them," I said. I could bear a Christmas without a man again.

No big deal.

Except it hurt just a little.

"We're going to spend the end of January and early February around San Antonio," I said.

"That sounds perfect. I can take the trailer to Dillon for Christmas and head down 15. I wouldn't mind some sun then."

I nodded. Logistically, it was all adding up. But emotionally? I wasn't sure about that.

By the time we reached the river, he'd agreed to meet us in Oregon again in the spring and drive back to Montana.

"That's a lot of driving for you," I said.

"It's more a lot of thinking time. I take voice notes about my book while I drive."

"How's that going?" I asked.

"I'm about two thirds the way through, which means I'm almost over that middle section. That's the hardest to write for me."

"I thought this was your first book."

"Oh, no. I have a drawer full of them. I started my first book in high school."

"What was it about?" I asked.

"You."

"Me?"

"Yes. It was a modern day western suspense. You were the heroine in trouble, and I was determined to rescue you. But you rescued yourself first."

"I never was good at waiting around to be rescued."

"No, you weren't."

We stared at the river for a while.

"What scares you so much about taking a chance on us?" he asked.

"The truth?"

"It's the only thing that really works," he said.

"That, ultimately, when I take my clothes off, you won't ..." I looked away, swallowing hard to tamp down the emotional pain rising within me. Larry hadn't wanted me, and he'd been my husband. I took a shaky breath. "I'm not sixteen anymore," I whispered.

I couldn't look at him, but my heart thumped so loudly I was sure he could hear it.

"Nothing could make me not want you," he said.

"Then why won't you ..."

"It's not you," he said, shaking his head. "Something happened ... I need to figure out how to tell you. But the problem is mine, not yours."

"Oh my god," I blurted out, turning to face him. "I knew it! You have ED!"

"What? No!" He burst out laughing. Soon he was laughing so hard he doubled over.

I couldn't help myself; I started laughing, too.

After a few moments, we both collapsed on the ground, the hysteria ebbing away to a few hiccups of laughter. He took both my hands. "Di, I don't have ED. I promise. And sweetheart, there is nothing wrong with you. You're beautiful, just like you always were."

He maneuvered himself closer and cupped my face with his hand. "Very, very beautiful." Then he kissed me.

I was afraid to move into it. What if he broke it off again?

But he was the one who deepened the kiss, his tongue teasing at my lips until I relaxed and let him in. I kissed hungrily, starved for this for so long. Long slumbering parts of my body awoke. My nipples hardened and desire built in my belly.

When he pulled back, it was gentle.

"I do want more of this, Di. I promise you I do. Is it so bad that I want to wait?"

On its surface, it was a reasonable request.

But ...

"Yes." I crossed my legs at the ankles and propped myself up by leaning against my hands. "We're not being driven by hormonal impulses we don't understand. We care a great deal for each other, don't we?"

"Of course."

"Is it the church?" I asked. "Do you believe having sex with someone who isn't married to you will condemn you to one of Dante's circles of hell?"

"No," he scoffed. "Although, Father O'Brian would be very disappointed that we were even discussing it."

"Father O'Brian. I haven't thought about him in a long time. He terrified me with his loud voice and those beads that rattled whenever he walked."

"Definitely pre-Second Vatican Council," Joe said. "I think he almost had a heart attack when some of those changes were announced." He plucked a blade of grass and twirled it around his fingers. "Seriously, though, it's not Catholicism that's stopping me."

He placed the blade of grass into his mouth and chewed the end.

"Then what?"

He chewed for a bit longer, then shook his head.

"I'm not ready to talk about it yet."

"Then when?"

"I don't know."

"Look, Joe," I said. "I know you had an almost perfect marriage with Patti, and I imagine your love life was perfect as well, but I didn't and mine wasn't. In the last five years of our marriage Larry almost never touched me at all. Do you know how that feels, Joe? Do you know how it feels?" My voice came out in a whisper as my throat tightened with shameful memories.

At one point I'd been on my knees begging him—begging my husband—to please, please make love to me.

I turned away and pushed myself to standing.

"You've got to understand. This is important to me. Is it a dealbreaker? I'm not sure. It may be. Thanks for dinner." I walked away from the river, leaving him there to listen to the frogs compete for their territory.

*Jug-a-rum. Jug-a-rum.*

~ ~ ~

We didn't say anything about our conversation when I joined him early the next morning for our planned hike. We were well-practiced at not discussing deep feelings.

After driving to the trailhead, we gathered our gear—water, hats, phones, camera—and walked a short distance to where the main loop began. Joe suggested we take the left-hand route which followed a boardwalk around to the top. Although it had staircases, it avoided the steep steps that led two hundred feet straight up to get to the top.

"This way goes past the pond," he said. "If we walk quietly, we should be able to see something, even if it's only a deer."

We walked through some fragrant-smelling juniper trees. Joe's hand motion slowed me as we approached the pool.

I swallowed my gasp. Nearby, the anticipated white-tail deer, plus a mama and baby bighorn sheep, were lapping up the shaded water. Joe pointed, and I saw the bandit face of a raccoon as he washed some food he'd gathered.

Using the boardwalk railing as a brace, I concentrated on the raccoon. There wasn't quite enough light where he was, so I adjusted the settings according to what I learned during my practice and prayed I remembered everything correctly.

He looked up at me, but must have decided I wasn't a threat. The deer was more wary, keeping a close eye on my movements as she drank. I was able to get some close-ups of her head and beautiful eyelashes.

The mother sheep had done a thorough assessment when I got close, but then proceeded to ignore me and nudge her young one in the direction she wanted him to go. They soon finished up and headed out, but I was able to get a few pictures before they left.

"Amazing," I said to Joe. "What I could see through the lens! See?" I showed him what I'd been able to get.

"Really nice. I'm so glad you got the camera. You really need a tripod."

"One thing at a time." I slung the camera over my shoulder.

"Do you want to go to the top?" he asked. "The views are pretty amazing. I brought some energy bars if you get hungry."

"Let's go. A month ago I would have said no, but I think Liz is rubbing off on me with this hiking thing."

"It's a kind of pleasant torture."

"That's one way to put it."

Conversation lagged as we continued the assent of Badlands Wall. Instead there was a low-level buzz of tension. I wasn't sure what Joe was thinking, but I was trying to figure out what had happened in Joe's life to turn him off sex.

Erectile dysfunction would have been easier to deal with.

The temperature was beginning to rise when we got to the top. I was glad Joe had suggested the early morning. Gratefully, I took the energy bar he handed me and gazed out at the scenery around me. The colorful mounds and shapes of sedimentary buttes and spires led off to the depths of the Badlands on one side, while to the other lay the prairie grasses of the White River Valley, extending seemingly to the horizon.

"This country is pretty diverse," I said after taking a deep gulp of my water.

"Yes. And you're going to see a lot of it," he replied.

"It's so dry in the West, but the East is lush with green and almost too much water."

"And it's changing all the time." He turned to look at me. "Just like us. I don't know about you, but I'm not overly fond of this part of life. Just when I thought I had my act together, my body starts slipping. Not a lot. Just a few things here and there. A cracked tooth. Skin sagging where it never did before."

"Peeing four or five times in the middle of the night."

He laughed. "That, too."

Some of the tension eased.

"Now, I don't know about you," he said. "But I could use a hearty breakfast."

"Yes! I'm starving!"

"Good! There's a place down the road that makes a mean biscuit. And stacks of pancakes dripping with butter and syrup."

"Yum!" It had been so long since I'd indulged in what I called fat food.

"And no fussing about calories or anything stupid like that," he said as we hustled back down the path. "You're a beautiful woman just the way you are."

My heart lifted and my feet flew over the path that had been a plod a few moments before.

# Chapter Thirty-Six

Once we returned to the RV park, Joe said he needed to do some work on his book. I was ready for some time to myself and I desperately needed a shower. We agreed to meet around two and plan something for the rest of the afternoon.

Although the hike and Joe's words had eased some of the tension I'd been feeling, there was still an edge to my sense of relaxation. I didn't know what he was keeping to himself or when he would get around to revealing it.

Had he taken a vow of chastity for the rest of his life? Was he a secret monk?

My imagination wasn't only running away ... it was galloping.

Once I had cleaned up and chatted with my sisters, I sat down with my computer and uploaded the pictures I'd taken. There were some good ones in the shots I'd taken by the pond, but I kept going back to the ones I'd taken of the restaurant owners. I pulled out the email they'd given me and sent a few of the best to them.

Moments later a reply popped up.

*Thank you so much!* the woman wrote to me. *We would like to use the one with us as a couple on the website. How much will you charge for us to use it?*

Charge? I hadn't even thought of selling my pictures. I was learning photography for my own enjoyment.

*It's yours,* I wrote back. *I enjoyed my meal and our conversation very much.*

*Thank you,* the woman replied. *Next time you come here, we will make a feast for you and your friends.*

I smiled. The invitation was better than any check could ever be.

With my mood light, I walked to Joe's spot.

"Hi there, gorgeous," he said, putting his arm around me and giving me a kiss.

On the lips.

My eyes widened, and he chuckled.

"I love to see that expression. I'm going to have to get more of that going."

"Okay," I said. "Who are you and what have you done with Joe?"

More laughter.

"Let's just say I'm a work in progress," he said. "How about a trip to Wall? I figure we've done enough hiking for the day. We can walk around, look at the kitsch, and have a burger. I'd love to treat you to a five-star restaurant, but that's a bit hard to come by in Wall."

"Wall's the place with all the signs on the highway, right?"

"Yep. 'Have you dug Wall Drug?'"

I laughed.

"What's interesting," he continued, "is that the official signs go as far away as Greybull, Wyoming, about four hundred miles. But people make up their own signs and put them all over the place. There were several in Vietnam during the war."

"Crazy."

"It gives you something to do on that long stretch of highway," he said. "So?"

"Sure." The kitschy town might be a brief respite from the intense conversations we'd been having.

~ ~ ~

And it was. We looked at all the tourist souvenirs, inspected the stuffed jackalope, and posed for pictures with wooden cowboys. Our free glass of water was thirst-quenching and the five-cent cup of coffee adequate.

The amount of stuff squeezed into the intersecting shops and corridors and tucked away into small rooms was staggering. The products ranged from painted wooden figurines, guaranteed to get lost in a closet within a month of the return home, to richly tooled cowboy boots.

"Those are beautiful," Joe said as I inspected a pair of delicately crafted golden feather earrings.

"Yes. Unusual." I moved on. They weren't expensive, but I didn't need to be foolish with my money.

I didn't think any more of it until we were at dinner when he pulled out a box.

"There are many more things to talk about," he said. "But I'm so glad you're here, willing to take this much time with me. No matter what you ultimately decide, I hope you'll accept these as a memento of the moments we had together."

With tears in my eyes, I opened the box and stared at the earrings. The light glinting off them made them even more beautiful than I remembered. I undid the earrings I had on and replaced them.

He nodded, his smile broad. There was a glint of moisture in his eye as well.

"Thank you," I said and reached for his hand.

His fingers grasped mine, and he rubbed his thumb lightly on my skin. For a while we sat quietly like that, savoring the moment, one of the remaining few we had left as life edged further into its second half.

That was the thing with being older. Time became more precious than it had ever been in our spendthrift youth. The right decisions had to be chosen carefully, but not so carefully as to leave no time for their enjoyment.

"Am I interrupting something?" the waiter asked as he stood there with our burgers.

We released our hands like giddy teens, and he put the plates down.

~ ~ ~

We sat on a bench watching the stars appear in the night sky before taking the drive home. Joe had his arm around me, and I was comfortable with my head on his chest.

"I've thought all day about how to tell you this. I haven't admitted it aloud to anyone before."

I put my hand on his chest, to reassure him. The warmth of his skin comforted me as well.

"Patti and I had a good marriage. I thought it was a great one. Right up until the time I found out."

Realization was starting to dawn.

"Patti lost her way," Joe said.

I stayed still.

"Apparently, she resented marrying so early. She felt she'd never had a chance to see what other relationships were like. She hated being tied down with kids so early. But she never expressed any of this to me."

I began to dread what he was going to tell me.

"One day at church, the marriage banns were read for one of the parishioners, a banker who'd been divorced ten years before he proposed to a young woman in his bank. He was a very active member of the church, serving as a trustee." Joe swallowed. "I thought he'd be single for the rest of his life. I suspected he was a player, fooling around with anyone who would take a chance. I just never realized he'd do it with my wife."

A sound like an injured puppy came from his throat.

"Patti was in tears when we came home from church that day. It took me hours to get her to tell me what was wrong. And then ... and then ... I was so angry ... I got in the car and drove away. I drove for hours. No idea where I went."

"They had an affair?" I supplied.

He nodded.

"Several years long." A tear made its way down his cheek.

"I'm so sorry, Joe. So very sorry."

We sat like that for a long while, deriving comfort from our nearness and the silence.

"I forgave her," he said. "I had to. For my sake and the kids. But it was never the same. And as much as I tried, I could never make love to her again."

"Oh my god, Joe. I'm so sorry."

We sat like that for a while, just holding each other, letting the night sky and each other's touch ease the agony we'd both experienced.

He shifted so he could look directly at me. "Making love to you is a hurdle I need to get over because you deserve it. And I'm determined to give it to you. I promise."

As he lowered his head to kiss me, both of us cried quietly for the pain we'd had in the past. Pain that needed to be released before we could step freely into the future.

# Chapter Thirty-Seven

We parted that night with a long, lingering kiss in front of my cabin before we reluctantly let go.

As much as I wanted to have more, we were exhausted.

The next day, my last in the Badlands, we spent in a leisurely way: time apart while he wrote, time together where we talked more in depth and more honestly about our pasts than we had before. Neither one of us had achieved perfection in our relationships. It probably wasn't possible with two intrinsically flawed human beings. The best we could do was be kind to each other and love each other the best we knew how.

Although neither of us had yet to say that word.

Love.

We still weren't sure enough of each other to say it.

He barbecued some chicken which we ate with fresh corn we'd found in a small market. Then we talked some more until the mosquitos began to have more of a meal than we'd had.

"How about I bring a bottle of wine to your cabin in a little bit," he said. "I've got a nice California red one of my students' fathers gave me for a thank you. It seems to suit this occasion."

"Okay," I said. Would wine in my cabin lead to anything else, or would it just be wine?

On the off chance it could lead to something more, I changed my underwear into something a little sexier. It was a small step, one grade better than granny underpants and a functional bra. Itchy lace had been denied entry into my drawers for well over a decade.

But maybe it was time to try it on again.

It would depend on how the night went.

Joe showed up on my doorstep, also looking freshly

scrubbed. He had the wine in one hand, a box of chocolates in the other.

We kept the pretense of two friends chatting over a glass of wine and chocolates going for a little while. Then I got tired of it.

"Well, are we going to do this?" I asked impatiently.

He chuckled and shook his head. "Impatient Di. Always wants it now."

"Now? I've wanted this since I was eighteen. You're the one who is slow on the uptake."

"Guilty," he said, putting down his wine.

He stood and helped me to my feet. "Yes," he said. "We're going to do this."

The kiss started slowly, but soon our bodies were pressed together with need, and our hands pulled each other closer. He disentangled, and we caught our breaths.

"Let me look at you," he said. "I want to see you."

"Naked?" I squeaked.

"Naked."

He unbuttoned the first button of my blouse, his gaze never leaving mine. Somehow that was sexier than the undressing going on. Soon he had all the buttons undone and pushed the blouse from my shoulders, laying it across a nearby chair.

It took every strength of will I had not to cover up my disappointing bra. At least it was covering up my sagging breasts.

He unhooked the bra and draped it over the blouse.

My nipples turned into hard nibs, and it wasn't from the cold.

"Relax," he said as he lifted my breasts. "You're beautiful." Then he used his mouth to nibble and suck the tender flesh.

I moaned as need filled me. The man obviously had skills the boy had probably lacked.

"Your turn," I said.

"What is this?" he asked. "Strip poker?"

"Something like that."

His chest hair was graying, and the skin was no longer

tight against the muscles, but I ran my fingers over him like he had done with me, growing more relaxed in my semi-nakedness.

"Bed," he instructed me.

Once there, he pulled off my jeans so I was down to the not-granny-panties.

He stripped down similarly, then pushed back the covers and guided us both to the surface of the bed.

"Beautiful," he repeated. He trailed kisses down my body from my lips to the tops of my panties.

I ran my fingers through his hair, unable to do much more as my body responded to his ministrations.

"I'd ask if you were really sure about this," he said. "But I already know the answer."

"Joe, don't stop now!"

My body hit a new fever pitch as his fingers slipped under my panties and slowly pulled them off, before standing and discarding his own underwear.

Erectile dysfunction wasn't going to be a problem.

After more agonizing moments of teasing, he finally entered me, once again his whole attention on me, as he learned what gave me pleasure and brought me closer and closer to our final release. When I came—with a scream that I'm sure the neighbors heard—he was right behind.

~ ~ ~

When we woke from our post-coital sleep, he gently touched my lips with his.

"I love you, Diane O'Sullivan. I always have. And I always will. Please come back to Montana when this trip is done. Let me show you how many ways I can make you happy."

"I love you too," I said. "As long as we can keep doing this ..." I gestured to our intertwined bodies. "I'll be happy to be in Montana."

"And when it's no longer possible?" he asked.

"I hear there's a little blue pill for that ..."

He laughed and pulled me close.

"Do you think Bug has room for one more at Christmas?" I asked.

"You'd come to Dillon?"

"If you think it would be all right."

"I'll make sure of it." His hand caressed my cheek. "I love you. I want you in my life. My kids will just need to get used to the idea."

"Then I'll be there," I said, grinning up at him.

"I'm so glad you and your sisters stopped at Yellowstone."

"So am I."

He looked at me with a grin. "Now where were we?"

I laughed as his hands reawakened my body. He lowered his head and kissed me.

Joy flooded my soul. The future was bright and Joe was in it.

It didn't get any better than being with your first true love.

# From the Author

I hope you enjoyed the first book in this new series. Yes! You will be hearing more about Liz and Kathleen, as well as catching up with Di and Joe.

The story about the elk chasing Di is based on an experience I had in my twenties. A friend and I decided, in the way you only can when you're in your twenties, to call an elk using an elk bugle, a device that allows you to sound like an elk who is spoiling for a fight. (Note, these are not legal to use in hunting in Montana.)

Well the thing worked and we found ourselves in a small clearing facing a large elk with a big rack. He put his head down. My friend yelled, "Run!"

I fled to hide behind the nearest tree while my friend waved his arms and shouted, "Stop! We're people!" The elk stopped, looked my friend over, and turned with a snort.

All kinds of things can happen in Montana!

Sincerely,

Casey Dawes

P.S. Reviews are always welcome by this author. Please feel free to leave one!

# About the Author

Casey Dawes writes non-steamy contemporary romance and inspirational women's fiction with romantic elements.

Her women's fiction series, Rocky Mountain Front, explores the five siblings from a ranching family living in Montana, the people who love them, and the characters in the small town in which they live. Previous to that she wrote a 5-book contemporary romance series about friends and family on the Central Coast. Her latest series features love between "seasoned" heroes and heroines in a small Montana town.

Currently, she and her husband are traveling the US in a small trailer with the cat who owns them. When not writing or editing, she is exploring national parks, haunting independent bookstores, and lurking in spinning and yarn stores trying not to get caught fondling the fiber!

*Promise Cove is my most popular series! To get a free novella,* Promise Cove Beginnings, *go to this link:*
*https://bookhip.com/VAKFSWN*

*You will be added to my newsletter mailing list: On the Road to Your Next Read ...*

# Other Books by Casey Dawes

## Promise Cove

*Return to Promise Cove*
*Spring in Promise Cove*
*Hope in Promise Cove*
*Winter in Promise Cove*
*Promise Cove Wedding*
*Summer in Promise Cove*
*Away from Promise Cove*

## Beck Family Saga

*This series revolves around a Montana ranching family—
women's fiction with a touch of romance!*

*Home Is Where the Heart Is*
*Finding Home*
*Leaving Home*
*Coming Home*
*Starting for Home*
*Finally Home*

## RV Park Romance Series

*Brand new romantic comedy series!*

*Grown-Up Second Chance*
*Her Son's Secret Father*
*Her Texas Cowboy*

**California Romance Series**

*Two mothers, two daughters, and one friend explore
contemporary romance on the California coast.*

*California Sunset
California Wine
California Homecoming
California Thyme
California Sunrise*

**Montana Christmas Series**

*A new adult contemporary romance series set in Missoula
Montana—just right for the holidays!*

*Sweet Montana Christmas
Montana Christmas Magic
Second Chance Christmas*